Parrot Under the Pine Tree

Surendra Pratap Singh

Invincible Publishers

First published in India in 2017 by Invincible
Publishers

Copyright Surendra Pratap Singh 2017
ISBN: 978-93-86148-55-1

Surendra Pratap Singh asserts the moral right to be
identified as the author of this work.

The views and opinions expressed in this book are the
author's own and the facts are as reported by him, and
the publishers are not in any way liable for the same.

All rights reserved. No part of this publication
may be reproduced, stored in a retrieval system, or
transmitted, in any form or by any means, electronic,
mechanical, photocopying, recording or otherwise,
without the prior permission of the publishers.

Invincible Publishers
G - 120, Sushant Lok III, Sector 57, Gurgaon-122002

Opposite Kasturba Ashram, Radaur Distt Yamuna
Nagar, Haryana- 135133

Dedicated to
Rashmi and Payoshni,
whose love for the mountains surpasses mine.

Acknowledgements

* * *

Foremost, I wish to express my deep sense of gratitude to our **God Almighty** for bestowing the wisdom and strength upon me to visualize and finish this book.

I'd like to thank Malvika Solanki for proofreading and editing the manuscript, Sneha Agarwal for designing the book cover, and Ajay Setia, the publisher for pursuing me doggedly to publish the book with him.

A big thank you and my heartfelt appreciation to Rashmi, my wife and Payoshni, my daughter for enduring my absence in their midst when I spent long hours at the computer writing the book. My heartfelt appreciation to Payoshni for the photo and cover design.

Finally, Kausani, a picturesque town in the Kumaon Himalayas deserves a special mention for turning a fleeting thought into the reality of a story.

Chapter One

***

From the pagans of the pre-Vedic period to the faithful of the post-Vedic era, only the Sun God hasn't lost its eminence in the daily lives of the human beings. Both the believers and the atheists hold it in reverence. Heliolatry has persisted from the prehistoric times. No natural phenomenon has captured the imagination of so many people as the sunrise, which has provided intellectual nourishment to the educated for generations.

And it was the sunrise of a divine kind that drew thousands of enthusiasts to a lesser-known place in the Himalayas. These were pre-dawn hours. From behind the snow-capped mountains, hidden under the veil of brume, the sun prepared to rise. It took time to climb those lofty peaks with precipitous gradients. In the valley below lay a sleepy little town.

A long road winding through effulgent valleys, dotted with huts and fields, approached Kausani, a quaint hamlet perched atop the ridgeline. Thereafter, it cut through the place splitting it in two unequal halves and then vanished into the Katyuri Valley, overlooking the white sentries. The two ridge-halves spread like the wings of a gigantic dragon. More huts adored the forward slopes. For centuries Kausani had loved and revelled in its aloofness. Throughout the year it covered itself in a blanket of obscurity as if it hated civilisation. Of late, the hotels and resorts like pockmarks had sprung up all over on the forward slopes and destroyed its beauty and tranquillity. Kausani resented their presence on their soil and often shed tears in the calm, dark hours, but each morning with a smile awaited the day's arrival for itself, its inhabitants and its guests.

The dawn here was long, the day longer and the night the longest. Here the Gods controlled everything and eternized tranquillity. It was their land. The local folks in reverence called it as the '*Devbhumi*'. In this land, time was its own master and not a slave to some conceited man.

So, the sun chose its own time to rise, its own time to set, day after day, month after month and year after year. And today was no different. The natives of this Himalayan state owed their existence to it. The sun not only brought light in their lives, but it also gave life to the forest, the land and the water- things on which their survival depended.

This place had its own world—the world of religions, the world of spirits. And it drew people of the material world to it, the majority for a short period but some folks forever. Here an indescribable bliss reigned and greeted all visitors. Unlike the other places, Sunday enjoyed no special status in the folks' lives here. It didn't differ from the weekdays. The distinction between days had blurred so much that one had forgotten which day was what. As one soaked one's soul in those heavenly environs in endless hours of idleness, one wished not to remember anything that in any way reminded oneself of time and bound to it.

Like any other day, Kausani with every passing minute emerged out of the darkness, tree by tree, house by house, street by street. Every rooftop was filled with folks,the locals and the visitors. The prospect of a good sunny day had driven the native women to carry grain, chillies and clothes on the roofs for drying. But the tourists' worries were of a different kind. For some, it was their last day in Kausani and hence they prayed for a great sunrise so that they could, for posterity, capture the divine spectacle in their cameras, in their hearts.

Also, in that motley crowd love stories, born in a short span of time, faced a bleak future as the reckless lovers readied to leave to different destinations. In spite of the uncertain future of their whirlwind romances, the lovers gave last-minute promises to *one another* and exchanged addresses, phone numbers and email IDs. Parting hugs and kisses filled their eyes. But misgivings remained in many a heart. For some, though, the love in such fleeting moments had been what it often was: a quick physical liaison to be had and forgotten.

As the darkness dissipated fast, the crowd rushed pell-mell on the rooftops, filling every inch of the space. Attired in colourful clothes, people with cameras—still and video—hung around their necks paced left and right, forward and backward in needless anxiety. Some women, smelling of cheap perfume that stifled the fresh mountain air, fidgeted in low quality, ill-fitting jeans that they had perhaps worn for the first time. Those in Indian dresses moved around without any constraints.

Jeans in the last few decades in the Indian society had become a great social equalizer; the rich wore it, the poor wore it. While the former wore it with diminishing vanity, the latter wore it with new found pride.

In a corner veiled in grey mist sat a young couple waiting for the dawn. The man had a quick glance around and then kissed his wife on the lips. A stunned woman hugged her man with a question in her eyes. Back home in the orthodox land where the men walked a yard ahead of their wives and where holding of hand in public drew snide comments and disapproving glances, a public kiss like this could have caused a mini-riot. In their five years of marriage this had been his most chivalrous act in public. It made her heart pound faster with thrill, expecting gallant actions in the privacy of the bedroom. The sound of footsteps forced them to break off their embrace.

On the next roof stood a young mother who post childbirth a year ago couldn't shed as much weight as she had wished for, though she had got rid of her face fat. With a sweater tied around her waist, she tried to cover her less attractive behind. She was a single female traveller.Many nosy parkers indulged in bizarre, unwarranted guesses. Unconcerned, she soaked her soul in those salubrious climes.

On the adjoining parapet sat a young woman, dangling her feet over the side and gazing at the misty mountains. The freshness and freedom of the place inspired her to hum a love song. Back at home, covered in black from head to toe when she moved in the company of other women, she felt her beauty go unappreciated, her smile unreciprocated. And when furtive glances presuming her an old woman slipped past her face, the beauty beneath the black sheath struggled to unshackle itself. Her heart suffered a sharp pang of regret for marrying into an orthodox family when she had a choice not to.

The cool breeze kissed her bare arms and cheeks, and unfurled her hair. The mind broke the shackles, setting her soul free. Like a bird, she flew into the nearby clumps and sat on the top of the tallest pine. From there she watched the mountains, the valleys and the folks. Every time the cold wind hit her, she shook her wings to keep herself warm. In excitement, she jumped from one branch to another, chatted and quarrelled with other birds. She was free to do anything she wanted.

'Oh, what a freedom!' the woman let out a huge

sigh.

The next moment she felt a tap on her shoulder. In a voluntary motion, her right hand went over the back of the head to cover her face with hijab. For a moment she felt several known eyes pierce her face with indignation, but she regained her composure when she looked back. Her husband had returned with tea, which she drank in unusual hurry. Thereafter, she remained edgy and her face alternated between the colours of joy and anxiety. Her man's repeated assurances failed to put her at complete ease.

On the first roof, fathers taught photography to their children. On the second, a few cameramen positioned the groups. On the third roof, a musician adjusted the strings of his guitar to compose the first song of the dawn. On the fourth, a man sat with the paper and pen to compose a verse. And on the fifth roof, devotees, with none of the above accessories, waited to offer water to the rising sun, a Vedic ritual that had survived several attacks on the oldest faith.

The upcoming divine spectacle had a different meaning to different people waiting for it for the last hour. A speck of redness from behind the holy peaks emerged. Then in a steady manner the Alpenglow spread upwards and sideways. The chill in the air ebbed away. A little later, the atmosphere was filled with a loud uproar whose echo reverberated in the Katyuri Valley below. The sun was rising. It seemed in no haste. From the moment people sighted the first outline, hundreds of cameras clicked non-stop and flashes exploded until it became a huge sphere. In less than an hour it lost its redness and became a blazing fireball, unfit to take pictures of.

Most kids clung on to their mothers who, unlike fathers, shared their children's joy. A girl of six when ignored by her father complained to her mother, she wouldn't talk to him and then walked away to a secluded corner. Reclining against the parapet and gazing at the mountains, she murmured to herself, "Wish we could stay in this place. It would be so much fun going to school here." It wasn't her wish alone. The hearts of other children, born and brought up in the concrete jungles, echoed similar sentiments when they arrived in the hills.

Some pine trees greener and taller than the others vied for visitors' attention but remained resigned to the fact that the holy mountains grabbed all the attention. But they drew comfort that a few leisure travellers would walk in their midst and sit under their shadows. A writer would gaze at them for hours appreciating their individual and collective beauty. The children would pluck pine leaves and brush them against their tender cheeks, and feel them between their palms.

A stone's throw from that crowd, a few makeshift teashops had come up in the wee hours. Their owners did a brisk business. Amongst them sat a middle-aged Kumauni man under a plastic lean-to that neither protected him from the rain, nor the wind. The tea seller with a freckled face and sunken cheeks looked older than his age. Poverty had stolen several of his youthful years. A worn out shirt and pant, and a faded sweater didn't diminish his pride. Out of a faded cap hiding his bald pate blew out his scraggy, grizzled hair in every possible direction. From the grey-white stubble it looked the man cared little for his looks. The man smiled with cracked lips whenever a customer came to him.

Beside him sat his sari-clad wife, the mother of two children, in a diligent supporting role. The ten-year younger woman had big blue eyes, thick lips and a sharp nose with a large circular ring. Bright lipstick, dark kajal, face powder and perfume were proof enough that she, unlike her husband, she took pains to look attractive. Her brocaded blouse, designed to cover the bosom and cleavage, failed once a while in its duty. As more customers thronged to the shop the woman, unable to handle the rush, panted and light beads of sweat dripped down between the cleavage of her perky breasts. Every time she bent down to pour tea in the glass, her cleavage flashed, attracting glances; some abashed, some unabashed. A few elders were sympathetic to her present existence but indignant that such a good-looking woman deserved a better fate. Unmindful of this, she went about her job as usual.

In between she stole a glance at a young couple that fed each other bun and drank tea from the same glass. It amused her. She remembered her husband feed her once during the marriage ceremony ten years ago. Thereafter, he ate alone and she ate with the children. This kind of love was alien to her and quite mystifying. What kind of feeling did a woman experience when her husband fed her? She stole a glance at the couple who were busy feeding each other. The sight filled her heart with a tinge of envy, which vanished when the couple left. If her husband ever fed her, she would bite his fingers, she thought. A naughty smile ran over her face.

A yard away the baby boy, sitting on a piece of tattered rug, had been crying for a while to draw her mother's attention. The spit oozing down the corners of his mouth had dried up, and so had his tears and snot. Unsatisfied eating tears, the hungry boy let out a huge cry. Concerned, the mother stood up to attend to him. Sitting on the ground with folded knees and back towards the customers, she lifted the boy and put him in her lap. The hungry boy with his tiny hands tried to raise the blouse, but failed and cried in pain and hunger.

"Wait," the mother admonished him, "You are as impatient as your father."

Then she, covering her breasts with sari, thrust the nipple into the mouth of the baby who after a few bites drew out milk. After a quick glance around when she saw no one watched her, she heaved a deep sigh. Every time the wind blew her sari off and exposed her golden legs, she pulled it down. The boy after the fill, fell asleep. And before she could have a breather, an unwashed four-year girl, with running nose and itchy head, shouted for help. She went over to her, wiped the girl's nose with her sari palloo, and then sat down to search her daughter's head for lice. In between the man looked at his wife and children. The customers' faces lit up when the woman returned to serve them tea.

Hours of hard work under the sun had weathered her skin so much that her normal eyes looked bigger and enticing. And whenever they fell on a man, even the strongest couldn't escape its magical spell. Some men at the teashop had more than one cup in the hope of getting her tempting glance. While the others were content with spending a few minutes more in her warm presence.

Over the years she had watched how young and old couples, hand in hand, hand over shoulder, walked around the place and sat in secluded corners expressing their love to one another. And she had learnt that people whispered, 'I love you' to the person they loved. So one night she put on her best sari, wore bright red lipstick and said 'I love you' to her husband, and waited in excitement to hear the same from him.

"Have you gone mad?" the man snapped back. "Today you speak their language, tomorrow you will wear their clothes and bring shame to the family."

"Forgive me," she apologised at once.

"*Arey, pagli*," his voice was calm. "Their world is different from ours. We are better off the way we are. We don't have to imitate them."

Those words made sense to her. That night her husband showed patience and care during lovemaking. Satisfied, she fell in deep thought.

But the poor woman didn't know that amongst educated people, longing and love were vocal, demonstrative and celebratory. In the poor folks' lives they were tedious and dreary. She recalled her husband saying she was beautiful on two occasions; one, when she dressed up for the marriage and two, when he made love to her. He spoke the word 'beautiful' as fast as he did the act. She had noticed that he always made love in complete darkness and with a sense of guilt, and wanted her to lie still during the act. Perhaps all men behaved in the similar way. Like washing clothes, working in the field, cooking food and raising children, sex too was part of her duty, she thought. What the city women thought about it remained a secret to her simple mind. And it was one secret she wasn't much keen to discover.

Theirs was a small enterprise run by the husband-wife team during the sunrise and sunset times. In between they cultivated a small piece of land in which they grew vegetables and farmed goats. The five-rupee tea served in a glass was an instant hit with the tourists. And for those not used to having tea on an empty stomach, they had a wide variety of biscuits to choose from. If the tea seller wanted he could have hiked the price to ten rupees, which people would have paid without a fuss, but he wasn't greedy like his brethren in the city.

Contentment was one thing the hill folks had in plenty.

Shivering from the cold, people thronged to him for hot tea. And a few old people, perhaps the second or third time visitors, sat with him for an abridged version of a folktale or two that he narrated to them with a smile and with no hindrance to his work.

Wrapped in layers of woollens, an old man, after holding the cup, commented, "A hot tea in this cold is a divine experience." Then his gaze fell on the broken wooden stool on which lay a crumpled newspaper. His eyes lit up. Reading newspaper with hot tea in the morning had become a habit since past several years. He stretched his hands and picked up the paper. For a second he forgot tea and flipped through the pages. It took him some minutes to realise the paper was almost a week old. With a shrug he put it down and picked up the tea gone cold.

"Is there a better place to watch the sunrise?" asked the second man, sipping tea. The question was directed at the tea seller, but he looked at everybody sitting there in anticipation of the answer.

"No. Though there are places higher than this from where one can get a better view, this place is the best as it offers hot tea," said the first man.

"Ah! What a way to watch the holy Himalayas rise from deep slumber with tea in hand," sighed the second man and dipped the biscuit that fell in the tea. After a quick glance around he took out the sodden biscuit with index finger and ate it. Then he sipped tea.

In walked a professor, rubbing his hands, and asked for tea.

The tea seller, putting the pan on the stove, said, "Babuji neither is Kausani's cold so biting, nor is my tea so refreshing. In the past five years things have changed."

"Yeah, things have changed," the old man repeated and had a large gulp, fearing the tea might go cold. "The summers have become hotter and the winters milder. Global warming is the cause of all this."

Unable to comprehend it, the tea seller argued, "Babuji, *Dharti Ma* is angry with us, because we consume more than she can produce. And on her complaint, the Sun

God is threatening to destroy us all. We've to have to change our ways."

What a simple explanation to a complex problem faced by the world! The retired professor thought as he gulped down the last sip, gone cold. The man was dressed in grey trousers, green shirt and a tie, and brown tweed coat and a Kumauni cap, as though he was going to the university to take a class. Even after eight years of retirement the man hadn't reconciled to the fact that he no longer worked. He missed the chalk and duster, and mushy ambience of the classroom. The old man missed his pupils more, his children less. Where every male was dressed in casual, the professor's formal attire drew people's instant respect. And today he seemed to enjoy every moment of it. He wore cap to hide his pate, which in recent years had developed in him a sense of inferiority complex and caused a severe decline in his libido. Here, in the salubrious climate of Kausani, he chose to forget this and many other stresses.

Who said the wisdom lay in books? The professor mumbled to himself. Then a few seconds later, he complimented, "You make nice tea. What special thing do you add in it to make it so refreshing?"

The seller, with a grin, replied, "My father told me about an herb with which he claimed to cure constipation, however chronic it was. A glass of the mixture for a week was enough, but he forgot to pass me down the formula. When I opened the teashop I thought of adding the herb to change the taste. My customers liked it and the tea became an instant hit. It's a rare herb that grows in this place."

Hiding disappointment behind a smile, the professor thanked and left. He had hoped to get the cure for the constipation that had slowed down his pace of life.

A newly wed couple in the late twenties on honeymoon trip had chosen to stay indoors and observe the sunrise from the privacy of the bedroom where a large window opened out to the snowy peaks. They were up at dawn and awaited the sun's arrival. The husband wore a lower and a cotton jumper, while the wife a top and jeans. Colourful bangles, interspersed with gold ones, dazzled from her wrist up to elbows and vermilion sparkled in her hair parting. On her body the oriental and the occidental cultures blended in a bizarre harmony. Those unwieldy glass bangles pricked him while making love, but his feeble protest to remove them were brushed aside by her who, like thousands of Indian brides, loved the sight of glass pieces on her forearms. During free moments she played with them as happy dreams filled her heart and soul. It was their eighth day in that place. Every day they awoke to the sun and had an exhilarating experience that it arose for them and no one else. It was a unique feeling they savoured, alone.

In tight embrace, they stood at the window to welcome the day. As the first rays fell on their faces, they with closed eyes prayed for each other's long life. They would have continued to be in that position had the door bell not rung. Both opened their eyes and looked down. It occurred to them then that they had forgotten something. He ran for the bathrobe, she in the bathroom. The waiter walked in, placed the tea on the table and went back. A little later they, sipping tea, watched the sun grow from a tiny crescent into a red fireball.

Their daily routine, as one would expect it to be of a newlywed's, had been predictable. After waking they did everything together; watching the sunrise, eating breakfast out of each other's hands and going for long walks in the woods. The sunset, on the contrary, was witnessed from the gentle environs of the pine forest, which for over a week had provided them with newer and wilder venues for their passion play. Small hillocks located behind larger mountains where local folks didn't venture out at that time of the year and where silver brume swirled through the maze of pine clumps and billowed after each shower, were the perfect love-spots. They, during their little adventures, had found a few such secret locales.

Between meals they were fed on the passion of unbridled kind; physical dimension of which had stifled the emotional component. Such was their love. Such were the lovers; mad and wild about each other. And they had constricted the whole world around themselves, to exist for them and them alone.

As the sun made its voyage upwards, the day heated up. By eight many visitors had boarded vehicles for the return journey. A small percentage of them, however, had stayed back and after breakfast loitered around the market. The honeymooners had slipped out of the hotel and made a dash for the forest. It was their last day in Kausani.

Ten days that they had been together they had spent the first day in knowing each other mentally and emotionally. In such a short time they wanted to savour the bliss of a lifetime, because they knew that once at home, the husband would be sucked into his family business and the wife into looking after his large family. In subsequent years they would get so caught up in their chores that they would get lesser time for each other. With greying hair and bulging bellies, he would end up devoting more time to the business, she to their children.

It wasn't their story alone; it was of so many others.'

Between this time and the evening nothing significant happened. The natives got busy with their daily lives. The visitors went around on a shopping spree, buying handicrafts and artefacts. The interaction between the locals and visitors made the one rich and the other wiser.

The day had begun to roll up fast. The clock struck

five. New sets of buses and cars started to roll in. In the beginning thin and warm valley mist, which glared against the weak sunlight, met them with feigned warmth. But on the upper reaches its cousin, denser and wetter, piggyback on the cool mountain wind, greeted everyone with a smile, full of genuine warmth.

The two mists revelled in their little rivalries.

And as soon as the new tourists arrived at the Chowk, the light drizzle sprayed them. It was an ecstatic experience for them, who were escaping from the sweltering heat of the Indo-Gangetic Plain. It was June, the hottest month in the northern India. But here it was pleasant, divine to be more precise. What an escape it was! Everyone thought as they alighted from the vehicles and strolled towards their accommodations.

"Oh, God! This place is a heaven," exclaimed a young male voice. It made several heads turn in his direction and nod in admiration. Their hearts echoed the same sentiment.

Intoxicated by the petrichor, the man stood there and let the rainy mist swirl around him. One moment he would show out of it to disappear the next moment. Had somebody not pulled him by the arm, he would have continued to play with the mist with which his relationship went back to his childhood days.

Escaping the monotony of the mundane, Vedanta had arrived in Kausani.

Chapter Two

* * *

Mesmerised by timelessness of this tiny town, India's most famous son, Mahatma Gandhi, the apostle of peace, during the tour of the Himalayas, had halted at this place and sought divine blessings for the freedom of his country. Enthralled by the beauty of Kausani, he had christened this hill station as the 'Switzerland of India'. And Sumitra Nandan Pant, another famous son, had sought inspiration to write some of the most memorable Hindi poetry, to whom Kausani hadn't disappointed either. Whoever came here, returned home with loads of everlasting soul-nourishing memories.

Seduced by its charm, a young Vedanta stood still.

"Come on, sir, let's move. You will be here for two weeks." He felt as if someone had poured molten lead into his ears. But he couldn't ignore those words. Miffed, he followed that voice. Walking through the thin fog he arrived in the hotel lobby where a young receptionist sat, chewing her lower lip in a thoughtful way. The sound of his footsteps drew her attention. She greeted him with a grin. Handsome customers often brought a broader smile on her face. Bending forward, she with a pleasant demeanour asked, "May I help you, sir?"

"Yes, Ma'am. May I've a room, please?"

"Do you have a booking, sir?"

"No."

"All right, any preference?" she glanced at him.

"Yeah, facing the Himalayas and without a TV."

"Room No 12 would be fine for you, sir. Don't switch on TV if you don't like."

"I might be tempted if it's there," he smiled.

"Strange," her voice had half curiosity, half mischief, "a young man is afraid of temptations."

"I've come here with a different purpose," he shot back. "I want to feel coldness of the day and tenderness of the night."

Her philosopher refrain was, "I can understand. You are here to experience things, which back home, you can only dream of."

"Like?"

"You want to touch the clouds, catch the mist in your fist, sit under the pine trees, and bathe in the rain," she spoke, with a smile of adolescent flirtation.

Her words were effortless, as if she were reliving those experiences. That moment she looked like a ten-year old child, full of innocence and exuberance, on a maiden visit to that place to enjoy the myriad beauties of Nature.

"Thank you so much for advocating my case so well," he grinned.

Her half-blush brought that conversation to a close.

"I've come here in search of my soul," he cherry-picked his words, in order to impress her.

"Or in search of a soulmate," she whispered.

"Both," he winked at her and started walking towards his room.

Her cheeks turned red, her smile sheepish. Her heart beat faster. Her gaze chased him up to the staircase.

"Excuse me," an elder's voice pulled her out of a daydream. And it was business as usual for her. Hopes in her heart had a short life.

For Ved, hot bath and hot tea followed in quick succession. After unpacking suitcase, he laid out his clothes in the cupboard. Then he drew out the curtains and opened the windows. A gust of fresh breeze rushed in and filled the room. It was so refreshing, so invigorating. The ambience lifted his spirits. The western sky was clouded. It would be futile to venture out, he thought. The dusk rushed in. A large fly hovered around the window. Two kids, groceries on their backs, ran down the slope. They were in a hurry to reach home in the valley. Through the window he watched things, both animate and inanimate, melt away in the dark. Half-hour later the night fell.

It was a typical mountain night, black, nippy and still. He switched off the air-conditioner. For miles he could see nothing, he didn't wish to see anything. That moment he wanted to gaze at the dark. It gave him a sense of fulfilment, a feeling associated with some kind of achievement. What? He didn't know. But it elated his heart and soul.

His thoughts received a jolt when the waiter asked him for dinner. He nodded and followed the man to the restaurant where he ate in the company of a few strangers with whom, he at that moment was in no mood to acquire any acquaintance. Later he came back to his room and sat on the window sill.

In the stillness of the night he took a trip down the memory lane.

Vedanta had a decent lineage. His grandfather, Manohar Prasad, a freedom fighter, had fought alongside Netaji as part of the Azad Hind Fauz. When he was sixteen and in the school, his grandpa had died. So most memories associated with the old man had started to fade away, but some, which had got embedded in his heart, were his grandpa's heroic exploits in the Battle of Kohima during the Second World War. Those stories had enthralled him, motivated him. For a young Ved, his grandpa was his greatest hero whose death had created a big vacuum in his life.

Then over the next few years the grandpa, whose stories he missed, whose pampering he missed, became a myth to him.

His father, Shashank, after retiring as a civil servant had joined a political party and served as a junior minister in the state cabinet. But all of a sudden, to everyone's surprise, he had left the politics and become a hermit. This transformation was brought about by his father's inability to adapt himself in the profession wherein people with heart seldom succeeded. One had to be heartless and shameless to climb the ladder of success. And Shashank was neither.

In his father ran the blood of his grandfather for whom honesty was a man's biggest virtue. Because of the obsession with honesty, his father could never rise beyond a commissioner whereas his less capable and corrupt colleagues had risen to the rank of the secretary. In politics too, he had been a miserable failure. Both the bureaucrats and the politicians, he thought, were servants of the people. But he saw none of them behave like that. The servants acted as the masters, feudal lords and kings, and supposed-masters of democracy begged with folded hands before the servants.

This evil force of democracy had disillusioned him. After retirement, he had become religious and spent most of his time reading Hindu scriptures in which perhaps he sought solace, or answers to his countless questions that life had hurled at him. Of late, his father had limited his material needs and become an out-and-out philanthropist whose activities often annoyed him and perhaps his mother too, but she, like a true Indian wife, didn't show it. He, at times, did.

In contrast Vasudha, his mother, was a realist. Unlike her husband, she had a more successful career. She started her career as a lecturer in a government college and rose to become the Vice Chancellor of a central university. After retirement, she lived in her own world in which several mini-worlds—the world of books, the world of husband, the world of sons, the world of friends and the world of servants—existed. To his surprise her world of materialism had some space for charity too. How did she strike a balance amongst these worlds, remained a mystery to Ved? Despite some serious difference of opinion with her husband, she had stood by him all these years, like the rock of Gibraltar. He had seldom seen his parents fight in front of him. Whatever problems the couple had, they like sensible adults had solved those within the four walls of their bedroom.

His elder brother, Srikant, a surgeon, worked and lived in Chicago. Three years ago, he had married a second generation Indian-American girl and last year he had acquired the US citizenship. The news had shocked his father who had hoped that his eldest son after doing the M.S. would come back to India and serve his own people. Nowadays, his father seldom talked about Srikant who in his world had ceased to exist. His mother, however, kept in constant touch with her elder son. However, Srikant and Vedanta shared a relationship that was formal but friendly.

Born of the same parents both brothers had the opposite traits. While an extrovert Srikant in college days was popular amongst girls, an introvert Vedanta was ill at ease in their company. As one changed his girlfriend every semester, the other could never get any. While the elder brother hankered after the money, the younger didn't.

While Vedanta was emotionally attached to his parents, Srikant wasn't. Their paths were different, their pursuits were different, and their lives were different. Ambition was the common loose thread that bound them together. In comparison to the older brother's soaring ambition, the younger one's paled.

Ved was the second son. The name Vedanta was given to him by his grandfather. Later, because of difficulty in pronouncing it, it was shortened to Ved. Now everyone called him Ved. The class teachers at the time of taking attendance addressed him by the longer version. So Vedanta had become Ved. Whether or not he liked this change? He wasn't sure. Now, of course, he had accepted it with a grudge. But whenever somebody called him Vedanta, it reminded him of his grandpa.

Next summer he was to complete his B.Tech from Institute of Technology, Kanpur. During the campus placement he had got several well-paying job offers from some multinational companies. But he had pended his decision. While shuffling through the books one day he had learned about Kausani, the place he had never heard of until then. Its anonymity had generated a huge amount of excitement in him. So during the semester-break, he packed his bags and boarded the first train to Kathgodam from where he took a bus to Kausani.

It wasn't a vacation trip. It was a soul-searching yatra. Here he, in the lap of nature at its best, wished to find answers to one question.

Of all of his parents' worlds, which one was his, or, which world did he belong to, or which world did he wish to choose?

Chapter Three

* * *

In the struggle for primacy, the man had forgotten that God and not he, was the master of this universe. Through the elements of nature, He controlled all forms of existence on this planet. One didn't have to be a believer to see it.

The next morning was cloudy. A light drizzle forced the valley-fog to rise up and cover up the Himalayas. It disappointed several enthusiasts who had waited for hours to get a glimpse of the rising sun. And many people, who had kept a night's halt at Kausani on their itinerary so that they could see the sunset and sunrise, were disheartened. This experience had been a heart-aching one; unlikely to be forgotten so soon, because none of them were sure, when and whether they would come there the next time. Bad luck had poured water over their plans.

And those staying back weren't going to have any luck with the weather either. The rain that had started at about eight in the morning with a drizzle turned into a downpour as the day progressed, confining people to their homes and hotels, and initiating a debate amongst them about its intent. The prospect of an early monsoon had enlivened the discussion. Their parched lands and parched hearts for past two months or so had been waiting for the rain. But the hills, unlike the plains, weren't dependent on the monsoon. The rain here was a local occurrence, not enslaved to any season in particular. Like other elements of nature, it too was its own master.

Vedanta sitting in the room watched the day's plans go awry. With not much to do, he went about shifting the furniture according to his liking. He drew the bed closer to the window from where, he sitting or lying could watch a portion of the valley and sky. A reclining chair by the bed added another option. All the while a lone bird flew past the window now and then. Sound of random vehicles plying to and fro to the valley interrupted the tranquillity of the place. If one moment the sun blazed to berate the city folks for the havoc they caused to the environment, the next moment the cool breeze reminded them there was still some hope left.

The closest cluster of pine drew his attention. It had trees of all shapes and sizes, as if it were a joint family of grandparents, parents, youngster and toddlers.

Admiring the beauty of nature, he celebrated the rainy day by gulping down umpteen teas with generous helpings of *pakodas*. After dinner, he prayed for a bright sun the following day. For a while he wrestled with incongruous thoughts. It caused him a huge mental drain. And he dozed off straight away. In the middle of the night he was woken up by a sudden gust of rain. He had left the window open to let the fresh mountain breeze in.

The rain fell without any pattern, creating a cacophony that at times was made pleasant by sporadic light showers. In front of the balcony stood a huge rose mallow tree whose branches overhung the railing. Its white, yellow and pink flowers covered a third of the balcony and brightened up Ved's every morning. And across the road was a gazebo that gave a 180 degree view of the Snow Mountains and where tourists spent quality time during snack and mealtimes. It was a preferred place for many travellers to watch the sunrise.

The raindrops on the tree, road and gazebo produced different sounds. The noise on the soft, large leaves was smooth, on the mud, rough and on the tin-roof jarring. And the farthest sound was the loudest. He put cotton in his ears to avoid its clanging. In a few minutes the soft sound died down; the rough sound ebbed and the jarring sound softened up.

Still sleep was hard to come by and so he sat up in bed and gazed into the black outside. The raindrops pattered on the windowpanes. Against the divine flashes in the distance, the gazebo looked like a giant ghost surrounded by several dwarf ghosts. The fog was out on a regular beat to guard the place from the demons, notorious for their attacks during the darkness. The clouds had begun to split and scatter, exposing several starlit tracts.

Quietness of the night produced a low single pitch, tone, causing a constant echo in the air. It was a musical lullaby, so sweet that it had put the whole countryside into a sound sleep. But he lay wide awake. In his ears echoed his father's words, said behind a mysterious smile, "Son, I'm happy that you, unlike your elder brother, have chosen to ponder before making the important decision about your career. Remember, you must know what you want out of your life and not what life can give you. And if you fail to find the answer, sit under the stars."

His father had said something so significant in such simple words that its essence had escaped his mind then. It had begun to make some sense now. He racked his brains, trying to recollect if his father had said something more. But when he couldn't, he fell asleep.

The next day Ved awoke to a chilly morning. The tap

water was freezing cold. It seemed as if June had borrowed a day from December. And this hired day was more loyal and colder than it was in its parent month. People had put on sweaters, coats and jackets. The older folks had worn an extra piece of woollen clothing. The arrogant day revelled in self-importance and showed off its new found power. In the month of December its existence was anonymous in the midst of colder and drier days.

The commotion in the hotel caught Ved's attention. He reached out for the watch. It had struck eight a moment ago. On inquiry from the waiter, who brought him morning tea, he could learn a little about the cause of it. So, he dressed up in haste and climbed down the stairs to the lobby, from where emanated the sounds of hurrying feet and confusing voices. A motley crowd stood in there. Many distraught faces said something serious had happened.

He pushed his way through the throng and noticed an old man lay on the couch, mumbling, "I wish to die in this holy land."

"Papa, *pagla gaye ho ka*," a male, in mid-thirties, blurted.

"*Chup*," an old voice shut him up. Then a corpulent woman bent down and whispered, "*Hahn*, what did you say?"

"Leave me to die here, please..." the ailing man mumbled.

"Have you lost your mind?" the old woman whispered in his ears loosening his loincloth, and then rising, told her sons, "Your father says, take him home."

A few minutes later the old man fell unconscious. Jittery, people looked at one another in needless anxiety and yelled, "Call the doctor, call the doctor." A nervous receptionist rang up the local medico whose clinic was located a few houses from there. After a while all eyes turned to a man, accompanied by a local boy with the doctor's bag, rushing towards them in an unusual hurry. As he came closer, the stethoscope hung around his neck, shone. "Doctor Sahib!" several sighs of relief filled the air.

Dinesh Joshi, a native had served as a nursing assistant in the army medical corps for over twenty years, with more than half his service in the military hospitals. A couple of years ago, he had retired as a havildar and made this town as his new home, though he hailed from a village in Chamoli District in the Garhwal hills. What he lacked in knowledge tried to make up with his diligence. Out of respect the locals addressed him as 'Doctor Sahib', though he had no formal medical degree.

A half covered veranda housed his clinic, while the back portion consisting of two bedrooms and kitchen, made up his modest house in which he lived with his wife. The two married sons served in the army and visited them during the leave. Apart from those months the couple lived a blissful life. Dinesh and his wife were a regular at every social function in the villages around Kausani. The government doctor at the local dispensary seldom stayed there, and so the folks relied on him for treatment.

Dinesh always wore an OG trouser, more out of necessity to use them till they were worn out than any pride. A shirt and a tweed coat in winters completed his attire. High ankle army boots that never failed to draw envious glances, made his walk easy on the slopes. The stethoscope was a gift from the army major with whom he had served before retiring and the satchel his own of the army kit. Emergency or no emergency; he treated every call as an emergency.

Pushing through the small crowd, the medico reached the old man. He bent down, put fingers before the patient's nose and with the tips of thumb and index finger opened the pupils, one by one. Then in a diligent manner the compounder ran the stethoscope over old man's chest, heart and stomach several times, trying to diagnose. As he gave the stethoscope a little push on the tummy, the old man let out a loud, smelly fart. People around made faces and covered their noses with hand. The medico turned his face away and smiled.

Then he stood up wiping sweat off his forehead with a kerchief and spoke to a burly man standing close by, "Don't worry, your father will be all right in an hour's time. It's a gastric trouble, which has caused sudden chest pain. It's not a heart attack. However, I suggest you show him to a medical specialist in Haldwani."

The hefty man, the patient's eldest son, in mid-fifties with streaks of grey in unkempt hair, when heaved a sigh of relief, his whole body in loose kurta and pyjamas shook. Then he, turning to his mother, spoke in soft whispers to seek approval for the decision he had already taken based on the doctor's advice. The old woman's affirmative nod eased out the knots on his forehead. The son lifted his kurta, put his hand inside the inner pocket of the bundi, took out cash, paid up the doctor's fees and expressed profuse thanks.

A few yards away two women smelling of sweat and cheap scent, one ten years younger than the other, talked, frowned and scowled at the crowd. From their knotted foreheads and arched eyebrows, Ved guessed them to be the patient's daughters-in-law. He closed in to eavesdrop. They chatted in a low voice and whenever their mother-in-law gave both a stern stare, they fell silent.

Both were upset by the old man's sudden illness, which in all likelihood threatened to cut short their trip. And this drove them mad. The young wives' grudges were many, but one that hurt them the most was their freedom to dress, like other women there, had been curtailed due to the presence of in-laws. In Varanasi with great enthusiasm both women had packed their Salwar kamiz, and jeans and top, but they had to replace them with saris when their husbands had told them that parents were also going to Kausani.

So, for the young mothers nothing had changed between Kashi and Kausani except that here they didn't have to do the household chores; otherwise both wrapped themselves in a six-metre sari and had to cover their heads with palloo before in-laws. What a vacation it was turning out to be? They bemoaned. And both, in their minds, had planned to deny sex to their husbands for some days as revenge for spoiling their holidays. But a housewife's capacity for such revenge was limited.

"I had told everyone at home not to get the old man along, but this *budiya* wouldn't listen to anyone. Our vacation is as good as over," blurted the younger daughter-in-law.

"Why blame her? It's the fault of our husbands who outdo each other in displaying their love for their parents," growled the elder one. "I don't know what these greedy men are after. It seems the old man has promised them some buried riches after his death."

"Yeah, look how subservient they are with their mother. Sometimes I wonder what she feeds them to wield such explicit obedience from them."

"This old couple won't die so soon."

"Yes, you are right. Both won't leave us until they have sucked the last ounce of blood from our bodies," spoke the younger daughter-in-law. "My sister is lucky. She lives with her husband alone without the burden of her in-laws. They go on long holidays every year, not like us once in five years."

Not to be left behind, the elder daughter-in-law bragged, "My sister goes on holidays twice a year."

"Thank God! They aren't married to the

shopkeepers," both spoke in unison, and sighed with relief.

Then a brief pause followed.

"Our utility is to raise children, do household chores and satisfy their physical desires," said the elder daughter-in-law, with disdain in her voice.

"Pray to God the old man doesn't die here, otherwise our husbands won't go anywhere for the vacation for a long, long time."

An old man, standing nearby, overheard that badmouthing, and looking at his wife, commented, "These days younger generation has no respect for the elders. I don't know where this world is headed to?"

"Hell," she shot back. "Where else do you think? Why lose peace of mind over things we can't change? Come on; let's go away from these evil women." Then she held his hand, and dragged him away from there. The old man's face puckered as if he would cry any moment.

The back biting went on and on, and got bitter. Ved didn't have the heart to hear it further. The women's anger was justified. With holiday spoilt, they were taking out frustration on their husbands and in-laws. A moment later, they were silenced by the old woman's stinging rebuke. She asked them to pack up the suitcases and be ready to move out within half-hour. Cursing their fate, the poor wives moved towards the hotel rooms. It was an end to their dream holiday; an end to an important wish. Those young hearts had hoped to get a week's relief from the dullness of the household chores, but even God had been deaf to their prayers. Why the old woman always dictated their lives? Why their husbands behaved like puppets? What had they done to deserve this fate? They fought tears and bitterness as they packed bags.

But their half-dozen children, four boys and two girls, who played outside the hotel, weren't that much shocked by this unexpected turn of events. Perhaps they had got an inclination about it when they had seen their grandfather fall on the floor, and hence were busy in making the most of it. A little later they were dragged away by their fathers and put into the waiting vehicles.

After some time two cars jam-packed with luggage and passengers moved down the serpentine road, straightening out in the valley below. Once they were out of sight, the crowd dispersed. Gossip filled the air in the lobby, in the corridors, and in the rooms.

The hotel staff breathed a sigh of relief. The manager's sigh was the deepest and loudest. A death in the hotel at this time of the year, peak tourist season, would have dealt a serious blow to his business.

As Ved was about to move away from there, he heard a voice, "Sir, sorry for the inconvenience. Everything's okay now."

His heard turned. It was an anxious receptionist, who shaken by that incident, still recovered from the shock. He walked up to her and said, "I think you need to take a break."

"Yeah, you're right," she gave a grateful smile and left the desk.

Ved returned to the room where Rakesh waited upon him and enquired whether he would have lunch in the room or in the restaurant. He spoke nothing. Perhaps his mind was still occupied by the incident. It had caused a minor disruption in his routine. Somehow he wasn't able to concentrate and was keen to know more about the old man. Part of his worries was related to the compounder's diagnosis that hadn't been convincing. The patient needed urgent care of a cardiologist. He prayed for the man.

"Sir, don't worry about the sick man. He will be okay once he reaches Haldwani," Rakesh tried to comfort him.

"I hope so."

"Sir, there is an interesting thing I forgot to tell you about the old man. Last evening when I had gone to serve him tea, he had expressed his desire to die here in the *Devbhumi*. When I asked him why he wanted to die in this remote place when every devout Hindu wished to die in Kashi to get Moksha? His simple answer was this land was as holy as Kashi's. But his wife and sons thought otherwise. They doubted the old man had become senile, otherwise why would he talk of dying in a place other than Kashi, where they belonged."

"So the family was from Varanasi."

"Yes, sir."

"You see some old beliefs, however wrong they might be, refuse to die down. It's a strong conviction amongst the Hindus that the person who dies in Kashi is sure to attain the Moksha. Saint Kabir, born in Kashi, was against this belief and hence he chose to fight against it and several such bad customs. He chose to die in Maghar, about 200 km from Kashi. It was believed that anybody who died in Maghar was sure to be reborn as a donkey. Though Kabir tried to convince the common folks that one would get the Moksha irrespective of the place of one's death, most people seldom believed him. So, how can one blame the old man's family? I feel sad for him."

"Sir, isn't God supposed to be present everywhere?" Rakesh gave an innocent look.

"Yeah, I guess so," was Ved's confused reply, "but I'm not too sure. I feel God favours the believers over the non-believers, the rich over the poor, the city folks over the village folks."

A confused Rakesh gave a questioning glance.

"If you go to a big city," Ved went on, "and see the

slums next to swanky apartments, you will experience His presence more in some places and less in others."

To a simple villager God was kind and just to one and all. He had been raised on this belief. Listening to anything about God that portrayed Him in bad light was blasphemous. But he could never be rude to the guest, as he believed in the ancient Hindu saying, 'Atithi devo bhav.'

"Anyway, I think whatever has happened is for the good of the old man," Rakesh tried to end the argument. "Sir, it's time for lunch."

"Yeah," said Ved with a blank face. "I'll go down to the restaurant."

Until afternoon the day was gone in the activities related with the old man's sickness. All of the hotel staff and the visitors had willy-nilly got involved into the incident to see its happy conclusion. And by the time they had lunch, the tourists were too tired to venture out and therefore, had chosen to take a siesta.

Vedanta stretched himself on the bed for a catnap, but in vain. A moment later he sat in the chair and resumed reading Homer's Odyssey, which he had started during the journey up to there. He laboured hard to finish the next two chapters as the angry wind banging the windowpanes often drew his attention outside to the mist and rain swirling down the hills.

Towards evening arrived the June dusk. It spread its warmth over Kausani. Under a dim sky the shadows lengthened in the valleys and then spread out to the hilltops. What a waste the day had been! He reflected. From dawn to dusk he hadn't been able to collect any positives. The clouds had precluded the sunrise and the sunset, and for better part of the day it had remained misty and overcast.

And nobody mourned the day's loss more than those travellers for whom it was their last day there. With pain of loss in their hearts, they went to bed early to be able to return home after the sunrise.

For Ved, though, it was going to be a long night of reflection. Since his arrival there, he had found serenity in his thoughts. At home their anarchy had torn his mind apart, and caused a great deal of distress, but Kausani's tranquil environs had a soothing effect on his turbulent consciousness.

Somehow he had an intuition that future days held a surprise for him. What could it be? In his mind many possibilities came and went. But one thought brought a smile on his lips. And it proved to be precursor of a sweet dream.

Excited, he hit the sack.

Chapter Four

* * *

A girl child's life in the Indian household is a story of blatant prejudice. The moment she makes her journey into this world out of her mother's womb, she suffers cold stares and cruel jibes. Too young to understand the meaning of either, she smiles at anyone and everyone who gives her a look. Her acts of smiling and crying go on and on as she passes from one lap to another. As she grows up she has to swallow the daily dose of discrimination with every morsel. At every family gathering and mealtime people make her feel she isn't a permanent member of the family. Often her parents tell her she is the '*paraya dhan*' and will one day leave for her real home, that of her husband's. At tender age when she should be playing with toys she is reminded about the marriage, a word alien to her innocent mind. As a result, her emotional and physical growth is faster than it should be in the normal case. In the process she loses her childlike simplicity and enthusiasm.

Yamini's childhood had been no different.

Being the lone daughter amongst three siblings she had an uninspiring upbringing. Most of her time, with two elder brothers, was spent more in squabbling than playing or caring. Denial of a glass of milk and an egg, or an extra helping of her favourite vegetable on many an occasion after a few years had stopped to cause her any hurt. When she talked with other girls in the neighbourhood and found their stories were no different from hers, she, in her innocent mind, had presumed that perhaps the boys were given better food because they were required to do hard manual work when they grew up.

As a young child she, sitting on the rooftop with text books, would often gaze at the mountains for hours in awe and draw inspiration from them. Once a while she prayed for a good job so that she could afford to eat plenty of chocolates, drink milk and eat good food. These small wishes formed big parts of her biggest dream with which she began her each day. As the years went by she grew up, but not her dream.

After some years the brothers got married and moved away to different towns in the plains; one for a good job opportunity and the other for business. The retired father had spent his entire savings in settling down his sons. For a few years, though, everything in the Bisht family remained hunky-dory. Every month the sons sent money home and came to visit their parents in Almora each year. But this didn't last long. After four years all of a sudden the money orders stopped. However, the father never forgot to visit the post office every month to enquire about it. After six months when his patience ran out, he called up both sons who gave silly excuses for not being able to send him the money. That moment the old man realised that his wife and he had become a burden on their sons. It was one thought he had dreaded all along, but never entertained in his mind because he had been sure his sons, whom he had given a good Hindu upbringing, would look after him in the old age. How could his sons turn their backs on their parents in times of need? How could they not emulate the example of the great Shravan Kumar whose tale of sacrifice so often was narrated to them? He had pondered for long hours and found no answers.

Narendra Bisht's emotional and financial investments in his sons had been so complete that their betrayal had shattered him from within. He felt as if the bank in which he had deposited his lifetime's savings had gone bust. In Yamini, a final year college student, he saw a ray of hope, but felt ashamed to think of living on the daughter's earnings, a sin considered by the old-fashioned Indian men. But he had no other option left. A small piece of agricultural land was sufficient to grow vegetables. His poor health prevented him from taking up any job. Pension was spent on the grocery bills. With sky rocketing inflation, he knew, it too would soon fall short. The medical bills were paid off with borrowed money.

Yamini, after completing her degree, came home and found the situation had turned worse. She extracted the secret out of her mother. It took her no time to realise her father had become an emotional wreck. She was pained by his deteriorating health. Like this, she knew, he wouldn't last for more than a couple of years. Mother was stronger. She knew father was too proud to ask her for any help. That night she promised her parents she would stay back with them in Almora.

It took her a moment to decide it, but several nights to get over the feeling this decision would require her to give up the scholarship for higher education and thus a chance for better job opportunities.

A month later her good looks and beamish smile got her a receptionist's job in a hotel in Kausani, a two-hour leisure drive from Almora. It had brought happiness in her parents' lives. It had fulfilled hers.

In five years her job had given her ample opportunities to interact with hundreds of people from different walks of life. In the peak tourist season she on a given day got to meet dozens of persons belonging to different states, religion and class. During the summer, people from across the country thronged Kausani, while the Bengalis came there during the Puja holidays. The winters were preferred by the honeymooners, the young couples and a handful of writers. But it was the Gujaratis who brought the maximum business to the place all the year round.

Over the years she had learnt to converse in Bengali and Gujarati more out of necessity and it had endeared her to the old travellers from these two states. The young generation, however, never forgot to flaunt their knowledge of English.

And there was yet another art in which her job had helped her to acquire mastery. She could read the language of eyes and detect in them the love, lust, compassion, contempt, empathy and apathy. From a glance she could make out the hidden intent behind the innocent looks, and fantasies playing in the minds behind the mischievous smiles.

It made her feel exquisite. It made her feel vulnerable.

Her affable manners and disarming smile made many a man, not used to these things at home, to stop at the reception longer in order to prolong chat with her. On occasions when men were accompanied by spouses, she adopted a businesslike tone. A millimetre increase in her smile was provocation enough to attract not-mess-with-me stares from jealous wives. The older women had no such life-threatening concerns, as they were convinced of their husbands' lack of charm to win over a young receptionist.

So her life had a smooth sailing until one October evening when a young and handsome man checked into the hotel. For the first time her heart missed a beat. For the first time she felt attracted to a complete stranger. For the first time she broke the employer's rule. And for the first time she fell in love.

It was love at the first sight.

Then for next one week they roamed the countryside hand in hand like childhood friends. During those sojourns she opened her heart to him, shared her disappointments and dreams with him. Those seven days were the best days of her life. His company had given her so much bliss she had hoped it to last her lifetime. Each day new promises were made. Each day love manifested itself in newer ways.

As the day of his departure drew close, she became edgy. To pacify her, he gave her the ring, which he had been carrying for a long time for his soulmate. For many moments she stood in disbelief. Then she accepted it as tears rolled down her eyes in joy. Next day he was gone but had left with her his phone number and address. The following day and days after when she rang up she got no response. A detailed inquiry revealed that the phone number and address were fakes. Helpless, she watched her world crumble into dust.

The poor soul had been too naïve to know the betrayal came in beautiful disguise and made the unsuspecting and vulnerable hearts its victims. The innocent love often fell prey to its charms and succumbed to its temptations.

Heartbroken, star-crossed; she would have ended her life had it not been for her old parents. Enraged, she threw away the ring in the river. Dumping the garbage of painful memories took longer, almost a year to get rid of those from her body and mind. The sight of holy Nanda Devi healed her soul.

Until Vedanta's arrival she hadn't been so frank and free with any other man. His eyes didn't speak the language of so many others'. She didn't know why, but in his presence she felt free from the shackles of formality.

And he didn't seem to mind it. So whenever she got any chance to tease him, she didn't let it go by.

Next day when he ran into her, she was in a mischievous mood, "Sir, any luck with soul-searching?"

Ved halted and replied with a playful glint in his eyes, "You know, one night I let off my soul to wander for a while out of the room when it begged me, but thereafter it never came back to me. I've been searching for it since then."

"Don't worry, sir. The holy mountains will protect it. You'll find it soon."

"May I know the name of my well-wisher?" he was hesitant.

"Yamini."

"Ms Yamini, you're indeed kind," he expressed gratitude.

"Sir, please call me Yamini."

"Ma'am, I'm afraid I can't do that. We don't know each other well," he went on, "familiarity often gives false hopes."

"I'm old enough to know every dark cloud doesn't bring in the rain," she spoke. Her voice had a tinge of sadness and a touch of reality too.

He saw disappointment writ large on her face. "Yeah, that's true but some clouds do bring in the rain. One has to wait for the right one."

Managing a faint smile, she queried, "Are you a philosopher, or a poet?"

"Neither," he replied. "I'm an engineer."

"Great words of wisdom coming from an engineer," she quipped.

"Why? Can't engineers be wise people?" he teased.

"I didn't mean that," she blushed.

He looked the other way and when his gaze

returned to her face he found sadness had reappeared in her eyes.

"Didn't someone ever tell you that you look so stunning when your smile is uncontrolled?"

After a brief hesitation, she replied, "A year ago a man did. It took me a while to learn he had told me a lie."

Those painful words came out from a tender heart that seemed to have recovered from the storm of betrayal. He chose to offer her some comfort.

"Do you know, what's the biggest crime a man can commit?"

"No."

"To hurt a good-looking woman like you," he went on, "and the man who has caused you so much suffering is sure to burn in hell. I believe the right guy is about to arrive in your life. Perhaps he is finding his way up to this place."

It brought a faint smile on her face.

"Keep smiling. This way you light up this place," he said handing her the chocolate.

"Chocolate!"

"Yeah, it's a bribe for putting up with my weird behaviour," he said with grin.

"Thank you."

"You can smile. There's nobody around to admonish you for it," he winked.

She burst into laughter. He joined her.

Chapter Five

❄   ❄   ❄

The word 'grandmother' brought to one's mind the instant image of an old woman with snow-white thin hair, face with wrinkles more than her age, sunken cheeks and bones occupying more volume than flesh. But with her ever-radiant eyes and sharp mind she sang lullabies and narrated stories to her grandchildren. With passage of time her persona in the minds of the children acquired a mystery. And the old woman who told countless tales, of all genres, became a legend herself in the stories of her grandchildren.

Nandini was one such grandmother. But she was much more than being an ideal grandma to Saranga, her favourite grandchild. She was Sara's best friend.

It was a great moment in her life. That evening her darling Saranga was coming home from the hostel during the semester break. Since five in the morning she had looked at the clock a hundred times. The red threads in her eyes showed she hadn't slept well last night. How could she? She was dying to catch a glimpse of her grandchild, kiss her and hug her. Every now and then this thought brought tears in her eyes. In an instant the memories of past twenty years flashed before her eyes, frame by frame, as though she were watching a bioscope. The first image of a day-old girl, spongy, vulnerable, wrapped in a cloth, giving a cute smile to everyone, was still so fresh in her mind.

The film ran in the fast forward mode. She had little time left. An hour later she was to go to the railway station to receive her. It was one duty she had been doing since Saranga had gone to the hostel four years ago, and she had won this after a hard fought argument with his son and daughter-in-law, both of who were reluctant to concede to her demand due to her poor health. The couple often found themselves helpless in front of her stubbornness.

She commanded unwavering respect from the second generation Dattas. Only one person in the household could question her and that was Saranga. The girl took so much liberty with her she treated her more like a friend than a grandma. And the family's great matriarch enjoyed this special equation with the youngest member of the family.

Theirs was a special relationship, separated and bound by a gap of two generations. With Saranga in her heart, she began and ended her day.

Today was a special day. She was going to see her grandchild in bone and flesh. On this day she without fail put on her best clothes. Since the death of her husband ten years ago she had lost any interest to look good. But for Saranga she did this. In her twilight years she lived everyday for her darling granddaughter.

In needless anxiety, Nandini sometimes looked at the watch and sometimes at the odometer, which oscillated between eighty and ninety. But to her it seemed as if the car moved slower than a bullock cart. Fidgeting in the seat, she every second urged the driver to move on faster. Between dutiful nods Abdul did increase the speed to bring it down the next moment as he had explicit orders from the master to drive her safely. But if there were no such instructions he wouldn't have driven her fast either.

Half-hour later Abdul wheeled the car into the parking and helped her get out. Both moved to the station and waited for the train, due to arrive in minutes, for which repeated announcements were being made. And as soon as the train pulled at the platform, her eyes welled up. The sight of Saranga made tears trickle down her wrinkled face.

A moment later, Sara got down and screamed in delight, "Dadi". Both got in a tight embrace. For several moments thereafter neither spoke a word. Their tears did the talking.

Then Sara, separating from her grandma, teased, "Dadi, your bones hurt. It seems you have been fasting a lot."

"Now that you are back I won't," replied the old woman, wiping her eyes.

On the way back, Saranga bombarded Nandini with a barrage of questions and wanted updates about everything. And once she had satisfied her granddaughter's curiosity, she, turning to Sara, said with a smile, "Since we left home Abdul must have asked me a dozen times when Saranga beti is coming home, but he is pretending as if you aren't travelling with us."

"I guess poverty makes people miser in their emotions too. They are fearful to spend all of it in one go," Saranga said.

The old woman gave the little woman a long admiring glance. Then both watched Abdul drive through the crowded streets. These were tensed times for him, they could sense it and hence, they didn't want to cause him any distraction. Therefore, they kept quiet as long as the din outside lasted.

And once the car pulled on an open stretch, Nandini resumed conversation, "Abdul is a third generation man from his family working with us. His grandfather, who then was a young man during the partition, was caught by a Hindu mob and was about to be lynched when your grandpa, who was passing by, stopped and told the mob he was his cousin and thus saved him. Later he started working in our household as a driver. And when he died, his eldest son replaced him. Some years back when Abdul's father's eyesight deteriorated, he sent him to work with us. Abdul says his son will replace him when he retires. The boy is quite respectful to me. One day he told me his family will continue to serve us forever as a mark of gratitude for saving his grandpa's life. Though we've told him many times that he is free to choose a better paying job elsewhere, he wouldn't listen."

Sara's heart was filled with respect for Abdul.

Nandini said with a sigh, "Perhaps he is unwilling to leave the comfort of our household for a few hundred rupees more."

"Oh, now I know why he is so affectionate to me," said Saranga. "That's the perk of being your favourite."

The grandmother gave a huge smile.

Fifteen minutes later they arrived home.

The moment Saranga set her foot inside the house, everybody's eyes lit up. Grandma halted her and gestured Alka to bring the evil eye remover; a paper packet containing red chillies, rock salt and a few more things. Nandini took the packet in her hand, closed Sara's eyes, waived it from top to bottom, and around her head several times mumbling mantra and then handed the packet back to Alka, who took it back to the kitchen to burn, and report the result to her mother-in-law. It was a ritual she performed every time Saranga came home, and also every week when she stayed longer.

And when Sara gave her an enquiring look, Nandini said, "Don't worry; I'll teach you how to remove the evil eye when you get married so that you can protect yourself and your husband from it."

"Dadi," Sara blushed and ran inside.

After a quick wash she, flanked by both women, sat at the dining table and devoured her favourite snacks, prepared with great care by her mother. A piping hot tea enhanced the taste of those delicacies. If her mother had her way, she would still be drinking horlicks. She ate as if she hadn't eaten for months. Her talks were cut short by Nandini who urged her to concentrate on eating. And once she was done she stood up and emptied her dirty clothes into the laundry bag. Then for next few minutes she kept herself busy with needless things as Nandini looked on.

After finishing, she caught her grandma's arms and both came out into the veranda, their favourite place. She sat down on the floor and put her head in the lap of grandma who ran bony fingers through her hair. And when the silence began to bite, she spoke, "Dadi, please don't cry. I'm back."

"All right," said Nandini, fighting tears. "Beta, you are the apple of my eyes. If I had my way I won't let you go away even for a second."

"Dadi, then you will have to keep me illiterate." Sara teased.

"*Dhat*, your dadi isn't a selfish woman," Nandini retorted.

After a brief pause, Sara asked, "Dadi, could you tell me why you named me Saranga?"

"Why? You don't like the name?" the grandma gave a questioning stare. "It's so melodious. When you say Saranga it seems as if Narada has strummed his Veena."

"No, no. I love the name but my friends keep asking me who was Saranga." Anticipating an exciting tale she got up and pulled her chair closer.

Nandini gave her grandchild an affectionate pat

on the head and began, "Sarang is the sun and Saranga its energy. As sun is the source of life to this universe, so are you, the source of energy and light in our lives.

"Great! I'm so humbled."

In walked Alka and whispered to her mother-in-law, "Amma, the chillies didn't smell at all."

The old woman gave her an I-knew-it glance and sighed with relief. Her wrinkles lit up. Then turning to Sara, she said, "Beta, the world is full of evil people. You should take precautions."

The sound of doorbell cut short their chat. Alka had returned to the door. Sara sprang up on her feet and ran towards the entrance. Her father was home.

"It's Keshav," Nandini shouted from behind.

"Daddy," she hugged him as soon as he stepped inside.

"Hi, how's my little sweetheart?" her father asked planting a kiss on her cheeks.

She complained, "Why didn't you come to the station?"

"An important business meeting kept me away but don't worry, my darling, we've full month to catch up on our common interests."

"No dad. Just a week."

"Why?"

"Ask mummy," she said taking the briefcase from his hands, and ran away.

An hour later they all sat together for dinner.

Turning to wife, Keshav asked, "Alka, Where is Sara planning to go on vacation?"

"She wants to visit Kausani with her friends."

"That's a nice place."

Alka wasn't enthused by Sara's idea. She was afraid to send her off to a remote place without any family member.

Looking at her mother-in-law to garner support, she spoke, "Amma, I'm scared to send Sara on this trip. Every day we read and hear about many horrific incidents. Demons, in human garb, lurk around every place and strike women of every age."

"I know we live in unsafe times, but still women do travel alone in connection with their jobs, or on vacations. Our Sara isn't alone. She has a dozen girls for company. They will look after one another. Moreover, the place where they are going is inhabited by good people," argued Keshav.

Nandini also came out in support of her son. She added, "Don't worry; our Saranga is a grown-up girl. She can take care of herself. The other day when I narrated Draupadi's story, she questioned me why didn't Kunti, realising her folly later, cancel her dictate to Yudhisthir to share Draupadi with his brothers. I was left speechless. And if this wasn't enough, she asked me, whether I as Draupadi's mother-in-law would have let this injustice happen. This question haunted me for days. How could a woman let another woman be shared by five men, as if she weren't a human being but some commodity? The way Saranga questions the wrongs of our scriptures assures me she has the confidence to face the world on her own."

By the time dinner got over the issue was settled in Sara's favour. Alka also gave her grudging consent. Keshav advised her to carry plenty of cash as ATMs were less reliable in the hills. Then for next one week Sara spent her time in the company of grandma and mother whose list of do's and don'ts kept increasing with every passing day. She knew their concerns for her safety were correct.

On the eight evening Sara and her friends boarded the train for Kathgodam. And on the ninth morning they caught a bus, which during three-hour journey passed through the green hills dotted with huts. The road ran along the river, carrying gurgling water that became noisier when squeezed by big rocks. The girls sang and danced, inviting giggles from the local passengers. And whenever the bus negotiated a blind bend, it let out a screech. The driver's forehead filled with beads of sweat. The man cursed in Kumauni if the incoming drivers forgot to honk. After a brief lunch halt at Almora, the journey resumed.

From there on the road after a while opened out into a large valley, on either side of which lay the fields where men and women in colourful dresses worked; some did the weeding, some planted the rice saplings, and some watered the ploughed lands. And some distance away, a pair of oxen, whipped from time to time by the master, dragged the plough across a wet, brown soil. The sparse mustard fields broke the hegemony of the green over the countryside. Onto the right, patches of tea plantation on hill slopes brought a surprise look on several faces.

"Wow!" one girl exclaimed, "I wish to settle down here and work in the field alongside my husband."

"And walk into the nearby forest whenever you two feel horny," the second girl whispered with a wink.

"Yeah, that's not a bad idea at all," the third girl let off a huge sigh.

"The air is so fresh," the fourth girl, lost in her own world, said, drawing in a large breath.

"This place is out of a classic novel, so romantic, so sexy," the fifth girl's voice was choked with emotion.

The sixth girl listened to that conversation in amusement, and enjoyed the beauty of the countryside.

"Hey girls, chill. We've full one week to enjoy this and many more things," Sara spoke, rolling her eyes in mischief.

The bus moved on, as did their talks. Worn down by journey, the local folks had dozed off in order to take some rest before reaching home where a host of domestic problems awaited them. The bus passed through Someshwar, the place bustling with life. The empty and filled vehicles passed through the place, in needless hurry. In less than half-hour, the bus climbed up a winding gradient, passed by a sleepy hotel, and then glided through the market buzzing with tourists. It halted at the Chowk. The driver called out to the girls to get down. Once Sara and her friends, and a few local passengers had alighted from the bus, the driver honked and drove away to Bageshwar, the last stop.

The girls with luggage stood at the Chowk, where the mist dancing through the undulating lanes had blurred the edges of the buildings. They screamed in ecstasy.

Saranga had arrived in Kausani.

Chapter Six

❅ ❅ ❅

Above the rosy horizon the sky was filled with white and grey clouds of different shapes and sizes. Beneath it, in the far distance, stood the snow-capped peaks, reaching out to the heavens above. Those mountains rose above a swathe of thick white clouds. Closest were the hard pine-forested rolling hills that lay subdued in humility. The two mountain ranges in between them had squeezed a large viridescent valley that was half under shade and half under light, and was dotted with dainty little houses. The fragments of fog hid in the folds. On to the right corner of the canvas was a small hillock on which was seated a young woman whose ethnic skirt billowed in the wind. With a broken twig, she seemed to draw sketches on the ground.

It looked like a 17th century Indian painting in which the sense of space was flatter, but the colours were brilliant and the delineation delicate. Imagery of the landscape seemed to have come from the creator's dreams. The canvas contained bright blues and greens that highlighted character of the land. Chiaroscuro characterised the creation. Beauty of the picture lay in its simplicity and its ability to encourage the viewers to imagine it was real, not colours on the canvas.

Could any ordinary mortal have painted this?

Vedanta, standing some feet away, asked himself. For long he marvelled at the creation. The woman's picture held his maximum attention. Her beauty was enhanced manifolds by the streaks of light falling on her face. She seemed in a pensive mood, perhaps reflecting on her past, or contemplating about the future.

Such incredible subjects never existed in the real world, but in the surreal world of the artists.

"Why did painters paint such unique subjects?" it was one question that always baffled Ved whenever he saw a nice painting. That moment he wished to put life into those lifeless subjects. But alas! He had no divine powers and God wasn't going to oblige him with them.

Then he felt someone give him a gentle push from behind. He turned back. It was the fog, which swirled around him and within minutes filled the area in front. It occurred to him then that he wasn't in any art gallery appreciating that painting, but stood under the sky watching the Master at work. And He was one painter who worked on the same canvas again and again, and kept no records of his previous works. His each creation that lasted for a few moments was a perfect masterpiece. Only the mortals indulged in imperfections.

As thick blanket of fog began to envelop the mountains and valleys his eyes searched for the woman who until a moment ago had adored the frame. The spot where she sat was empty. He rushed towards it but the fog beat him. The whole area was swallowed up by it.

"Was she for real, or some ghost?" doubts had started to cloud his mind but whoever she was, he had no doubts, she was a gorgeous woman. Finding the track through the mist wasn't easy. Half-hour later he hit the main road and breathed a sigh of relief. Lost in thoughts, he found his way back to the hotel through bad visibility. After a while he bumped into a man.

"I hope you are okay," an anxious voice asked him.

"Sorry sir. I wasn't looking at the road," Ved expressed regret.

"Don't blame yourself. It's so dark out here," the man said. "Something important would have brought you out in this bad weather."

"No, no. When I came here the weather was fine. Then in minutes it packed up. It has become scary now," Ved replied. "But it seems you left Kausani a few moments ago. You could have waited there for the fog to clear away."

A brief silence ensued. As the visibility improved, he had a close look at the man, dressed in saffron. A sense of awe overwhelmed him.

Inching closer, Ved commented, "So, I'm in august company."

"No, no. I'm an ordinary mortal."

"You are being modest."

The man laughed. Ved felt as if that laughter was meant to assure him that stranger wasn't a saint, the likes of who wandered the holy lands in the Himalayas.

Bending forward, the man stared at Ved's face in deep study. His act made Ved nervous and uncomfortable. Then stepping back, the man said, "Deep lines on your forehead tell me your mind is in turmoil."

"Yes, but how do you know that?"

"The first time a young mind goes through this is when a person moves out in the world to achieve something, and the next time when he has achieved everything. And between these two stages a person lives several lives, often forgetting to live a true life," the stranger remarked. "But your predicament is different."

"What?" Vedanta was taken by surprise.

"You are here in quest of something," the man's

voice was calm.

"How do you know?" Ved asked, with growing interest.

"It's written on your face, your forehead."

"Come on, you can't be serious."

"Yes, I'm. Perhaps you don't know physiognomy is an ancient spiritual-psychological system of understanding a person's character by reading facial features and predicting future. In ancient India there were a few blessed souls who by looking at people could predict with high levels of accuracy. In today's world to some folks it comes as a siddhi (power) and to others it comes out of experience."

"You mean the ancient Hindus knew about it."

"Sure. Most of the ancient civilisations had a good knowledge of this. I've acquired it of late and I'm hopeful to unearth several secrets hidden in our scriptures on my way to finding the truth."

To Vedanta it sounded a little less convincing and a lot more interesting. He found hard to contain his excitement, "What else can you predict about my future?"

The man read a few more lines on Ved's forehead, and then sat down in contemplation. Ved waited.

"This place would provide answers to all your questions and also end your quest."

"Quest?"

"Yeah, quest for the soulmate."

"But it wasn't this I came here for," Ved's objection was mild.

"My son we all embark upon the journey to seek a particular thing, but by the end of it so many things about which we had never thought of, come our way. Your destiny has brought you to this place. Hers will follow suit. A fairy tale romance will culminate into marriage. But then ....," the man hesitated.

"Then what…?" enquired Ved, getting anxious. "I'm dying to hear everything you know about me."

"I'm afraid it's not so positive, but since you insist I shall tell you this too. After a few years a severe storm will hit your life and tear apart not two but several lives."

"What will cause this destruction?" questioned Ved, not believing a word of what he just heard.

"Maya."

"Maya?"

"Yes, call it illusion but I prefer Maya. Didn't Kabir say, '*Maya maha thagini sab jani*? (Maya is the greatest deceiver). It appears in different guises to different people. And its favourite disguise is greed."

"If I were to believe you, what could be the remedy for this?"

"I can't think of any. Keep away from Maya."

"What if I don't fall in love with the girl?"

"Can you do that?" the man quizzed. "Your eyes tell another tale."

Vedanta blushed. He hadn't taken his mind completely off from the woman he thought he had seen in the painting. Whatever might be his credentials, this man wasn't a simple person but someone who possessed divine powers.

"So, I'm condemned to a broken marriage," Ved murmured.

"Don't worry, there's hope, though. You will have to come back to this land for penitence and forgiveness. It's tough to predict the outcome now but if any miracle were to happen, it would happen right here, in this place."

Those words had replaced anxiety with hope. Ved breathed easier. With poise, he asked, "How will I recognise the love of my life?"

"Don't worry, your heart will," the man said.

"Remember, every quest comes loaded with two elements; fear and surprise. And it's up to the seekers to choose which of the two they want to burden themselves with."

"And which one's burden are you carrying?" Ved was curious.

"Surprise," was the banker's prompt reply. "Fear has long banished from my mind."

"I guess I'll have to carry the burden of both."

"Yeah," the banker stood up to leave. "It's time for me to resume my journey."

Vedanta took out a hundred-rupee note from the pocket and tried to give it to the man, "You will need this."

"Thanks," the man refused. "I long lost any requirement of these papers. When I was your age, I had a great yearning for them. I've seen them in different colours and designs. As a banker I earned millions in America and Africa."

"A banker!"

"Yeah, you heard me right. There was a time in my life when I was so obsessed with money that nothing else could give me greater pleasure. It gave me power to acquire anything I desired. The luxurious suites, the costliest wines, the expensive clothes and watches were a call away. Awash with wealth, I embarked upon the journey through the spiritual wastelands of the west to seek happiness in decadent and immoral things. It was a futile quest for everlasting bliss in the materialistic pursuits that lasted for a limited period. And therefore, it proved so thin, so temporary. Devastated, two years ago I freed myself from the bondage of avarice and came to the Himalayas in search of truth. I've trekked in the Alps and the Andes, but nowhere did I find the tranquillity that I find in this place."

"What made you to take this drastic step?"

"It's a long story I've no intention to burden you

with. Suffice to say I had to earn wealth to win over my love but when I had acquired it, I had lost her."

"Oh, so like Siddhartha you abandoned everything in search of the truth."

"I think we all have a bit of Siddhartha in ourselves," the man was philosophical. "It was easier for me to make the decision but afterwards the going became tough. It wasn't any easier for the great man too. As I search for my knowledge tree I need no wealth. All truth seekers have to lead a spiritual life because spirituality enables a man to see things, which are invisible to the physical eye. It enables him to learn lessons from the past and see future in the present. What I need is perseverance in the penance."

"You make me think if I were to renounce the world, I should do it now."

"My intention wasn't to influence your young mind in anyway. I explained the circumstances that led to my decision. The paths leading to the truth can be many. If Siddhartha chose the renunciation, then King Janak chose the opposite path to seek the truth. And both achieved it. So, you have to seek your own path. Until then consider honest living as the penance. Let deceit not be your Menaka."

"So, you consider truth-seeking the preserve of the old people."

"No. I think one gets His call for this."

"That means He considers me a sinner."

"That's a terrible thought, young man. You have more positive qualities. Don't let the demons of doubt cloud your mind. Remember, the battle between evil and good isn't fought on the battlefield, but within human minds. If each one of us fought this within ourselves and won, the world will become a peaceful place. In truth lies peace. And peace we all must seek, but perhaps time isn't ripe for you yet."

"So, I stand at the end of the queue of truth seekers."

Vedanta hadn't intended it to be a pun, but alas it had turned out one. It made him feel so small. How could he be so ungrateful to the man for his words of wisdom? He stole a glance at the man and found him calm, as he battled the turmoil within.

The man stood up. Their chanced meeting was about to end. He wished it had lasted a little longer.

"Kausani will give answers to all your questions. You won't have to venture far. Take this and save a happy moment each day in it," the man said, handing him a wooden box."

"Why? Won't heart suffice for this?"

"Don't we all live in this delusion?"

A puzzled Vedanta sometimes looked at the box and sometimes at the banker.

"Learn it yourself," The truth seeker smiled, turned back and then set off northwards.

"May I know your name, please?" begged Ved, raising voice.

"Call me Fakir," the stranger shouted without turning his head. The past was past and a hindrance in seeking the truth. Hence, he looked ahead at the Himalayas as he moved on.

From a banker to a vagabond what a transformation it has been? Ved murmured to himself as he watched Fakir disappear into the fog. Never before in his life had he encountered such an eventful day. Ever since the dawn the day's activities had unfolded in a mysterious way where each following event had been stranger than the one preceding it. It was one day he could have done without. It was one day he would like to forget, but he knew he wouldn't be able to do so. He pondered as he walked back to the hotel. On reaching the lobby he kept his head down and made a dash for the room.

Rakesh who had been waiting on him since long asked, "Should I get you lunch, sir?"

He nodded and entered the bathroom. The hot water calmed down his nerves to some extent. After lunch he asked Rakesh, "Do you believe in ghosts?"

Timing of the question took the waiter by surprise. But he had known tourists to ask weirder questions. So, he maintained his poise and answered, "Yes, sir. This I'm saying based on my personal experience and not on some heresy. Would you like to hear it?"

Two shockers in the day had been sufficient to disturb his peace of mind. A third one would have torn him apart from within. And he wasn't in the right frame of mind to take that risk.

So, he gave an excuse, "Sure, but today I'm so tired. May be some other day. Please get me tea at six."

The waiter nodded and left. Ved lay down on the bed to get some rest, but in vain. His mind was so cluttered up that it took him the whole evening to get rid of unwanted thoughts and by the time some success came his way, the night had fallen. He skipped dinner and instead, preferred to have a glass of hot turmeric milk, a famous grandma's recipe that in the past had helped him with sound sleep. But even this failed. He tossed and turned in the bed. The lonely night teased him, tormented him.

A lone dog, in the valley below, barked expecting other canines to share his concern for the village safety. But the other dogs slept in peace, assured that thievery in their village was a thing of the past as the last theft had happened about a decade ago. The unrequited old snarls got smothered under the weight of the night downpour.

Minutes later Vedanta too, listening to the whisper of the rain, fell asleep.

Chapter Seven

* * *

The morning-after was cloaked in quietude. In reluctance, the snow peaks showed up one by one. A thin white haze lay over the valley. Onto the right corner, a hummock, forested with pine trees, appeared like an island in the lake of white fog. The morning chill was pleasant. The houses, scattered on the slopes and in the valley, emerged. The last things to show up were the tea gardens. The stillness, untroubled by a low jungle buzz, promised to last the whole day. The lazy night had made a slow exit.

Rubbing sleep-swollen eyes, Ved awoke with a bad head. Though, last night before going to bed he had tried to put bizarre events out of his head, the dreams had turned out weirder and creepier. Perhaps a pre-dawn walk might lighten his head; he thought and after a quick shower rushed to the forest where he wished to observe the sunrise and where he hoped to find the woman of the painting.

Wish was driven by hope.

On arrival at the spot, where a day ago he had witnessed the most stunning spectacle of his life, he looked around for the girl. But alas! She wasn't there. The other settings were almost unchanged. If yesterday the same landscape breathed life, today it was lifeless. Leaning against the tree, he hoped for her to appear from behind one of those hills. As he looked around his eyes fell on a parrot sitting under the pinetree. The bird looked sad. It screeched time and again. A moment later another parrot flew in and sat beside it, and both exchanged loving glances. Hungry, they picked seeds. Ved wondered which of the two was female. A few minutes later the parrots squawked and flew away together. The light had become intense and beads of sweat pricked at his temples. His enthusiasm began to ebb away and he didn't stay there long.

Since six in the morning Rakesh had made a dozen rounds of the room, each time with a fresh cup of tea but had gone back disappointed. And when the clock in the corridor chimed ten o'clock, he got worried. How could he find Ved's whereabouts? The man carried no cell phone.

Clutching his head in despair, he sat down on the stairs and waited.

Rakesh was born in Dharchula, a village close to the Indo-China border. The pilgrims to the Man Sarovar Lake and the Mount Kailash made it a bustling place during summer months and gave its inhabitants business. His father ran a small hotel and made decent money. Often he had heard his parent's dream of constructing a hut and buying a piece of land of their own. That time he was seven years old and washed utensils in the hotel, while his mother did the cooking. When returning pilgrims narrated their heart-warming experiences of seeing the Kailash and taking a dip in the holy Lake, his young heart was filled with reverence. Listening to those tales he wondered whether some day he too would be able to undertake that arduous journey and see the abode of Lord Shiva. "What did his palace, built on the lofty Kailash, look like? What did the lake look like? How did its water cleanse people's sins? And what were the sins?"

To his uncorrupted mind it was difficult to decide

which human acts came under the category of sin. But one sin he was sure about. Sleeping with a woman, not your wife was considered the most despicable sin. He had heard several village elders say this, and those wise men could never be wrong because they predicted the rains, the landslides, the crops, etc. A few amongst them, in their younger days, had made the pilgrimage to the Holy Kailash as porters and so they were blessed souls.

During one such pilgrimage when a wealthy man made a lucrative offer to his father to carry the man's luggage, he couldn't refuse. Leaving home and hotel to his wife, his father left. Rakesh roamed the streets like a proud son. That season his father was the lone villager to undertake that journey. Then one day, after about a fortnight, the bad news came that a batch of sixty returning pilgrims and porters had died in a landslide, six miles short of Dharchula. His father was one of them.

A moment ago he had owned the whole world, a moment later his world had crumbled into pieces.

His mother cried day and night. When his tears dried up he tried to wipe hers. After the cremation of his deceased father the behaviour of his grandparents, uncles and aunts turned hostile. They abused his mother and him in the filthiest possible language. They beat the widow holding her responsible for her husband's death. The poor woman had no place to go. Her parents were too poor to support their widowed daughter.

To such destitute souls God offered solace. A small temple, located half-mile from the village, became her sanctuary where she often spent her daytime. But alas! This little happiness in her life was short-lived. One afternoon when her younger brother-in-law found her alone near the temple, he tried to rape her but when he didn't succeed he ran to the house and told everyone that he had caught the widow with another man. They all believed his lie right away, but no one spared a minute to hear her truth. She was branded a low woman and along with her son banished from the house. The cruel relatives had dispossessed her of her husband's share of property, the cruel fate of her dreams.

That night they slept in the barn of a neighbouring house and next dawn they hitched a ride in a truck and reached Almora where they stayed for some years before shifting to Kausani where he got a waiter's job in a hotel.

The sounds of hurrying steps broke his thoughts. Ved had entered the lobby. He sprang up on his feet and ran to him.

"Where have you been so early in the morning? Sir, I brought you tea at six and when I found the room empty, I got worried," Rakesh complained. "You should have taken the umbrella. It's a hot day."

"Sorry dear, I forgot to tell you. Also the weather surprised me," Ved pacified, placing hand on Rakesh's shoulder.

"Yeah, tourists who visit this place think it's free from heat and dust, but they don't know that weather in Kumaon in the last two decades has undergone a drastic change. Summer temperatures, which earlier never touched twenty, now often cross thirty-five degree Celsius. Earlier the houses had no fans, but nowadays every house has. Earth is becoming hotter day by day. Mother Earth is angry with misdeeds of her children who are causing her immense pain."

"Yes, you couldn't be more right. Next time I'll keep your advice in mind when I go out."

Opening the door for him, Rakesh ran back to get him tea, to be brewed in a special way. Tea leaves were crushed and mixed with sugar. Paste was then put into half-boiled water. A few minutes before straining, crushed ginger and tulsi leaves were added. Tea was served in a steel glass. It had taken him two days to perfect the technique.

"Refreshing tea," said Ved with a smile as soon as he had the first sip.

"Thank you, sir." Rakesh's eyes became moist.

"Yesterday I saw a young girl alone in the forest. It surprised me. Is it safe for women to roam around alone in lonely places? Ved queried.

"Was she carrying any basket?" Rakesh tried to clarify his doubt.

"No, to me she didn't look like a village girl."

"Oh, I see," Rakesh gave a smile. "People often like to spend some time alone when they are here. Since women are safe in our state, we receive a large number of single woman travellers. I think she could be one of them."

"But her dress was too gaudy for a tourist," Ved expressed doubt.

"Sir, perhaps you don't know, people tend to do stranger things in privacy here."

This failed to convince Ved whose inquiring glances perturbed Rakesh. He wanted his favourite tourist to have a good time and not be burdened with absurd things. It then occurred to him that woman could be Divya.

"You said she couldn't a tourist," Rakesh went on, "and I'm sure she wasn't a local girl. Then that leaves us with one possibility. That woman could be Divya."

"Divya? What Divya?" Vedanta became inquisitive.

"It's one story we hill folks avoid to recollect, or recount."

"Why? Is it tragic?"

"Yes, and perhaps much more," Rakesh, with tears clouding his eyes, began, "About twenty years ago a woman, who had gone to the forest to fetch firewood, found a little child wrapped in a cloth lying under a pine tree. The child was hungry and crying. She picked up the child and breast-fed her. Then she looked around for the child's parents. She shouted for them but surrounding hills sent back her echo. When she became sure that someone by design had abandoned the girl, she brought her home. Everyone in the family accepted the little wonder as a gift from God. The girl was named Divya. She was raised with a lot of love and care. The family guarded Divya's secret from the villagers. The mother told them she was her sister's daughter. Since the couple didn't have a child of their own, they had brought her home. Raising relative's children was a common practice amongst the local folks and hence, nobody had any reasons to doubt them.

By the age of eighteen Divya grew into a lovely girl. People thought God had sent down an *Apsara* from heaven. Her presence evoked opposite but intense sentiments in both genders. The young boys chased her all day long. The young girls burned with jealousy. The words about her beauty spread far and wide. And when every heart in the village was ablaze with love or hatred, she one night disappeared. Next morning when the villagers awoke to this bad news, there was shock and disbelief all around. Her parents searched her everywhere, but in vain and then they sought the police help. But that didn't change the result. Where could she go? This question puzzled several minds. Her mysterious disappearance had broken many a heart. A couple of boys had been driven to suicide, some had started smoking marijuana and others had become emotional wrecks.

Every week a new story circulated amongst the villagers and was discussed at great length in the fields, forests, shops, homes and streets. Some folks said she had been poisoned by a jealous wife, while others felt she had been killed by a failed lover. But the majority believed she was an evil spirit who had come to their village to destroy young men. After some time so many versions, most of which were hurtful to the locals, floated in the air. The folks became fearful to talk about her. The village elders declared she was a devil and debarred people from talking about her. She couldn't have been a human being after destroying so many young lives?" Rakesh murmured.

Thereafter, both fell silent. The mystery still occupied their thoughts but for different reasons. It was hard for Ved to believe the story. How could he? He had seen the woman in bone and flesh.

Looking into Rakesh's eyes, he probed further, "Is that all you know about Divya?"

"Yes, but there is a man who perhaps knows more."

"Who?"

"The caretaker at the Anasakti Ashram. I'll take you to him but after you eat something."

"As you wish," Ved smiled. "Bring me lunch in the room after an hour."

Rakesh left. He was happy Ved had heard the story without passing any judgement on it and had agreed to have early lunch.

An hour later he brought Vedanta to the Anasakti Ashram where he introduced him to the caretaker, a man in late fifties. From a distance the greying hair, sunken cheeks and eyes, and thin hands made him look several years older, but from near he, more or less, looked his age. He wore a blue pant faded at knees, a dark cots wool shirt torn at the collar, and a black coat bearing several weather beatings. The black rimmed spectacles were put on whenever somebody approached the man. With a pride, acquired by guarding something so important, the man's face glowed.

The caretaker expressed surprise that a visitor had approached him for Divya's story in which nobody in the past had shown any interest. The locals had their own version to contend with. However, it was difficult to say if anybody other than the old man knew more reliable version. At least that's what he thought.

Sitting on the bench, the caretaker, with a strained smile as he struggled to find acquaintance in Ved's dishevelled countenance, asked, "What do you want to know about Divya?"

Ved told him everything he had heard it from Rakesh. Then he gave a puzzled look. The old man's smile seemed to hide a dark secret. In the meanwhile Rakesh begged leave of them and left. The two then for a brief moment shared many glances. Ved was getting uncomfortable with the stillness that seemed to lengthen into eternity.

And when he was about to urge the old man to unravel the mystery, he heard a deep sigh. The caretaker, turning to him, began, "Nobody in the hills knows what I'm going to tell you now. The girl picked up by the village woman in the forest was a dead child, abandoned by a midwife."

"What? She was dead?" Ved almost jumped in fright.

"Yes, the little girl was dead. She was an illegitimate child that had died during delivery. The midwife took money from the mother to bury it in the forest. So she, in the dead of the night when passed through the woods got so scared that she put the body under a pine tree and ran away from there. She kept hearing terrifying voices until she reached home. Not all visitors know that hills and forests in this region are inhabited by hundreds of spirits. At the base of the Trishul Peak lay the '*Roop Kund*', a frozen pond in which for over seven hundred years countless human skeletons have been preserved."

"Who could those people be and what were they

doing in those icy mountains?" Ved interrupted.

"There are many theories about sudden disappearance of such a large body of human beings. Some believe they were pilgrims on a holy trek in the Himalayas, while others say it was an invading army from the plains out on a mission to capture a Himalayan Kingdom. Had earth not heated up, those human bones would have remained a secret. God knows how many more secrets Mother Earth holds in her bosom? Those spirits are roaming all over the place. And one such spirit, when it found a dead child lying under a tree, entered its body. So by the time a woman sighted a crying baby in the forest, the spirit had taken possession of the body. You know everything what happened thereafter."

"All but one thing," Vedanta asked, with deep anxiety. "Why and where did Divya disappear?"

"This mystery has been troubling my mind ever since. I wish I had the answer. I doubt anyone else has."

"So, it would remain an unsolved mystery."

"Unless somebody gathered courage to solve it," the old man said, staring at him.

Import of those words wasn't lost on Ved who had already made up his mind to get to the bottom of it. Divya's tale was too human to be a ghost story. And he didn't mind to accept the challenge. Without hurting the narrator's local sensibilities, he said, "I think I should be able to solve this riddle."

"Be watchful, young man," cautioned the caretaker. "Don't leave windows open in the night."

Ved gave him a grateful smile and was about to leave when his eyes fell on a figure inside the Ashram. It was she. He couldn't miss her. With joy his eyes filled.

"Divya," he shouted and ran inside.

Chapter Eight

＊　＊　＊

Above the horizon was spread out a reddish orange band from one end to the other. The orange and red clouds lay scattered across the entire width, above which hovered the scraggy grey clouds whose underbelly shone in the reflected orange. Below the horizon, the dull white clouds were scattered in a jagged outline giving it a shape of a ridge line. In front lay the actual snow peaks, which for a moment paled before the fake range. Between the snow peaks and Kausani lay a series of mountain ranges which darkened as they came closer to the town. The farthest range was the brightest and the closest was the darkest.

Perched atop the flat piece was a twelve by ten feet barrack with tapered roof, wooden walls, a door and a small veranda in front. Inside, about a dozen people of all ages and gender watched Mahatma's black and white photos, arranged in order on the inside walls. The photos depicted Gandhi's lineage, his childhood, his education in England, his struggle in South Africa and the 'Namak Andolan', the 'Champaran Satyagraha' and some other events related to the freedom movement in India. His two large portraits adored the wall opposite to the entrance. From the veranda one got a magnificent view of the Himalayas. The building was called 'the Anasakti Ashram'.

Outside, a parapet wall encircled the whole complex, which had a few other structures too. The tall deodar trees added to beauty of the place, where Mahatma Gandhi in 1929 had planned to halt for two days during his tour of India, but he was so smitten by the place that he had stayed there for fourteen days, and wrote the 'Anasakti Yoga' based on the Gita.

A girl stood alone before a photo showing a young lawyer being thrown out of the train on the platform in South Africa. It was one event in the great man's life that filled every Indian's eyes. She was so glued to the photo that she didn't notice when a man came and stood next to her.

"Divya," she heard an impatient male voice.

"Sorry, do I know you?" she asked, sounding peeved. "I'm not Divya."

"Oh, I should have known that," he mumbled to himself.

"What?"

"You couldn't be Divya."

"Who's Divya?" she questioned, getting curious.

"It's a long story you need to know," he said in a serious tone. "Can we move outside? People might get disturbed here."

"Okay."

With a grudge she followed. Outside in the backyard, they sat on the parapet under the shade of the deodars.

"I'm Ved," he held out his hand.

"I'm Sara."

"You mean Saranga," he smiled.

"And you must be Vedanta," she smiled back.

Both were given names by their grandparents. Those were wonderful names but had been shortened by their families and friends, who found the names out of sync with time, and also hard to pronounce. By now both had reconciled themselves to being called by their shorter names, but missed the melody of the sound of their actual names.

For a moment they glanced here and there before looking at each other. Their nervousness had reduced to a level where they could talk to each other.

"Did you go to that hillock two days ago?" he asked, pointing in the direction of the mountain.

"Yes, I was there in the morning that day."

"I saw you there and when I approached you, the fog took you away."

"Interesting," she said, raising her eyebrows. "I didn't know I was being followed."

"No, you've got me wrong. I'm a nature lover and that morning I was out early to capture the subtle hues of dawn. Sunrise was so mesmerizing I thought I was watching a painting."

"And the lady in the painting looked so enigmatic that you started an earnest search for her," she interrupted him.

"Yeah," he resumed. "During my search I stumbled upon a scary tale. Two local men told me you were a ghost and your name was Divya."

Then he narrated to her the entire story. She listened in rapt attention. And when he finished, she burst into laughter. Her eyes gleamed, her cheeks reddened and her dimples deepened. That moment she looked so pretty, so human, so vulnerable. The admirer from a foot away wondered whether Saranga was the girl the Fakir had talked about.

The young heart then stirred and missed a beat. He had found the answer.

After a while she commented, with a mischievous glint in her eyes, "The trip to the mountains can't be fruitful unless you heard a ghost story or two."

"Thank God," he sighed.

"A fascinating story," she said, getting up.

It made him anxious. He wanted to spend some more time with her but it would have been bad on his part to disrupt her schedule. However, he did hope to meet her sooner and for a longer time.

"When can we meet next?"

"Why?" she said, with a thin smile. "You want to tell me another ghost story?"

"No," he replied. "An interesting human tale."

"You appear to be in a tearing hurry," she said, with a tinge of sarcasm in her voice. "I'm not. Don't forget we are still strangers."

"How could we?" he objected. "Now we know each other well."

"How well?" she shot back. "People spend their lives together and still remain strangers to one another. Our acquaintance isn't an-hour old."

It caused him huge embarrassment. He hadn't expected such cruel assault on his sincerity. But Saranga was no ordinary girl. The beauty and the brains coexisted in her persona in perfect harmony. And she knew which of these attributes to use when, where and in what measure. If her beauty had cast a spell on him, her intellect had made him curious. He didn't want to say a word, or make a gesture that could offend her and drive her away.

After giving the matter a careful thought, he spoke "We need to meet soon. I've something important to tell you about your future."

"Another exciting story," she said, with a wry smile. "In Kausani a boy sees a girl and is infatuated with her.

In order to get close to her, he tells her a fanciful tale and when this doesn't impress the girl, he uses the master stroke. Informs her he can foretell her future for which they should meet soon. It's an original idea and impressive too, but in my case it's flawed. Like others, I should have been a fatalist but I'm not."

"I swear I'm not lying," he pleaded.

"I need time to convince myself."

Then she walked back inside the Ashram to her waiting friends to suffer their taunts and stares. She looked back at him and smiled, but said no words. Upset, he left the place.

The meeting had left him puzzled and angry. It was something he hadn't expected to happen so early. Seeing Saranga in flesh and bone had relieved his mind of a huge burden, but it had disappointed him too. Some thoughtfulness from her would have brightened up his day. But that wasn't to be so. The burden of a vain meeting was sure to linger on in his mind for some days.

At dusk, the day had handed over its worries to the night and gone home. In the dark, enthusiasm had turned into apathy and hope into despair. Demons of doubt had started to raise their ugly heads and torment his soul. His mind was losing peace and he was losing sleep.

A dreadful night brought in a dreadful dream.

A week later when Saranga insisted they make a trip to the base of the Trishul Peak, he relented. It was a risky venture to undertake without proper snow clothing and equipment. But he couldn't say no to her. How could he? The men in love took bigger risks than this. During the journey they shared their disappointments, their dreams. With joy in their hearts they faced every difficulty with a smile. En route, they passed by the Bedini Bugyal, whose unending green grass captivated them so much they halted there in a gaddi hut. After a few days they reached at the base of the Trishul. The place was freezing cold. As they stood admiring the haunting loneliness, Saranga heard someone call her name. Mesmerised, she walked towards the sound. Vedanta tried to stop her, but to no avail. She seemed under a magical spell. After some distance the ice on which she walked caved in. She crawled on her hands and knees up the bank, and screamed for help. He held her hands and tried to pull her out, but the thin ice melted under his feet too. Both started to sink together. Why was this happening to them? They had committed no sins to deserve this. Under those icy waters, a hundred hands pulled them inside the lake that would consume them like it had thousands of people centuries ago. It wasn't the death he feared but its moment, its anonymity. With Saranga in tight embrace, he waited for the inevitable.

All of a sudden the rain lashed against his face. Terrified, he sat up in the bed. Thank God he wasn't a somnambulist. What an awful dream it was? He wiped the face and looked at the window that played with the wind. How did it open in the midnight? He remembered having locked it before going to bed. It reminded him of the caretaker's advice.

He smiled and peeped into the dark outside. A blissful calm prevailed in the air.

Thought of nightmare made him feel as if it were real and they both had been saved by some divine intervention. Between dream and reality his mind swung like a pendulum and it took him some time to realise it was a dream. Was it an omen of disaster? He pondered and then arrived at a conclusion that his fixation with Divya's story could be responsible for this.

Satisfied, he switched on the lamp and looked at the clock. It was three. At that ungodly hour he couldn't get tea to calm his nerves. Since coming to Kausani, he recalled, that he had started drinking more tea than he did at home.

With sleep gone and dawn still two hours away, he picked up the book and resumed reading it. Odysseus had escaped from Polyphemus, the one-eyed monster but had lost a few of his companions. The homesick sailors had great yearning to return home. With remaining crew he set sail for Ithaca, his kingdom, where Penelope, his beloved wife, with their son waited for him. Their memories filled the great warrior's eyes. Every moment of the voyage he had dreamed of one thing that soon he would reach his homeland and reunite with his family. Longing for Penelope gave him strength to face dangers on the sea. Hugging her hand-woven blanket, Odysseus fell asleep. And when he awoke he observed a huge red ball emerge out of the sea.

Dawn had broken in Kausani too.

Sipping tea, Ved wondered how an ancient Greek King could love his wife so much that he spurned every temptation the Gods enticed him with. In those days women were treated and traded like a commodity, or trophies to be won in the battlefield. Because of its uniqueness this love story, over the centuries, had caught imagination of the writers and lovers alike.

If God were to grant him one wish that moment then he would ask for Odysseus' faithfulness, he thought, as he finished tea.

The sunlight had driven away the night's demons. It always did. He felt calm within. An hour later he, after breakfast, came out in the lobby and found a cheerful Yamini waiting for him.

"A boy delivered this in the morning," she informed, handing him the envelope.

"Who sent it?"

"I don't know. The messenger didn't tell me her

name," her smile grew as she spoke.

"How do you know it's not him," he asked, hiding excitement.

"Because the writing is so beautiful," she replied. "Go and meet her. The Gods are collaborating to bring you both together."

He grinned.

"By the way, how attractive is she?" she queried.

"More than I had imagined," was his instant reply.

Then he realised his mistake, he blushed and slipped away. She closed her eyes and thanked God for bringing bliss in his life. It was a cryptic message, which said he should come to the place she frequented the most. Outside the lobby, he halted and tried to recall if she had indicated her favourite place during their brief chat but he couldn't. He headed straight to the Ashram but didn't find her there. Where could she be? He thought as he came out from there. That moment he didn't want to entertain the absurd thought she could be Divya. In an involuntary action his legs moved towards the knoll where he had seen her for the first time.

And his joy knew no bounds when he noticed her waiting under a pine tree at the same spot.

"Saranga," he shouted in delight.

"Vedanta," she gave a surprised look.

"Why? Did you have any doubts?"

"No, I was sure you would come."

"Why?" he was puzzled.

"Because you were looking for me."

Her self-confidence, her attitude compelled him to ask question to himself why he wasn't like her.

"Aren't you interested to know about your future?" He asked, regaining his poise.

"Doesn't my presence answer that question?" she

said, with a smile.

Grappling with curiosity, both lapsed into silence for a while. The narrator was condensing the story to make it engaging for the listener, and the listener was readying herself to hear about that part of her life to which she, till now, had given no concrete shape. Her dreams were hazy, her desires confused. Some knowledge about the future could help her to give them a definite shape.

So, she waited and waited.

Without any preamble he narrated the circumstances in which he had met the banker, out in the Himalayas seeking the truth and how that man had predicted his future and its linkage with hers. He told her every detail of the story and stopped short of telling her the tragic end of their marriage.

"Is that all he told you?" she asked in unconvincing voice.

"Yes."

Though, he did look honest, the tale made her uncomfortable for the fact that she, that moment, was in no mood to believe that she was going to fall in love with a stranger during the trip. Her heart wasn't prepared for such a shock. It wasn't her idea of love; it couldn't be of any normal girl's. And she was a normal girl. At least that's was she thought about herself.

But destiny had planned her love story to unfold in a different way.

"Do you believe in this tale?" asked Vedanta.

"Should I?" she gave an inquiring glance.

"I'm not sure. Like you when I heard it for the first time, I too was taken aback, but later on I realised perhaps ours couldn't be a chance meeting. In this holy land nothing moves without His consent."

"Is it His consent then?" she parted, with a

mysterious smile.

Bewildered, he watched her climb down the hillock and disappear into the labyrinth of hill tracks.

Chapter Nine

* * *

The air of enigma, left behind by her, grew thicker and thicker with every passing minute. Her smell hung in the air. And Vedanta, staring in the direction in which Saranga had gone, wondered whether fate was conspiring against him. A moment ago she was there with him and a moment later she was gone, without any promise of future meeting. Why was she doing this to him? He asked himself.

Perhaps the women were meant to be enigmatic, he thought. God after creating them had added enigma in abundance in their nature. It was this quality that made them so desirable. The more enigmatic a woman was, the more power she possessed. This enhanced her physical beauty and added an element of intelligence in her.

Immersed in her thoughts, he gazed at the mountains to get answers to many questions that tormented his mind that moment. Far from getting any solace, his agony continued. And when his limbs started aching and his heart getting heavier, he stood up to return to the hotel.

"Sir, any luck with your quest?" Yamini's honest question greeted him as soon as he stepped into the lobby.

It hit him hard. He was in no mood to reply to that but her ebullient face brought a change in him. After all, she was his lone well-wisher in that place and he couldn't afford to offend her. Forcing a smile, he spoke, "It seems the misfortune has developed intense liking for me. It doesn't leave me alone even for a second."

A deep melancholy ran through his words. She was seized by utter helplessness. A sad heart was seldom equipped to comfort another sad heart. But sometimes melancholy did comfort melancholy.

"That's unfortunate. I know why it hasn't knocked at my door for some time," her voice choked.

"Come on; don't make me so selfish. I'd hate to light up my world by bringing darkness into yours."

She knew her argument would cut no ice with him, so she changed the topic and told him that half-mile down the road there was a private library wherein he could get some exciting books and a few hours there could brighten up his mood. Also, its owner was an interesting person with whom he could have some intelligent conversation.

When he showed curiosity to know more about the owner, she was evasive. As he was about to depart, her encouraging comment was, "A pleasant surprise awaits you there."

He thanked her and left.

The word surprise lifted up his morale and pulled his mind out of its self-imposed inertia. His heart began to pound faster. Could it be she waiting for him in the library? He thought as he raced down the hill. Sweet snow and cobra lily petals littered the serpentine pathway. During the short journey, several thoughts mostly optimistic ones cropped up in his mind. Engrossed in dreams, he overshot the library. He stopped when it occurred to him the house should be somewhere close by. A quick survey of area brought his gaze at a secluded house. He moved towards it.

As the house approached, he caught its full view. It was an old bungalow nestled in the midst of sylvan oaks. The lawn was mowed freshly. The red, white and pink flowers of bougainvillea ran in a haphazard manner over the arched entrance. The architecture was medieval and Indian. A large veranda, dotted with chairs and decorated with hanging plants, encircled the house on its three sides. The house was well maintained. He turned back and looked. The nearest house was so far away and if the bungalow owner shouted for help, the sound wouldn't reach the village.

Ved rushed to the entrance and looked for the door bell. When he didn't find it, he banged the door knocker.

"Who's there?" he heard a feeble voice.

The wait lasted a few minutes. A woman, in late eighties, opened the door for him. Smiling through her wrinkles, she asked with affection, "Come on in, son. What brings you to this desolate place?"

A white woman's presence has come as a surprise to him. He had expected somebody else to be there. Perhaps she could still be inside the house, he thought as he grappled with that shock in his mind and disbelief on his face.

"I'm Vedanta," he held out his hand.

"Call me Gomati."

"Gomati!"

"You look unsettled seeing me here?" she asked as soon as she had offered him a chair. "Two things seem to have taken you by surprise."

"What!"

"My age and colour of my skin."

"No, no. I'm fine," he tried to sound calm.

In a minute she was back with a glass of water. Handing it to him she sat in the opposite chair and waited for him to finish. Picking up the glass, she asked, "What would you prefer, tea or coffee?" and without waiting to hear his choice, she said, "I think hot tea would be ideal for a good chat," and went inside.

He looked around. It was a large living room, rectangular in shape, whose walls had windows, opening out either to the veranda or to the adjacent rooms. Family photographs, black and white and coloured, of different sizes adored the white walls. Four wooden cupboards, with glass doors, covered the empty wall space and in them numerous books were stacked. Outside each self, a slip was pasted indicating the genre of books it housed. On an empty wall a large portrait caught his attention. He rose and paced up to it. A young woman with pink cheeks and big dreamy eyes, dressed in a colourful gown sat by the lakeside with a castle in the backdrop. He stood still, mesmerised by her sublime beauty. Its resemblance, except for the colour of the skin, made him inquisitive. Who could that woman be? He wondered.

"It's me," he felt an affectionate pat on the back. "Come, let's have tea."

"I was a good looking woman in my younger days," wrinkles on her face turned pink as she spoke, "that's what many men in my village thought."

"You are still so beautiful," he quipped.

"You naughty boy, trying to flirt with an old woman," she burst into laughter.

Then both fell silent for a while.

"Your presence here gives me as much surprise as mine would be giving to you," she said sipping tea.

"I'd be lying if I thought otherwise," he replied. "When I saw this house from a distance, I had visualised its owner to be, at least, a male. Don't you feel unsafe living in a secluded place, so far away from any help?"

"Not at all. I'm safe here," she replied. "God has been so kind to this valley. The Kumaunis are so honest and caring that I never, for a day, feel I live amongst unknown folks. They deserve our appreciation for keeping themselves insulated from the outside world, which in the last few decades has become violent. Of late, intolerance in the society has shot up and violence's new demon, terrorism is threatening to destroy the civil society in every country. However, this place remains unaffected."

It put all his doubts about her safety at rest. A comforting pause followed.

"But the purpose of my visit is different. At this moment, it's of lesser importance than your reasons for choosing this Himalayan townlet as your eternal home."

Tears filled her eyes as she prepared to take a trip down the memory lane and evoke a sense of her most cherished experiences, tinged with sadness at their loss. Since the death of her husband nostalgia had been her steady companion. It had lessened the burden of her loneliness. She was aware that the past carried the baggage of unpleasant memories, some of which it kept to lament and some it passed on to the present to introspect. Still, she decided to relive those memories and so she took time to arrange them in a way that it didn't burden the young man.

"It's an old tale," she began, "I'm not sure if it would enthuse a young man."

"You wouldn't know how excited I'm to hear it," he bucked her up.

It lit up the old woman's eyes. Nobody ventured that side. A maid and a gardener were two individuals with whom she shared her time and loneliness. But, with neither of them could she share her intellectual anxieties, her fading memories. Since the time she had been desolated by death of her husband fifteen years ago, she hadn't met anyone who had shown so much interest in her life. Sundry village folks, who sometimes came to enquire about her health, did hear her story but in parts with the purpose of filling gaps in the story they were so well conversant with. Forty years ago her love story had been the most talked about thing in the Kumaon hills. Her physical beauty, with passage of time, had lost its lustre and so had the tale lost its juice. Nobody found an old woman's love story exciting. New times had given birth to newer and juicier tales. To young generation these stories had every element of human drama in them. Thus, a simple love story of a German woman and a local man had got lost in the mist.

In a few moments an extraordinary tale awaited to be resurrected by the woman who had lived it for last so many years. Four decades ago she had travelled thousands of miles and come to India to research for her book, and had stayed back, forever. Before leaving Germany she, in her wildest dreams, had never imagined that she wouldn't return to her home in native Bavaria.

"Please begin, I'm all ears," Vedanta spoke when he found her waiting.

The story began with her childhood. She was born in a village in Bavaria in Germany. After her initial schooling in the village, she went to the University of Munich to study anthropology. During one organised tour she, along with her friends, got the opportunity to visit India. In the last week of their stay, they, as part of the plan, toured the Himalayas to study the nomadic tribes there. On a professor's recommendation they made Kausani the base from where they planned to operate.

That tiny place fascinated her so much that she prevailed upon her friends to extend their stay by a week. On the first day in Kausani she met Kishore, a local boy who could speak broken English and she hired him to act as their interpreter. Kishore had thorough knowledge of the customs, traditions and dialect of every nomadic tribe in the region. He knew which tribe would be where at any given time. As winter was about to set in, most of the tribes were expected to be at the foothills.

The girls interacted with some of the tribes and on a few occasions stayed overnight amongst them. The experience was exhilarating. They collected valuable data and over next few days sat down in Kausani to compile it.

During long trips to the foothills, Kishore used to regal them with folktales and jokes. His simplicity had touched everyone's heart. Angelika was the most impressed. With time her appreciation of him turned into liking and she began to find reasons to spend more and more time with him. The other girls paid no heed to this development as they thought it to be a stupid case of physical attraction.

On the penultimate day Kishore told them there was an ancient temple nearby where unmarried girls went and to fulfil their wish tied a thread. And the wish of any girl who tied the thread never went unfulfilled. Such was the power of the reigning temple God. When queried what the most girls wished for, he replied that all of them, without any exception, wished for a good and caring husband.

It excited the girls who were too keen to see the temple and some of them did have a wish. Next day after two hours of back-breaking journey in a rickety jeep they arrived at the foot of a knoll, covered in dense undergrowth. As they moved inside the temple precincts, a strange fear gripped them. The moss-eaten walls had cracked up at several places out of which black and brown wild weeds hung down. The place was filled with smell of burning incense sticks. Under a small canopy lay God's statue, smeared in red. Threads hung all over the place, on the stone pillars, on the trees trucks.

The place was creepy. They all, with folded hands, stood before the statue as long as Kishore chanted mantras. And once he had finished he urged them to wish for anything and then tie the thread. From his pocket he took out a bundle and handed them a piece each. Whether or not they had asked God for fulfilling their wishes, he couldn't know but he did see everyone tying the thread as per his instructions.

It pleased him a lot.

They were back in Kausani by noon. While a few girls mocked the whole incident, the others remained in awe of it. The visit had impacted Angelika the most. Inside the temple something strange had happened to her. It was churning from within. She felt as though she wasn't what she was but somebody else, someone who belonged to that place and not some distant Bavarian Village. Though she hated to admit she was a person possessed, she felt the same.

In the dream that night she found a strange voice calling her by a different name, Gomati and telling her the holy land was her real homeland. Thereafter, stranger things followed in quick succession. By next morning she found herself in love with Kishore. For a few days her friends made light of the whole incident but when they found Angelika serious, they got worried and tried to reason out but Angelika remained firm. Later, they wished her luck and left. Angelika stayed back.

"A young Bavarian girl falls in love with a Kumauni boy and makes a Himalayan village her eternal home. So, in brief, this is my love story, stranger than fiction," she sighed with relief.

Spellbound by that tale, for several moments, he remained silent. Before him sat an old woman whom, forty years ago, destiny had brought her to Kausani where true love awaited her. Was love so powerful that it could force the people to forget their countries, their religions and their loved ones, forever? Was love so selfish?

"I know what's going on in your mind?" she interrupted his thoughts.

"What?" he was surprised.

"How could my love story survive the odds?"

"Yeah."

"It wasn't easy. We came from different cultural backgrounds and so it was important we understood each other well. In the beginning the communication between us was difficult because he didn't know German and I didn't know Hindi. In six months I learnt broken Hindi and he broken German. It took us another six months to attain fluency. Thereafter, life became easy. Knowledge about each other's customs and traditions developed mutual trust and respect. After our marriage we made many sacrifices but neither of us changed our religion. He practised his and I practised mine. Thus, our love, despite many sceptics writing its daily obituary, survived."

"Whose decision was it to make Kausani a home?"

"Mine," she shot back. "He would have been too willing to migrate to Germany if I had wanted but I chose this place."

"Why, if I may ask so?"

"Because the air in this land is filled with spirituality. Though my native village is prettier, it is spiritually starved, as are many western towns and cities. Here I feel I'm in a world of eternal bliss, I experience presence of the gods. Who knows one day I might attain the moksha," she smiled, solaced by memory.

He gave her a questioning glance.

"Well, you could say I acted selfish in this regard but my decision was endorsed by my husband and later by my two daughters, who now live abroad but never forget to mention, whenever they call me, that how much they miss their birthplace. I don't know what but there is something unique about this place whoever comes here falls in love with it."

The statement brought a smile on his face. His

mind raced back into the corridor of memories. A week ago he hadn't heard about Kausani and now he enjoyed its breathtaking beauty. She was so right. Anyone could fall in love with such a wonderful place?

"Do you know what brought you here?" she spoke in a mysterious way.

"What!"

"Love," she repeated, "like me, it brought you to this quaint place. You never realise its immense power until you are struck by it."

"I'm yet to feel its full impact. Perhaps in these difficult times love has undergone a definition change," he said in a serious tone.

"You say this because of emotional stress and not because you believe so," she continued. "Since the days of Adam and Eve, love hasn't changed a bit. It retains its purity, innocence and simplicity. It transcends national boundaries and human barriers of race, colour and creed. Even today it inspires millions of people the world over, as it did thousands of years ago. It made many kings to abandon their thrones and live ordinary lives. It converted several ordinary people into saints. If love is the cause of celebration, then it is the cause of destruction too. If not harnessed it becomes a monster. Love is so powerful it can change destinies of individuals and nations. It demands forgiveness and sacrifice. It abhors revenge and retribution. It's one human emotion that has remained unaffected by the changing times."

The wise argument sounded convincing to Vedanta. After all, he was yet to fall in love to know anything about it. The old woman had experienced it for forty years. Then it occurred to him she could hold the key to understanding the complex mind of a young Saranga.

After hesitating for several minutes, he asked,

"Could you help me in unravelling the mysteries of a woman's mind?"

"Sharp guy," she continued. "Your intelligence compliments your handsomeness. But like your generation, you are a man in a hurry. In one meeting you want to know the complexities of a woman's mind for which people spend a lifetime to understand. If this subject were so simple then there would have been no failures in love. Only God has the answer to your question. I'm a mere mortal."

"You mean to say, you can give me no advice," his voice dropped in frustration.

"Be sincere. Be patient," she went on. "But you came here for books. Didn't you? Yamini gave you my address."

"So, you know Yamini," he almost jumped in surprise.

"Yeah, she is a girl with a golden heart. Once a while she spends time with me. But she isn't your girl. Is she?" the old woman gave a mysterious smile.

"Why?"

"I can see it in your eyes. Her name didn't stir your heart."

It astonished him. But the gloom descended on his face soon after.

The old woman, in a quick glance, caught both those expressions. "You needn't get disheartened," she resumed. "God willing, one day you will succeed in your pursuit."

"I wish your words come true soon," he said. "Often I get a feeling I'm chasing the mist."

"It happens," she sighed. "When you're in love sometimes you get a feeling of being stranded in the middle of nowhere and you're driven to despair. But true love is never easy to achieve. One has to overcome several difficulties. You should know the path to love is tough and a long one. It was no easier in my time. So negotiate it with caution and patience. God willing, one day the girl will understand your sincerity."

"Hope, God listens to my honest plea," he murmured.

On that positive note, he thanked her and left.

Chapter Ten

✳ ✳ ✳

Adolescence is the bridge, which a child has to cross before reaching adulthood. This brief journey is strewn with enormous challenges. A child had to shed its innocence before embarking upon life's toughest, yet fascinating odyssey. During this phase the mind and body go through many complex changes, some of which are difficult to deal with. At this crossroads, a young mind often entangles itself in a web of confusion wherein the adolescent takes one hesitant step forward and two confident steps backward. It's such a phase of life where the child isn't a child, and is yet to become an adult.

This period is characterised by intense mental churning. In some minds this churning lasts a few years, in several minds it lasts many years longer. For girls the bridge of adolescence is the longest. Often the most girls carry their childhood, tucked inside their hearts, over into many adulthood years. For women their childhood is the emotional reservoir out of which they draw their strength in times of distress.

During this crossover, girls remain attached to the childhood activities, such as sleeping with dolls, crying while watching cartoon films, eating more chocolates than chapattis, and talking about boys in hushed tones. As they move ahead, they look back afraid to let the freedom slip out of their hands so soon. Every step forward takes them a mile away from their childhood. Unlike boys, this is tougher for them.

Saranga's experiences were no different.

Until now hers had been an uncluttered world, inhabited by simple folks—a select group of friends and family members. She, surrounded with dolls, dreams and dadi's tales, lived in her little world, unmindful of the complexities of outside world. Sudden intrusion by Vedanta had broken the rhythm of her life and set panic in her heart, for she knew he was in love with her. She was fearful he would soon express his feelings. She was fearful because she wasn't ready to hear those words. She was fearful because she didn't know what love was all about.

The nearest she came to understand its meaning was when she, from her grandmother, had heard the story of Shakuntala, daughter of the sage Vishwamitra and Menaka. The newborn was left in the forest where the baby, surrounded by Sankunta birds, was found by Kanva Rishi. He thus named her Shakuntala. King Dushyanta met her during a hunting trip. And both fell in love with each other and got married in a 'Gandharva' ceremony. The king left for his kingdom, promising to come back soon to take her with him. One day, Rishi Durvasa came to the ashram, but lost in Dushyanta's thoughts, Shakuntala failed to greet him. Incensed by this slight, the Rishi cursed her that the man she dreamed of would forget her altogether. When the sage realized harshness of his wrath, he showed mercy and said the man would remember everything again if she showed him a personal token given to her. As time passed, Shakuntala wondered why Dushyanta hadn't returned for her. So she, with her father, set out for the palace. On the way, they crossed a river in a canoe, where the signet ring fell in the water when she was running her fingers through it. At the palace, Shakuntala tried to remind Dushyanta she was his wife but without signet ring the king didn't recognize her. Humiliated, she returned to the forest with son, Bharat who grew into a strong youth, playing with tigers and lions.

Meanwhile, a fisherman found the royal ring in the belly of a fish and took it to the palace. Seeing the ring, Dushyanta's memories of Shakuntala came back to him. At once he set out in her search in the forest where he saw a young boy open a lion's mouth and count its teeth. Amazed by his courage, the king asked his name and was surprised to find it Bharat. The boy then took him to his mother, and thus the family reunited.

It was one legend that had a profound impact on Sara's young mind. She asked, "Was Shakuntala king's first wife?"

Grandma's nonchalant reply was, "No." And before a young girl's next question could tease her mind, she said, staring at the sky, "The rich took as many wives as they wanted; the poor as many as they could. For a king it was customary to have several wives for several reasons."

"How could the king divide his love between several wives? Is love divisible?"

The question unsettled the old woman. How could she explain the intricacies of love whose true meaning she was yet to understand? A simple question, how could a man divide his love amongst many women, was so hard to answer. She had never thought about the subject. It was important she gave a satisfactory answer to her granddaughter. After a brief pause, she spoke from the heart, a woman's heart, "Love for a woman is sacred, sharing sacrilege. I'm not sure if it's same for men. They are so hard to understand, more so these days. For me, love is divine and eternal."

For many days, thereafter, Saranga pondered over

the lives of two women; Shakuntala and Savitri. It occurred to her then it was the woman who always made the sacrifice. Both had to use the patience, grit and intelligence to win their husbands back. As per her grandma the challenges before a modern-day woman were far greater. Like in the ancient times, the male species always looked for several females to mate. The sacred bond of marriage didn't hold him for long. He was always on the lookout for opportunities. The role of other woman hadn't changed with time. Only her name had changed. Saranga was aware a woman today had come to terms with the fact that her husband might not always remain loyal to him. So secrecy was loyalty to her.

Through the amorous lands of adultery, a modern woman had to undertake a treacherous journey and find a man who would hold her hand and her heart, forever. Loyalty for Saranga wasn't another fancy word to be talked of. It was the essence of her life.

Vacation in Kausani was more than a pleasure trip for her. In the serene environs of the place, she wished to find answers to questions that often troubled an adult mind. Relaxing in the balcony from where she could see the valley in front, her eyes surveyed from left to right and near to far. Kausani in fading light looked like a woman, with firewood on her head, rushing home where her angry husband and children waited to be fed. She had a long list of chores to do before she could snatch a few moments for herself. If her days were long, her nights were longer. Which of the two she liked? She wasn't sure.

A light chill had crept in. Sara went in and returned with a sweater. Manjari followed soon after. Both friends shared childhood memories, adolescent anxieties and future dreams. In the city's polluted atmosphere it was tough to think anything positive. Corruption, pollution, murder, arson, looting and rape occupied the maximum space on every newspaper and channel. The positive inspiring stories got lost in the smoke of negativism.

Here the air was pure. Under a clear Kausani sky, both wished to find hope for a better future. Sometime later both dozed off. Sara lapsed into a dream.

Savitri cried her heart out as the Yama carried the soul of Satyavan, her husband. Her pleas went unheard. She waited for him to grant her one wish so that she could ask him to bless her with a child and then trick him into releasing her dead husband's soul, and bring Satyavan back to life. But nothing of that sort happened. Was he a real Yama, or an impostor? The Yama stopped, turned back and said, "Hey Savitri, you are a virtuous woman, rare in this 'Kalyuga'. And it becomes my duty to protect such a woman because only women like you can give birth to pious progenies. The man you wish to protect in unworthy of you. He has cheated you several times. And he hasn't spared your best friend. His sins are beyond any reprieve. Hence, I can't grant you any wish. Hell should be his abode and not your home. If he is allowed to breathe anymore on this earth he would produce dozens of sinners."

"Then what should I do?" asked Savitri, shedding copious tears.

"Go and find a pious man, marry him and live a happy married life."

"What if he too starts cheating after some time?"

"No, that won't be possible."

"Why?" asked a confused Savitri, wiping tears.

"This is one wish every woman everyday prays for fulfilment. But not every woman's wish is granted by God. But you needn't worry. This is one wish I grant you," the Yama said and turned back to leave.

A bewildered Savitri watched the god of death, with his buffalo and Satyavan's soul, fly and vanish into the clouds.

"Satyavan a philanderer! Satyavan a philanderer!" mumbled Sara in dream.

Saranga had known Satyavan to be a faithful. How could the Yama say he was a philanderer? Had the god of death cheated Savitri? Satyavan wasn't a philanderer, Satyavan wasn't a philanderer. Sara started crying. Perspiring, she sat up in the bed. It was well past midnight. Why dream had given a bizarre twist to her favourite Puranic tale?

"Satyavan will always be a faithful man, in every age, in every era," mumbled Sara.

Death couldn't cheat Savitri, but dream had cheated Sara. Against the night lamp's dim light, she looked at sleeping Manjari; her best friend with whom she had chosen to share the hotel room during their stay in Kausani. She felt a pang of envy at the sight.

Thinking of Savitri, she dozed off.

Chapter Eleven

✳   ✳   ✳

The twenty first century had added swiftness in everything. In the age of computers, the love had become swift, short and slipshod. Relationships were made, unmade and erased from the memory in haste. It was the age of experimentation. People experimented with everything and anything. Marriage was experimented with live-in relationship. What however hadn't changed over the years was the quest for true love? Several lives were wasted in its search, and several were lost.

And the change in air had swept across people from all walks of life; the young and old alike. Every minute several marriages got sacrificed on the altar of ego. In each household, big or small; poor or rich, a storm raged that threatened to tear apart the lives of those who dwelled in them. In some houses the folks succeeded, in others the storm succeeded leaving behind debris of human relationships.

And one such storm that had raged in Manjari's house for several years, one day succeeded.

Fights between her parents leading up to the break-up had been long and bitter. Memories of a happy family had been fewer and vanished. Father had sent her elder brother, six years senior, to a boarding school to insulate him from acrimonious home environment. After a few years, mother sent her to aunt's place in Patna, but after uncle's death a year later, she was recalled as her aunt had fallen on hard times. So, bliss in a young girl's life didn't see the second spring. Thereafter, she was back in hell.

And hell it was.

Earlier she had witnessed her parents fight in open, often hurling accusations and abuses at each other at the slightest provocation. But after her return from aunt's home, their fights had turned violent. They hurled crockery and cutlery at each other, causing physical harm. In comparison the dog fight on the street below was more civil. Every night she prayed it to end soon, but her prayers went unanswered. God wasn't on the side of a helpless little girl; she had pondered gazing at the roof during long nights.

And when her mother couldn't cope anymore, she left the house to live with her parents, and filed for divorce. Two years later after making countless visits to the court and spending a fortune, she was freed from the bondage. Manjari was happy for her mother; for father she had no emotions. Her mother and she moved out to live in a new house. It was much more peaceful after going through a harrowing time in her father's house.

Safety of new home emboldened the mother to bare her heart to the daughter. She told Manjari that a woman had snatched her father, who had been having affair since five years after their marriage. So, it was the other woman who had wrecked their world. On one occasion she happened to her mother naked and found her quite attractive. As a bride she was sure to have been a stunner. Any man would have been proud to have such a lovely woman as his wife. Why then his father has gone after another woman? Was she more beautiful than mom? It was one question that troubled her young mind for days and in her quest to find its answer, she stole the woman's name and cell number from father's laptop, and then searched her profile on the social sites.

A rude shock struck Manjari like a thunderbolt. The woman, in late forties, was a childless widow, and with short height and round face she looked ordinary. In many photos she looked ugly. How and why had his tall, handsome dad fallen for such a female? She was at her wits end to guess the truth. Perhaps the woman practised black magic and had cast an evil spell on his father.

Father's absence had made a void in her life and she had hoped her elder brother to fill that. So, on a few occasions when she had tried to share her feelings with him, she found him indifferent. The boy's refrain about parent's break-up was, "It's a common occurrence amongst the couples nowadays." Perhaps his brother wasn't much concerned as long as parents funded his studies. Thereafter, her interaction with him had got limited to birthday and New Year wishes. And whenever she called him up, his answer was that he was busy and would call her back in five minutes. But those five minutes lasted till eternity. So, she caught up happenings in his life on the internet and found him engrossed in his own world in which his little sister didn't exist.

Both males in the family had moved on after the storm, leaving the women behind to collect the debris of their dreams. That moment, the little girl in him promised to herself that she would never ever wreck anybody's world. She knew her mother was a *devi* who couldn't harm a fly. It was her father who had been at fault all along. So, the father, every girl's hero and her hero too, had turned into a demon. A black widow with her black magic had done that.

From then on darkness had filled her life. And that black widow, without fail, every night came in her dreams and threatened to take her mother away from her. Afraid, she didn't confide this in her mother for the fear of losing her.

After the break-up, the mother had to take up a job to raise her children, though her husband paid alimony. Fighting all odds, Manjari studied hard and qualified for the B.Tech. A month prior to departure for the college, she noticed a change in her mother, who had lost a few kilos and trimmed her tummy. A pinkish Glow had returned on her face. Was mother seeing somebody? A fleeting thought cropped up in the daughter's mind, but then she admonished herself for such a sinful idea.

On the penultimate night before departure, she while searching her certificates in the drawers, unearthed the secret of her mother, who had chosen a colleague to share her loneliness with. So, after all these years of abstinence, her mother too had succumbed. Was it for revenge, or for pleasure? Her father had built his new life, her mother was on the threshold of building hers, but doing so both had destroyed the lives of their children.

A day later, a heartbroken Manjari stepped inside the hostel room, and found a girl sitting on the opposite bed.

"I'm Sara, your roommate," the girl stood up and gave her a hug. It was so full of warmth and love, that for a moment she forgot the rancour of the home.

"Hi, I'm Manjari."

From that moment, they clicked as friends. To rid of nostomania, they went to the cafeteria and gorged on pastries and patties. On the way back to the hostel, they were intercepted by a group of seniors and given a quick dose of ragging before the warden came to their rescue.

In coming months Saranga filled the void in Manjari's life. As a father she pampered her, as a mother she fed her well, and as a brother she gave her shoulder to cry on. And thus in no time she became Manjari's trusted confidant. Their closeness in some quarters was talked about with ridicule. A few students thought them to be gay. But rumours didn't trouble them. With each passing day, their friendship blossomed. So, when during the semester break Saranga expressed desire to spend a week in Kausani, Manjari jumped in delight.

Chapter Twelve

* * *

A week after summer solstice the nights had begun to lengthen. A few minutes of gain had made them livelier. After months of struggle, night had snatched its pre-eminence from day. In the dust free atmosphere, billions of twinkling stars had added charm and beauty to it. Each one tried to outshine the other over these lands to please gods, but took care not to be too bright to wake up their masters and face their wrath, and like their little brother, moon face banishment for half of every month.

After living in the dark for two long weeks, the moon had shown up in the sky. Fearful of awaking gods, it had chosen lesser mortals to engage in pranks. Less of glitter but full of mischief, it looked around for the rain and wind, both waiting, and then together the three moved over a sleeping Kausani. Tip-toeing from one window to the next they moved until they found one open window, through which the moon peeped in and found a young girl smile in her dream. Conspiring with the rain, the wind crept in and blew her pyjama up. The rain wet her naked feet.

In pre-dawn hours their mischief continued. Each time the wind moved her pyjama up, she pulled it down. Every passing second the rain climbed a few inches up on her legs. This went on for a while until she felt fingers move on her thighs. Jolted out of her slumber, she sat up in bed and gazed out. The greedy moon licked her legs. A gleeful rain, piggyback on the wind, wetted her. Any girl in love would have frowned upon this amorous indulgence, but this was a celestial act. It could make any girl feel special; it could make any girl feel beautiful. And Manjari was no different. It was the proudest moment of her life, and she wanted to savour it forever in her heart.

And before a fresh gust of wind could sneak in, she stood up, wiped her legs off and searched for the kettle. A little later she returned with black coffee and gazed in the dark, which at any other place would have brought back painful childhood memories, but here God had taken the sting out of the dark whose benign presence had a calming effect on her mind. Relaxed, she watched the darkness dissolve bit by bit.

The next sip of coffee, gone cold, shook her. She stood up. The chair creaked under her weight and stirred Sara from sleep. Rubbing her eyes, Sara queried, "Is the sun up?"

"It's about to," Manjari replied, "Get up, it promises to be a great sunrise."

Minutes later, after getting ready, both ran upstairs and sat on the rampart. All roofs were filled. Their faces lit up when the waiter brought them hot tea. Shivering, they held mug in both hands to get warmth, and awaited the sun's arrival.

And the night's weariness melted away when they sighted the sunrise, the prettiest in the past month, told by the hotel staff, which also was glued to that divine wonder.

The sunrise lasted about twenty minutes, after which the crowd dispersed. Back in the lobby Manjari asked the waiter if Kausani offered anything interesting for breakfast. The waiter looked around and then replied in a hushed tone. "At the Chowk there's a sweet shop that makes hot jalebis and samosas, and I'm sure you will love them."

And before the girls could pose another question, the waiter darted away. They looked at each other and smiled.

The Chowk, marked by a cemented roundel holding an electric pole, was waking up to a quiet morning. It had four roads converge onto it. The first road arrived from the plains, the second moved northwards to the Himalayas, and the third and fourth roads moved along the either spurs. All four roads shared equal space and equal attention at the Chowk before departing to their different destinations.

The shutters were pulled up one by one. The owners after doing the ritualistic *puja*, opened the account book, jotted down something, drew a line and wrote the new date underneath. Then they touched the book with their eyes, moved it over the photo of gods thrice and replaced it in the drawer. The shopkeepers were readying up for the arrival of tourists, expected to come in hordes as it was a weekend. A couple of shops sold vegetables, a few sold clothes, while the maximum shops were makeshift restaurants. And one sold ice cream too. The small market catered to needs of both the locals and the visitors. The junction had more hoardings than the humans.

Laid off by the employer for a day, three to four labourers from the Indo-Gangetic plains, stood leaning back against the retention wall at the Chowk. Dressed in faded and torn shirts, pants, sweaters, jackets and shoes with mufflers thrown around the head, they wiled away long lonely hours.On the bodies of those dull looking creatures with unkempt hair and scraggly beard the one thing that glowed was their eyes. The shameless men stared at every woman that passed by or halted at the Chowk. Like poverty, they had inherited ogling eyes from their forefathers. Back home in the village the men folk loafed around and stared at the women walking to the pond/river to fetch water, or to the field to collect fodder, or to the yard to bring cowdung cakes, and passed lewd comments. Like several social injustices the poor women suffered this insult often without a fight.

In the land where a woman's body remained wrapped in a sari and face under a veil, the man got to see the full face and half body in the dim light while making love. So, any opportunity to see a woman's body in full bloom of youth with its accentuated curves was grasped by the labourers with glee. It aroused curiosity, sensuality and jealousy in their minds. Impropriety of the act was too high sounding a word to cause them any moral bother. Their eyes feasted on curvaceous bodies, their minds fed on many fantasies. A little later a man came and took them away.

Saranga and Manjari, dressed in jeans and top with a cardigan, ran down the stairs and arrived at the Chowk, which was gathering life. The shop at the Chowk had sweets stored in a glass rack, and stacks filled with assorted drinks and mineral water bottles on its either side. The owner was frying jalebis and putting them in a tray. The sight made their mouths water. Manjari knew it would take about five minutes for jalebis to be soaked in the sugar syrup and be ready. Both decided to take a walk down the road towards quieter slopes before coming back for breakfast. It was a short leisure walk. For a few seconds their attention was drawn by a park, covered in the rainy mist, which, it seemed, was unwilling to expose the govt neglect and spoil the girls' mood.

The teashop had a few jalebis lovers, more locals than tourists. As soon as the girls entered in, two men stood up and offered them their seats. The girls thanked and sat down. The owner, with a smile, asked their choice for breakfast. After a brief discussion the girls settled for jalebi, samosa and tea. When Sara asked for some more jalebis, Manjari cautioned, "Watch your tummy, girl."

"These are for long staircase back to our room," Sara shot back. "Moreover, there's nobody to give our tummies an admonishing look."

Both friends enjoyed jalebi, samosa, tea and tranquillity. From behind the turn a squad of NCC cadets; boys and girls, dressed in starched khakis, marched past them. A few boys turned back and finding two lovely girls at the Chowk, waved and smiled. Manjari and Sara waved and smiled back. Thereafter, they moved along the market, buying ice cream, chocolates and toffees. A few moments later stopped an army truck. The co-driver hopped out of his seat, went back and opened the tail board, out of which some men in combats jumped down. The soldiers, in a drill square movement, surveyed everybody present at the Chowk. As their gaze rested on the women a few seconds more their minds went back to their wives waiting back home. Their hopes of meeting them were thin as the next leave wasn't due until after some months. This thought deepened the longing and hurt the hearts more. With a heavy heart they moved towards the vegetable shops. Before getting back into the truck, the more homesick amongst them stole a second glance at the women tourists.

Both Manjari and Saranga wondered what the army was doing in such a desolate place; the China border was hundreds of miles away from there. Neither the shop owner, nor people present there could satisfy their curiosity. "The army does strange things in stranger places," cryptic remark of an old man laid their anxiety to rest. The girls stood up, paid and strolled back to the hotel room.

But stranger things awaited them at the hotel.

Chapter Thirteen

***

Next day a weary sun arose and moved up the sky. The grey and white clouds in close vicinity grouped up and rushed to cover it from every direction. But the sun, dodging them, showed up through tiny gaps every now and then. In this, sometimes the sun won and sometimes the clouds. Thus, the game went on and on. The wind was amused and lay still. The Kumauni women, however, weren't amused, as they had prayed for a strong sun to finish off drying of grains and clothes.

Two young people sat in different hotel balconies, separated by a few hundred metres. Both gazed at the valley ahead and tried to comprehend what love was all about? Deep down in their hearts they felt that there was something that attracted them to each other. Was it love? They weren't sure. Infatuation was a petty word for that sentiment. But they liked each other's company. Could this feeling be the seed of love, waiting to germinate? They pondered for long.

Lost in Ved's thoughts, Sara finished tea and put the glass on the table. With intense glow the sun had driven the rufous clouds away and blazed. The beads of sweat appeared at her temples and then trickled down to her back and breasts, and wet her shirt that had begun to scald. The shadow of the glass on floor caught her attention. It was dark and cheerful. After a few minutes the shadow grew pale and began to shiver. She picked up the glass and moved in. And when she turned back to take a quick peek at the valley, she was hit by a surprise shower.

As a subdued sun moved up, she moved inside. She removed her wet shirt, wiped off her body with towel, and changed into a fresh shirt. After a light make-up she moved out. It was time to see Vedanta and seek answer to the all-important question.

Minutes later Sara and Ved arrived at the Chowk where several disapproving eyes and begrudging voices met them. But minutes later the folks' conversation turned to the domestic problems. Barring a few young men, the majority didn't seem interested in gossip. Perhaps they had seen tourists in more inappropriate poses. Sara had a quick glance around and found impassive faces engaged in one to one, or in group talks. Comforted by the situation, Sara nudged Ved, and both hurried towards the forest. And after half-hour's silent walk both reached at the spot that gave an excellent view of the valley and the Himalayas.

Sitting on the rocks, located on either side of the path, for several moments they looked sideways at each other. The words failed to escape out of their mouth. The human silence had been seized by silence of the wild. A stubborn stillness reigned. The inhabitants of the wood waited to listen in to the lover's conversation. And unmindful of this, both waited for the other to take the initiative.

Sara, after dithering for a while, spoke, "I don't know why, but I feel like believing your tale. Last night I thought a lot about it and came to a conclusion that our meeting in Kausani can't be a happenstance. Perhaps, the gods have planned this."

Vedanta couldn't disguise his glee.

Gazing into distance, she continued, "But for me things are confusing at the moment."

Those words held no promise. Sara wasn't an ordinary girl. So, it would take a lot of efforts by him to woo her, Ved had no doubt about it. However, her decision to see him had bolstered his confidence a bit.

Turning to her, he asked, "What should I do to win the heart of beautiful girl sitting opposite me?"

She gave a wry smile, "Don't worry, I won't ask you to jump off the cliff in front to prove your love. Two words: honesty and fidelity will please me. I know this sounds simple, but it's so tough to follow these qualities in life. Will you?"

Tempted to say 'yes', Vedanta held back and was lost in a deep thought, trying to understand the import of her words. Then peeping into her eyes, he queried, "What makes you think I won't?"

"A question in answer to a simple question and that took a delayed one," she snapped back. "I was right in my assumption of you. A present generation boy would speak something like that."

"No, no. You got me wrong. I didn't mean to say what I said," he fumbled for words, sounding unconvincing even to himself.

Those fumbling and mumblings reflected the helplessness of an innocent mind. It raised a smile on her lips and pity in her heart. The silence crept in. In nature's overbearing stillness, echoed the melody of two restless hearts. It was the one music that was to resonate in their minds for a long, long time.

"Inconsistent thoughts and insecure emotions last longer in a young man's mind. How could you be any different?" she spoke, in a grave tone. "I suppose all men are the same."

Vedanta couldn't afford to let this chance slip away. Battling confusion, he spoke with a degree of self-assurance, "Sara, how can you judge me when you haven't even tried me?"

"Oh," She gave a wooden smile, "Love has to pass through many tests every moment of its existence. And your love is still tied to umbilical cord."

"What?" he murmured, half in surprise and half in self-doubt.

"Did you say something?" she asked.

"Yeah, what's going to be my test?"

"Don't worry," she grinned. "Like Menelaus, you won't have to wage a war to win back your love; like Napoleon you won't have to write love letters on the horseback in the battlefield." A subdued sigh didn't escape her attentive ears. "It will be simpler, but not easier."

A question could derail her thought process, and perhaps upset her. So, he chose to hear her out.

"I like love wrapped in layers of mystic and purity. Pettiness tears it apart in no time. Infidelity kills it in an instant," she paused.

Love stirred in those restless young hearts.

In one; it was subtle, sublime and celestial. It was tender, eternal but anxious. In the other; it was obvious, usual and earthy. It was coarse, transient but anxious. And it was the anxiety that bound those two hearts that moment.

Both young hearts were filled with love for each other; but neither had the courage to speak those three fewest words. While one feared the impatience of a 'yes'; the other feared the prudence of a 'no'. In the grip of anxiety and fear, both lapsed into a long silence.

Those were moments of hope and moments of despair; those were moments of belief and moments of doubt; those were moments of tranquillity and moments of anxiety. And love waited to blossom in those unsure hearts.

Then through the rustling of trees, her words emerged, "I'm an old-fashioned romantic. I hate emails, Facebook and whatsapp for expressing one's sentiments. For me, emotions between two individuals are private and sacred, and they ought to remain so. It's blasphemy to share them with the whole world. It's like baring oneself before the strangers. The flow of words on a piece of paper touches your heart. The written letters carry the writer's smell and heartbeats. When you read the letter, you feel their presence around you."

Vedanta listened to her in rapt attention because every word she spoke told a thing or two about her psyche, which might give key to her heart. And with that key he hoped to open the vault of her heart and make an entry into it, and plant his love therein, forever.

Choosing his words, he remarked, "I love gazettes, but I still like to write letters to loved ones."

"Good, at least we've one common liking," she spoke through a smile. "But my idea of romance is different."

"Like?"

"Like you catch a cloud in your fist and whisper your love into its ears, and then ask it to carry the message to your beloved."

A nonplussed Ved couldn't hold his nerves, and questioned, "Sara, are you serious? Isn't it a weird thought?"

"I knew it was coming," she shot back. "Lovers can't be doubters, and doubters can't be lovers. Before the internet, people communicated with one another through letters, written on papers, and before the discovery of paper, people wrote on dry leaves and animal skins. Didn't Moses write the commandments on a stone tablet? Imagine the time when folks didn't know how to write on the stone. Didn't people in the ancient India use birds to send messages? So, why couldn't people before them use clouds as messengers? However incredulous it might sound, sending one's love messages through clouds might be possible. Isn't it the most romantic idea?"

Vedanta saw dreams float in those calm, hazel eyes.

"Have you read the Meghdoot?" she asked, her eyes fixed at far away hills.

"No."

"It's a must read for the lovers. In heaven there was a Yaksha who worked for Kubera, the treasurer to the gods. But this Yaksha was so besotted with his wife that he ignored his duty for which he, one day, was caught by Kubera, who cursed him and banished him to earth for a year. A disheartened Yaksha spent eight months on earth remembering his wife. Then one day the monsoon arrived on earth and he saw a rain cloud pass by. He requested it to carry a message to his wife, living in Alkapuri. The Yaksha described the route in an attractive way so that the cloud was inspired to take his message. The emotions described are so beautiful, so exclusive. It's my kind of romance."

For a few moments, Ved was speechless. Seated before her was a person, who he had thought to be a normal modern girl. But those words had proved him wrong. Inside her chest beat the heart of an unusual girl. And by no means, his task was going to be easy.

After a pause, he managed to say, "Sure."

"I want my lover to send me messages through clouds when I'm away from him, even for a short while. I love the rains and I love the clouds, and I love the million romantic messages those multi-coloured clouds carry for the lovers."

"How will you read mine amongst those?" Vedanta teased.

"Don't worry; I know how to read. First you learn how to write," she snapped back.

Perhaps that question was ill-timed; it occurred to him and he thought it wise to keep silent. The silence seldom has failed to resolve some of the greatest conflicts of human minds.

"What's your life's ambition?"

Timing and content of the question took him by surprise. It never occurred to him that anybody outside the interview room could ask him that question. To interviewers his answer would have been to head a multi-national company. But it wasn't the answer Saranga expected of him. And what she expected, he had no clue. Then he realised that he was in Kausani in search of it.

"I'm here in quest of the answer to this question," he replied.

"Your honesty impresses me."

Turning towards him, she resumed, "You will never understand my love for the mountains; perhaps nobody will. It has been my dream to own a house here in Kausani and spend a couple of months each year."

Ved spoke from heart, "I love the hills too. My quest brought me to this place a fortnight ago. Then I wasn't aware that one day I'd fall in love with this place."

"I didn't know you already have a sweetheart," she teased.

"Our father of the nation too had fallen in love with this place. I'm an ordinary mortal," he quipped.

It brought a smile on her face. Then she spoke, acquiring a serious countenance, "But my love for the mountains goes deeper. My heart belongs here. It's my life's greatest desire to own a piece of land, and construct a house. When I retire, I'll settle down here, grow fruits and vegetables, and spend my twilight years listening to the melody of dawn."

"Sara," he whispered, coming closer. "It's my dream too. Let's make it our dream."

Those words created the magic of a thousand mandolins, whose melody filled her lonely heart. For a while she listened to that music. It soothed her, it encouraged her.

And then the unexpected happened. Sara inched closer to him and whispered, "Ved, will you make it happen?"

"I'll," said Ved and then in same breath, whispered, "I love you, Saranga."

She gave him a curious glance. A brief pause ensued. Then she, through a thin smile, asked, "You want me to say I love you too."

"No," he said, after a quick thought. "You should say when you feel in your heart."

"Did you feel it when you said?" she asked.

The question put him in a quandary. Often he did and said things in impulse. Whether his heart had the same feeling for Saranga as his mind, he hadn't thought about it. So in a defensive tone, he replied, "Perhaps."

"Perhaps?"

"No…. yes. I mean I feel love for you in my heart."

"I'll have to ask your heart whether you are telling the truth."

"Who is stopping you?"

Then in an abrupt action she brought her ears close to his chest. Her sweet smell filled his face. His nostril inflated, his heart pounded like a rail engine. Her heartbeat too increased. Then she withdrew herself. For several minutes thereafter they said no words, but looked at each other, as lovers did when they met after a long separation.

Consumed by a moment of madness, Ved pulled himself closer to her and kissed her lips. With a bewildered look on her face, she kissed him back. Their lips had met, and so had their hearts, which that moment got flooded with a thousand dreams.

That afternoon the doubt had lost; the love had won.

As the dusk was about to fall, both returned to their hotel rooms. It was their penultimate day in Kausani. Manjari, who had been waiting for her friend in the hotel, ran out when she heard Sara's footsteps in the corridor.

"Oh, I'm so happy," Manjari shouted, hugging Sara. "You found your love."

"*Dhat*, how do you know?"

"Darling, the mist in your eyes," Manjari went on, "Tell me, how did it go?"

"Shut up," Sara cut Manjari's hopes of gossip short, and walked inside the room, "We need to pack up. It's our last day here."

That was the longest night for the lovers. In the long silent hours they dreamt, and dreamt. Dawn came loaded with hope and happiness. For the last time, they stood in their balconies and had a close look at Kausani, its valleys, its mists, its hills, its paths, its shops, and its folks. They wanted to savour those things in their hearts, forever. At last, they gazed at the Holy Himalayas in reverence and thanked gods for making something special happen in their lives.

Outside the lobby, both for the last time hugged each other, and bade a tearful farewell.

The lovers had left. Kausani, in several years, had become sad.

Chapter Fourteen

✳ ✳ ✳

Of all human emotions, love is the most magnificent. It's as strong as a diamond, as brittle as a dewdrop. It's as pure as gold, as sublime as dawn. All other emotions, victims of the circumstance, get born and die by time. They are transitory in nature, and seek reward and retribution. Love is above them all. It transcends every conceivable human barrier. It thrives on honesty and decays on deceit. Sacrifice it its oxygen.

Love is eternal.

And blessed are those who are in love. Saranga and Vedanta had been blessed in the land of gods. Back home, their parents were surprised to notice a change in them.

Once Saranga had hugged her grandma long enough and both had shed copious tears, they wiped off each other's eyes, and separated. Then over tea began a brief question-answer session followed by a eulogy to Kausani by Sara. The grandmother listened to every word in reverence as if she were listening to the Ramayana. The old woman was smart enough to pick up subtle changes in Sara's behaviour.

Later Sara went to her room, Nandini to her son's. Sitting on the bed, she spoke, "Keshav beta, do you know? Our Saranga has changed after coming back from Kausani."

"Amma, she looks tired."

"No. I mean she is in love."

"Come on, Amma. You are imagining things."

"Leave it. You won't understand," she said, getting up. "How will you? Yours was an arranged marriage."

Unsatisfied, the old woman stormed out of the room and went to kitchen in search of Alka.

The word 'love' unsettled Keshav. It often did. His marriage with Alka had been arranged by his parents. The month long period after the ring ceremony hadn't been enough to know a few things about Alka. Both had fallen in love with each other afterwards. Or, at the least, that's what he had thought so. But their mutual admiration had been infectious. Like mature lovers they had cared for each other and shared a few romantic moments every day.

In the school Keshav was a bright student, and hence the most sought after. His meticulous notes written in beautiful handwriting earned him every teacher's admiration, and every student's envy. The class room had a number of girls; two amongst them had requested the class teacher to put the boy Keshav in the middle of the desk with a capacity for three. This had infuriated many boys in the class and reduced his already dwindling friend list.

Brilliance in studies paid beautiful dividends, he had learnt early in life. Every minute spent in the company of those girls—one was fair and the other dark—was joie de vivre. A big handsome boy, the nephew of the local doctor one day came to the school riding a motorcycle. Where the poor students came to the school on foot and the rich on cycles; a bike rider was straight out of dreams. Since that day a different wind blew in the school. During the interval, the students begged the big boy for a ride, which was seldom acceded to, but the girls, one by one, got a chance to ride pillion. A few girls became his favourites.

With a deep sense of loss, the boy Keshav saw his two desk mates, after the biker's arrival, spent no time with him during intervals, and in the class he didn't get time to talk to them. His relationship, which earlier seemed to be headed in some direction, lost its way. Now it got restricted to their demand for his notes, which he gave. As time went by, rumours did rounds in the school linking the biker boy to some girls, including his desk mates. It broke his heart. He couldn't muster courage to ask them about it for the fear of losing their friendship.

And then after a year he lost contact with them as he moved out of the city. Why did he remember them whenever he heard the word, 'love'? It was one secret the boy Keshav never shared with the man Keshav.

In the kitchen, Alka was cutting vegetables and humming an old Lata song. It often came on her lips when the word love was uttered by her husband. She was born in a middle class family and had a strict upbringing. In the college she avoided boys, but one day she was shocked when a handsome boy in the college gave her a red rose as keepsake, which she kept in the history book. But one day when her mother entered her room for dusting, she snatched the book from her, turned back and swallowed the dried rose with spittle. Then she replaced the book.

"What was that, Alka?" the mother queried, in a headmistress tone.

"Candy, Mummy."

"Candy?" the mother muttered. "Alka, I'm fed up of it. You keep candy all over the place; in the skirt, in the pencil box and in the books. Haven't I warned you enough?"

"Sorry, Mummy," Alka apologised, catching her ears.

"Go, take a bath. Lunch is ready."

Thus, a storm was averted. Alka's mother had a

bad habit of sharing everything with her husband, for who love before marriage was the greatest sin a young boy and girl could commit.

Was that love? She wondered till date. Recollecting those days she stopped humming and she didn't notice her mother-in-law walk in.

"Alka, did you notice anything strange in our Sara's behaviour today," Nandini, asked stepping inside.

"Nothing, she is tired."

"No, you didn't get me. Doesn't she seem to be in love?"

"Nahin, Amma. I don't think so. If she is, she won't tell anyone about it except you. Nowadays Sara doesn't confide anything in me," the mother rued.

"Oh, why am I wasting time with you guys?" the old woman mumbled and moved out.

A few hundred miles away Shashank and Vasudha sat in the lawn and chatted. It was a Sunday forenoon ritual, both followed whenever husband was at home.

"Good morning, Mom and Dad," Ved emerged from inside, with tea tray in hand.

The father gave a surprised smile, but the mother got worried, "Ved, wait. I'm coming. You'll drop the cups."

Shashank gestured her to remain seated. Ved mollified his mother, "Mom, don't worry. I'm not a kid. I won't drop it."

A beaming Vedanta put the tray on the table, and for the first time made tea for both. Shashank put hand on his wife's and winked. Taking tea, he asked, "How was your trip to Kausani?"

"Wonderful."

"Did my son's quest give him what he had desired for?"

"More than that, Dad," Ved sat with them and

talked about Kausani, omitting any reference to Saranga. Vasudha listened to him in rapt attention, while Shashank pretended. He knew what went on in his son's mind that moment, and he was certain that Ved had met someone special.

After Vedanta had gone inside, Shashank inched closer and took Vasudha's hand in his. For a second Vasudha felt a chill run through her body. It was the same feeling when he had held her hand the first time they had met. The boy Shashank was mad after her in the college and chased her like a shadow. After a year she had relented and agreed for a date when she had become sure of his sincerity. Their courtship had lasted over two years during which both had kept their relationship a secret from their orthodox parents.

And once both were settled in their jobs, they told their parents, who agreed and they got married. Since then it had been a blissful life up to now. Like others, they had their quota of squabbles, a few fights that were forgiven and forgotten. Srikant and Vedanta were brilliant students and brought immense joy in their life. From God, they couldn't ask for more; they didn't wish any more for themselves, except that Ved married a good girl and settled down. Srikant had married and made Boston his new home. This decision of his eldest son still rankled him and had left traces of hurt in his heart.

Coming out of trance, Vasudha asked, "Why this ……....?"

"Will time hold me hostage for this?" he smiled.

"You have way with words. Why don't you gift me a verse on my next birthday?"

"Why wait for so long? You might get a surprise within a week?' he pressed her hand.

"What's making you so romantic today?" she queried.

"Because our son is in love."

"Come on," Vasudha retorted. "Shashi, you are imagining things."

"No, I can see it in Ved's eyes. When a boy wakes at dawn and shares some of the household chores with his mother, think he is in love."

"Did it happen with you?"

"Yeah, but you weren't there to notice it."

Vasudha, after a brief silence, spoke with a sparkle in her eyes, "It's good Ved has found someone to share his life with."

"I hope he is as lucky as his father," Shashank spoke with misty eyes.

"No, he will be luckier. Our daughter-in-law will be a unique girl, out of this world."

Their dream was cut short by a phone call. Vasudha walked in to instruct the cook to make special dishes for breakfast to celebrate Ved's homecoming. Shashank got busy with his business call.

In this house and the house thousands of miles away two lovers waited for the clouds with abated breath.

Chapter Fifteen

The clouds since time immemorial have caught attention of the mankind. Nobody; the young or old, man or woman, rich or poor, has been able to escape from their magic. At dawn and dusk they are at their best when they appear in a myriad of colours, shapes and sizes. Inspired by them, many poets and writers have written volumes in their praise. In the heart of every lover, they always have held a special place.

Vedanta since childhood had a limited view of clouds. For him it had two shades; white and black. The white clouds floated in the sky from September to June and brought no rains; while the black clouds hovered for remaining months in which they brought rains. Since he had fallen in love with Saranga in Kausani, he had begun to see clouds in many shades and colours.

The first reading of the 'Meghdoot' had changed his perception about those divine wonder. They weren't the rain carriers, but could be perceived as the messengers. The power of wandering mass of smoke, so well captured by Kalidas in his book, had astounded the modern poets and writers alike. The book had no parallel in literature. But on lesser mortals like him, the book worked its simple magic.

A night prior to the onset of the monsoon, Ved sat in meditation and tried to ignite the feelings of a Yaksha in him. The following morning the rain poured, bringing joy on the faces of the farmers and other folks, reeling under the shock of the heat wave. His face lit up and thought of summoning clouds so that he could send message to his beloved. Thus, he called out aloud:

O, the handmaiden of Hera
Take leave of queen for a day,
The black clouds are thirsty
Drying crops are in disarray,
Go deep down into the sea
Bring pure water from below,
Fill up clouds' empty bellies
Long lost has been their glow,

And then he waited. After some time a huge, bright rainbow stretching from sky to earth appeared. Looking at it, he pleaded:

Oh Iris, my beautiful Iris
Send down red-orange clouds,
Each night goes in vain
In pain each day shrouds,
Far away from here my beloved lay
My heart wants to say,

Moved by the lover's plight, Iris sneaks away from the palace of Hera, and summons the clouds, fills them with water, and then sends them to the wailing lover. Ved was delighted when he saw dark clouds in the sky. He ran upstairs to the roof and stood mesmerised. Amongst black clouds hung a lone red cloud that seemed to say, 'I'm ready to carry your message to your beloved'. Looking upwards, he spoke:

Oh, heavenly messengers,
Servants of beautiful Iris,
Steel your hearts and minds
'Cause not easy is journey this,
Oh, beautiful, wonderful clouds
Carriers of pure, white rain,
You look tired, take some rest
Let your energy not drain,
No ordinary message to carry
No ordinary love is mine,
Blessed was our meeting
In the land that is divine,
To my beloved take my message
Of unending love and longing,
I lay on the bed of melancholy
Fearful thoughts come thronging,
Lay the land of my beloved
Far away in the foothills,
A river flows on its east
On the west, are the windmills,
O, clouds! Go tell my beloved
Of a thousand dreams,
Not a wink of sleep gets her lover
Wakes up in the night and screams,
Arrows of melancholy pierce
His heart's ramparts redoubt,
Him, hold fear and agony,
Not let a moment pass without,

As soon as the message was read to them, the red cloud stored it in the heart and lifted up to a great height, and then moved north towards the foothills, where Saranga's home was. Filled with empathy for lovers, whose plight they couldn't see and so they moved at a great speed. En route, they passed over the parched lands on which stood several folks, looking upwards praying for the rain. Taking pity, the clouds halted and unloaded the part load and then continued with their journey.

In the meanwhile Zeus sent down strong winds to give them speed. A hundred mile they covered in a day and chose not to rest until they arrived over the Mount Vindhya, where they, as requested by the lover, rested for some time to regain energy. Rejuvenated by the rest, the clouds resumed the trip. Next day in the afternoon they passed over the large expanse of the great Indo-Gangetic plains, which was filled with a sea of people.

In the centre of a curious gathering some saffron-clad folks sat around a square pit and chanted mantras while performing the *puja*. And some feet away from them, two children dressed in loincloth rolled over the wet earth as some men threw bucketful of water over them. Over a stretched rope walked a fun ambulist covered in mud. People clapped and looked on at the ongoing tamasha. The clouds taking pity on the poor boys' pitiable condition, poured down the rain, and then moved on.

"What's this, Papa?" a boy, sitting on his father's shoulders, asked.

"It's a ritual to invoke God's favour for bringing down the rain," replied the father.

"But why are the poor kids made to roll over on the slush?" the boy inquired. "Their bones must be cracking and their bodies aching."

Father perturbed by that sight, spoke with a tinge of sadness, "Son, this is the rich folks' world. It has no place for the poor and the destitute. In their world the statues that can't eat are fed more than the poor who sleep empty stomach. Let's leave. A moment's stay further will fill your heart with grief."

"Okay, Papa, let's move," the boy was disturbed.

Fired by mission, the clouds thereafter didn't halt whether it was dawn or dusk, or day or night. Without a break they moved on until they arrived at the foothills of the Himalayas.

Over thousand roofs, they searched and searched until they sighted a lone girl sitting on the parapet and gazing at the sky. The description given by Vedanta matched with hers. The clouds then began to descend and when they reached within a hearing distance, the rosy cloud asked, "Girl, are you the beloved of Vedanta?"

"Yes," Sara stood up, wiping her eyes. "Do you carry a message from him?"

"Yes, we do," said the messenger and then read out the message. And when it finished, tears of joy streamed down the beloved's eyes.

It has been days since she had received Ved's last letter. Her heart yearned for a letter a day. But that wasn't possible for a normal person to write a love letter of substance each day. And he wasn't an incurable romantic.

With a lump in her throat, Saranga spoke, "O, the messengers of love, wait for a while. I'll give you my message for my lover. Keep this message in your heart. Carry it to my lover. And then she dictated her message:

O, wonderful messengers
Coming from distant lands,
With glowing, smiley faces
Attired in colourful bands,
Go, rush to the land of
My beloved, this very day,

Listen carefully and tell him
What now I say,
"Come, claim your beauty that lay beneath,
In the night's melancholic sheath,
Insomnia that witching hour unleashes,
And your dreams, hour of the wolf ceases,
Dawn for a while holds me in motherly embrace,
Through window the light winks at my face,
Long afternoon fills my heart with deep longing,
In helplessness, I watch fearful thoughts thronging,
Weary afternoon hours are seldom soothing,
Few happy moments are wiled away in brooding,
In colourful attire, arrives the golden dusk,
Its face is gaiety; its manners are brusque,
Night with open fangs waits to attack,
My sleep, my peace easy to ransack,
Night's melancholy east winds quietly smother
Agony of consciousness bygone moments hardly
bother,
Each moment of my living I suffer your memories' cruelty,
Against the demons of doubt, I guard my thoughts' fidelity,
Come my beloved; Hold me in your trusting arms,
Fill my empty heart with your faithful charms,
Before despair engulfs my heart in its eternal haze,
Come, let's relive those magical Kausani days,"

With the message loaded in the heart, the homesick clouds embarked upon the return journey.

Like this, the exchange of messages continued between Vedanta and Saranga during monsoon months. And on the night of the last rainy day, Iris came in the dream of both and spoke, "Hey, the dwellers of my favourite planet; the lovers of Kausani, from next dawn onwards I'll not be able to summon clouds in your service as Zeus has ordered them to go to distant lands to bring rains to the parched fields there. Therefore, I beseech you both to get married. I bless you both."

The rays fell on their faces, heralding a new day. Rubbing eyes, both sat up in bed. Iris was gone, and so was the dream. A daydream always had come true in their lives.

Two days later, Ved was surprised to see Sara's parents in his house. He knew the purpose of their visit. Both their parents, in consultation with the priest, fixed the wedding on an auspicious date that fell a fortnight after the Diwali.

Chapter Sixteen

❋ ❋ ❋

The Hindu marriage is akin to a long stretched canvas filled with riot of colours and anarchy of emotions. Under the twin weights, it sags. A close look at it reveals a band of bright colours, interspersed here and there with shades of black, grey and green. The work is characterised by chaos and confusion in which extravagance of emotions borders on vulgarity. Every human being; young or old, child or adult, man or woman, rich or poor, paint their emotions in a brazen manner. The result: the painting capture snot-so-subtle hues of every known human emotion. The canvas is painted in love and hatred, in jealousy and contentment, in compassion and mischief, in care and indifference. And whenever the bride would inquire about any dark emotion in the canvas, her parents would cover them and comfort their little darling with smiles and hugs. The mollified bride would then walk away and the parents would heave a sigh of relief and get busy with their work.

During a Hindu marriage the list of ceremonies runs over a few pages, guest list over several. Scores of people from close relatives to the family priest are involved in every activity; big or small. It isn't a simple wedding ceremony. It's a festival.

And how could Saranga's marriage be any different? A month prior, her grandma had called for an all-important meeting with the family priest in which she decided to match the horoscope of both, the bride and the groom. Keshav's half-hearted protest was brushed aside by the old lady, who had taken upon herself to oversee all arrangements. The eighty-year old family matriarch had a few years left, and Keshav had let her have her wish. Raghav, his son was settled in the U.S. and had married an American, antagonising everybody in the family. And so, it was the grandmother's wish that Saranga be married according to the Hindu customs and traditions. And nobody in the family could dare to defy her. After all, Sara was her favourite grandchild.

The grandma from her steel trunk took out an old frayed diary, dusted it and then sat down with Keshav and Alka to decide on the guests. It was a thirty-year old list, which she and her husband had made for Keshav's marriage. Her memory was sharp and she knew who in the list was alive and who had passed away. She took care not to leave anyone out. New guests, the friends of Keshav and Saranga were added. Nandini kept adding until the total crossed five hundred. Euphoria of seeing her darling Saranga in a bridal dress had energised her so much that she slept fewer hours than her son or daughter-in-law.

The grandma sat in the living room surrounded by the family members and the family priest. Laid on the glass table were a dozen old wedding cards. Search for exclusivity was tough and long drawn, stretching over two days. Suggestion flew thick and fast. The old woman heard every idea and those present there knew well that she would have the last say. In between Sara was called out for her inputs, but she told them she would go with the majority view and moved away to resume gossip with her friends.

Her maximum time was spent in chatting with Vedanta. There was so much to talk to and so little time left before marriage, she complained.

As the wedding day neared, the relations poured in and were put up at a hotel close to the house but most of them insisted to stay in the house, as the women didn't want to miss the fun. After much persuasion by Keshav, some relatives did agree to stay in the hotel. For him, it was tough to satisfy everybody.

In the house, each room was filled with additional mattresses and bed linen. Except for the master bedroom and Nandini's, all others were adjusted to house maximum people. Men and women slept in separate rooms. Sara had never attended any marriage before, and hence was amused to see all this. Every relative, old or young, had some advice or other to offer to Keshav and Alka.

The pendulum of advice swung between mischief and concern, depending upon the age of the advice giver. The young ones were full of naughtiness, while the elders were concerned. But there were exceptions on both sides. Everybody had something to say to Saranga. Like a good girl, she pretended to hear them and put up a serious face not to offend anyone.

Initial days for the bride were interesting but after some time it got boring, and a week later she was pissed off. When she wanted to spend more time with her grandma, she found her busy in never ending ceremonies. The old woman whenever passed by her pecked her on the cheek and blessed. Sara noticed that her grandma was the last to sleep and first to awake.

A few days before the wedding day, it occurred to Nandini that she gave no time to her darling Saranga, and she had so much to talk with her. It was well past midnight. Thought of a long separation from the little one filled her eyes. Winding up the day's events, she sneaked into Sara's room and found her on phone. The familiar sound of knocks on the door drew Sara's attention.

"Come on, Dadi. You don't have to do this." She sprang up off the bed, rushed to the door and held her Dadi's hand. Making her sit on the bed, she sat down on the floor and placed her head in the old woman's lap. Nandini ran her fingers through Sara's hair. For a long time, both said nothing to each other. In Dadi's lap Saranga let weariness of months melt away in minutes.

But the silence didn't last longer.

"Dadi, do you like Vedanta?"

"Pagli, too late to ask. Your decision can't change even if my opinion is any different."

"Dadi, if you say 'no'. I won't marry him."

"How can I break the heart of my life-giver?" Nandini pinched Sara's cheeks. "I find traces of your grandpa in him."

"Then he will be a good husband." Sara spoke, lifting her head.

Nandini took Sara's head in her palms, and whispered. "He better be. But don't worry. To me, he carries the best of your father and grandfather."

"Dadi, tell me. Who else in the family had a love marriage?" a curious Sara wished to know if she was making a family history.

"Sorry, you will be disappointed to learn that you are not alone. A couple of your uncles have had love marriages, but theirs wasn't half as romantic. Yours is god blessed, and hence very special." Nandini's eyes sparkled in pride.

"Dadi, tell me something about grandpa. I wasn't lucky to play with him." It was the last thing Nandini would have wished that moment. But she couldn't say no to

Saranga. So, she, from the forgotten memory heap, dug out a few of her husband's.

With a twinkle in her eyes, she said, "At a relative's wedding a young man met me and asked me my name. I blushed and ran away. But he chased me until I gave him my name. For several minutes he stared at me. It reddened me. Then we heard some footsteps in the corridor. And before I turned to leave, he held my hand and told me that I was the most beautiful girl he had met in his life."

"What did you do, then?" asked an excited Sara.

"Afraid to get caught, I ran away from there, but the image of the man didn't leave me. It gave me dreams, beautiful dreams. Then we met after a month and after a few meetings at some funny places, we fell in love. The man was smart. He sent a marriage invitation to my father, who accepted it. Three months later we were happily married."

"Dadi, you never told yours was a love marriage."

"It hardly was," Nandini looked out of the window. "But you never asked me. And before you naughty girl wish to dig further into your old Dadi's past, let me tell you. We didn't get physical until our wedding night."

Sara gave her grandma a tight hug and kissed. Inquisitive, she asked, "Dadi, how did the married women cope with life in your time?"

"Beta, the life of a married woman has never been easy. Even our Sita mata had to undergo the fire test. A married woman in our times lived in a perpetual fear of her husband being snatched away by the other women, the nautch girls and prostitutes, who solicited openly. In our times a marriage lasted for three to four days, during which the *baarat* stayed in the mango orchard where during the day, the nautch girls were brought in to entertain the men folk. The women never accompanied the marriage party then."

"Thank God! Marriage is a shorter event nowadays," Sara breathed a sigh of relief.

"Saranga, remember, the evil woman, the wife-snatcher has existed since the dawn of the civilization. In my time they came as the nautch girls. In your time they wear sophisticated garb of a secretary, a friend's wife, a neighbour's wife, a colleague at the workplace, etc. This is the wife's biggest threat that would exist forever. And every wife will have to wage a battle against it to ensure that no evil woman takes her husband away. Nor that in our time men weren't adulterous, but they were bound by strong family values and fear of the society. In a joint family every member kept a watch on one another, and this stopped men from going astray.

These days this protective umbrella is gone. In a nuclear family where both spouses work, it's difficult to keep a tag on each other's movements. The freedom increases vulnerability to temptations. Nowadays, the evil woman comes in different garbs. In ancient times, these women lived as the nautch girl, tawaif, devadasi, etc; the fanciful names for the other woman, whose sole aim was to break a married woman's heart and her married life. Whatever you people might call them, I call them as the husband snatchers. They are vile, vicious and scheming. They break hearts and homes. In modern times they come in several disguises. And men are men. They have always been so since the dawn of civilisation; amorous, adulterous, ready to jump into bed with the next beautiful woman."

"How do you tame them?"

"Saranga, I'll tell you a secret. The most men like strong women, who can tame them. And the husband snatchers are strong women."

"How was grandpa as a husband?"

"He was no different. My mother-in-law shared

his secret. She told me that her son was fond of watching the dance of nautch girls, and she asked me to be tough with him. One day I confronted your grandpa and gave him a stern warning that he had to stop his activities. And he did."

Sara looked at her grandma with pride, and said, "I know, my Dadi is a strong woman. A married woman can't afford to be weak. But you don't have to worry about Vedanta. He's a good boy. Moreover, I've a *taviz* that will protect you from modern-day witches."

Both heard the door's sudden creak. Keshav and Alka stood at the door. Stepping in, Keshav said, "Amma, what secrets are you sharing with Sara?"

"Why?" asked Nandini. "Are you both jealous I'm taking away your share of love?

Alka came closer and sitting beside her mother-in-law, spoke, "Amma, you have the first right on Sara."

Keshav urged his mother, "Amma, it's late. Get some sleep. Tomorrow will be a busy day."

"Beta, these old bones have not gone brittle. In fact, mine are stronger than yours."

"Who can deny that but even the strongest need some rest."

Nandini stood up. She kissed Saranga good night, and left. Keshav moved out. Alka stayed for a while and tucked Sara in the sheet, kissed her forehead and went to the kitchen for the last look before returning to her bedroom.

And three days later, Saranga and Vedanta were married in a grand and solemn ceremony attended by hundreds of relatives and friends. The ceremony lasted until wee hours of the morning. After a few hours of rest, the family prepared for the send-off to Saranga. Next morning Sara left her childhood home for a new home, her husband's home. Her tears never stopped. She cried clinging to her grandma, mother and father; for a long time.

At the in-law's house the newlywed were accorded a grand reception. The day was spent in numerous ceremonies that tired the couple out. And next afternoon they headed to Bangkok for a week long honeymoon. Hectic days followed after their return from there. For some time, both spent a few days at Sara's place, then at Ved's, before both boarded the train to acquire a home of their own. Excited, they embarked upon the journey to a new world, their world.

Chapter Seventeen

✳   ✳   ✳

The city of gardens; the epithet rattled the outsiders, but the locals still called it more out of nostalgia and glory of the bygone era than any pride. Two decades later the city had turned into a concrete jungle, like several others in India. The Bangalore skyline, not in distant past was full of greenery and gardens, now was dotted with skyscrapers. And amongst those high-rise buildings was the Akash Homes, spread over a few acres. The complex boasted of many facilities such as a swimming pool, an ATM, a shopping complex, a walking plaza and a coffee house. The rich could afford to buy or take a house on rent in it.

Most of its residents were rich. Ved and Sara moved into their flat on the fourth floor. Opposite to them lived Manjari with her husband. Both friends shared the same office and homes on the same floor. However, their husbands worked in different companies, located in the IT Park. On weekends whenever they could get some time for themselves, they spent on shopping for household goods and on setting up their home, which had become their small world in which both couples lived their dreams, one by one. These were the happiest moments of their life.

The night prior to a holiday was the busiest and the

most sought after. Evening was spent on watching the latest Hindi movie, followed by dinner in the favourite restaurant. They returned home with cars filled with household goods. Till wee hours they consumed numerous cups of coffee, argued over setting up things in the house and then made love; and into each other's arms fell asleep and slept until the maid rang the doorbell at ten the next morning.

Sunday or holiday morning air in the Akash Homes was still and if someone happened to visit the complex during this time, they were in for a mild shock because except for a security guard, they could see no other human soul. The shops opened after ten. Most visitors there often got confused and looked at the watch again and again to check if their machine worked.

But holiday or no holiday; a woman, in late forties, on whose face the anxiety of years had added a few more wrinkles, but hadn't been able to diminish her beauty a bit, awoke before dawn each day. Those shining wrinkles had added a sublime grace to her face and enigma to her persona. Everybody called her Aparna auntie. And whoever met her couldn't escape her charm. Her two secrets a few women were privy to. One, she was an excellent cook, and two, who her husband was.

Awaking late on a Sunday morning, Sara found no sugar in the house. Against her will, she put on a light sweater and moved down the lift to the provision store on the ground floor. Her eyes turned around and fell on the middle-aged woman, sitting on the bench in the park. There was something about her that held Sara's attention and drew her towards it.

Inching closer, Sara asked, "Ma'am, are you okay?"

The sound made the woman's head turn. Next moment before Sara stood a tall, fair woman in late forties with streaks of grey in her hair that reached a slender waist.

Her face carrying wisdom of years glowed in grace. Sara for a moment glanced at the woman's well-maintained figure and was forced to look at hers and it gave her a complex. She needed to work on her body, a thought flashed in her mind. A cream salwar kurta enhanced the woman's sublime beauty. Sara could have continued to gaze for some more time had she not felt a tap on her shoulder.

"Yeah, I'm Aparna," the woman said, with a golden smile.

"Hi, I'm Saranga, call me Sara. I got curious to see you alone here and so……….."

Aparna cut her short, "I was missing my husband so much that I sat down here for some time. When he is here on leave, we often sit on this bench for hours, and relive our beautiful moments. His call woke me up in the morning and since then I couldn't sleep. Two months in a year for thirty long years is too little a time between the spouses to share their grief and happiness with each other."

"Why? Where is uncle?"

"On the Bangladesh border. He is a BSF officer and stays there with the troops. So we decided to buy a house and shift here. My two children are married and settled. We stay together whenever he is posted to a peace station. So, for me it's a lonely existence, which gets broken when my children come to me, or I go to them."

"Call me auntie. Here everybody calls me so." She said, putting the young woman at ease. Overwhelmed by that rare Indian etiquette, an oddity amongst the new generation, Aparna opened her purse, took out a silver coin and said handing it to Saranga, "Beta. Take it. It's *shagun*. God bless you both. I think we need to celebrate our new found friendship with coffee."

Then Aparna gestured to the coffee shop nearby and they both walked in there. Saranga looked at Aparna in whom she found some glimpses of her grandma, except the woman sitting opposite her was years younger.

"So how do you find this place?" asked Aparna.

"Auntie, we are still settling down in our new home, and don't get time to explore this city," Sara replied between sips.

"Sara, your eyes are beautiful and speak your heart's language. You miss your folks, don't you?" she queried.

A mist settled in Sara's eyes. She nodded, closing her eyes. Then she felt a hand on her shoulder and heard an assuring voice, "Don't worry, I'm your own. Drop in at my place wherever you feel homesick and want to have home-made grub. And I wish to share a secret with you. I'm a good cook. My hubby says so. And I need a regular confirmation of that."

"Sure, auntie we will drop in. I'll let you know when we are free next week," she thanked her and came back home.

As Sara entered the elevator, she asked, "Where is uncle coming next?"

"Next month. Until then I'll wait for him. It has been a long wait this time," Aparna's voice was weighed down by sadness.

Sara was moved by her situation. She held her hand, and assured, "Auntie, don't worry. From today you have a daughter here. Call me whenever you feel like."

Aparna smiled. Sara smiled back. Later she returned home. That place had lessened some of Sara's homesickness. Thereafter for several days she got busy and didn't meet Aparna. Then on a Friday morning she got an invite for lunch on Sunday.

And on Sunday she entered Aparna's house with a bouquet, and was surprised to find Manjari with her husband. "Wow, that's great." She hugged Manjari. Their husbands exchanged 'hello' and sat in down in the sofa.

"Sorry boys, you will have to endure coke. My husband would have offered you a beer," Aparna said handing soft drinks to the boys.

Manjari watching from the sidelines smiled at her husband, "Auntie, it's good we came here; otherwise these men won't leave any opportunity to drink beer on Sundays."

The girls then picked up their glasses and went to the kitchen to help Aparna who didn't let them help, but chatted with them nonstop. The smell and taste of home cooked food was something that the young couple had missed since long. And what a luck it had been? In auntie they had found image of their mothers. The boys on the pretext of office work thanked Aparna and left. The girls, on auntie's insistence, stayed back for a little longer.

"Auntie, how you spend your time?" asked Manjari.

"I'm a busy person, though people think otherwise. My day starts early with an hour long prayer. Then I've breakfast. Forenoon time goes in reading. After lunch I spend some time in the park with children and evening with my favourite TV programmes. So passes my day. Evenings are seldom spent alone. Somebody from the building drops in everyday."

"When is uncle coming?" asked Manjari.

"Next month," replied Sara.

"Auntie will get busy for a month then, and nobody will get to see her," Manjari spoke with a wink, looking at Sara.

"No, it's not that. You guys can come when uncle's around. He will be happy to meet you both."

"Auntie, we will come and look him up."

Thereafter the three women chatted on various subjects over coffee and in the evening Manjari and Sara got up to leave.

"You girls are like my daughters and you can come to me any time," Aparna said hugging them.

Sara and Manjari came back to their flats.

Aparna, after marriage with Joydeep had moved into their flat in this building. The Chatterjees had two children; a daughter and a son, both after doing their MBA had taken up job in multi-national companies; the son in Japan and the daughter in Singapore. Two years ago both had got married in a glittering ceremony, after which they had moved away with their spouses. Twice a year the daughter visited Aparna; sometimes with her husband and sometimes alone. The son also came to India once a while to look her up. But neither could lessen their mother's loneliness. Her husband tried during short leaves. After his retirement, she expected Joy (her husband) to share her solitude of years.

In bliss, days passed and months passed. And in the second year Vedanta and Saranga were blessed with a baby boy, whom both on the advice of parents named as 'Dhruv'.

"Like a North Star, Dhruv will shine and bring glory to our families," Shashank's eyes shone with pride.

Vasudha and Alka took turns to stay with Saranga and help the new mother to raise the newborn. Ved and Sara felt proud every moment they looked at their son, who had brought immense joy in their life and given it a new meaning. It was bliss, they experienced every waking moment, dreamed every sleeping moment. And until Dhruv was three years old, both didn't get good sleep. Sara's maximum time was spent in care of Dhruv. At times she felt she neglected Ved, but she couldn't help it. Perhaps every woman went through this phase in her married life.

For initial days Ved was understanding, but as the time worn on, so did his patience. He missed Sara by his side.

He wanted to cuddle up with her, hug her and make love to her. But often their son awoke Sara at odd night hours, and he had to sleep often alone, killing his libido. In the night when Sara sneaked under the blanket, he could never know. Their bundle of joy was creating a space between them.

Chapter Eighteen

* * *

The conniving night had ripped off an hour of twilight. The lazy sun didn't complain. A restless dawn broke on a cloudless March morning. One fist above the horizon in an endless sea of grey, a lonely moon set. Not far from it, the morning star shone bright and teased the big brother. The wind had fallen into deep slumber. The glitter of the kingdom of heaven was gone. A few hours ago the billion dazzling stars had perplexed the million minds: how vast was the universe and how small the earth. The dark banished the human vanities; the light brought them to the fore.

Then the first rays fell on the high-rise building, one of the many that dotted the city landscape. The fifth floor of the Akash Homes had four flats facing east. And in one of those lived Ved and Sara. Through a large window whose curtains were pulled aside, the light beamed in the bedroom and fell on Saranga. The sun rays travelling through the glass had become hotter and sharper, and pricked her tender face. Beads of sweat had begun to appear on her forehead.

Unable to endure the sting any further she sat up in bed, ran fingers through her hair and palm over the face. Then she stretched her hands out and yawned. Her eyes fell on the alarm clock, a pre-independence piece his grandfather had brought from Lahore during his maiden visit there and gifted it to his wife, who as a young bride had often found it difficult to wake up in the morning. The polish had peeled off at places and gave the clock an antique look. Ved had made fun of it once, but a stern look from her had kindled a liking for the clock in his heart.

Last night she had forgotten to activate the alarm and drawn the curtains. After all, I've two hands and household chores are endless, she said to herself and cried. Then she jumped off the bed and rushed to the adjoining room where Dhruv was fast asleep. She shook him up, "Beta, get up, you will be late for the school."

"Mama, please……. let me sleep for five minutes more," the boy pleaded, showing a stretched palm.

"No, nothing doing. You're already late. Take your brush and get going," she lifted him up, and said handing him the toothbrush.

And she watched Dhruv whine and walk inside the bathroom.

"All right, Amma. You can go, I'll get ready," he assured her brushing his teeth.

She smiled and left. Dhruv addressed her by different titles like Mama, Mummy, Ma, Amma, Mother, etc. The boy was sensitive and caring far beyond his age. He would grow into a good husband, she thought. If Ved had learnt a thing or two from his son, perhaps their lives would have been much better. She came out of the bathroom and found Ved snoring. Unconcerned, he slept upside down on his stomach.

"Ved, get up," she shouted. "How many times should I tell you? For God's sake, please don't sleep in this position. You will suffocate."

Then she went to the kitchen and brewed a strong

ginger tea. Holding a cup in her hand, she came out on the balcony. Leaning over the railing, she sipped tea. From that height the world down below looked small. People moved from one side to the other; some in needless anxiety and some in genuine hurry. The vehicles sped past. The pedestrians waded through the food and tea pushcarts that had encroached upon the footpath on either side. Littered were the berms with paper cups and plates, plastic wrappers and leftover food. Now and then a whiff of foul smell rose to the balcony. Stray dogs, beggars and rag-pickers loitered in the streets, scavenging for food in the garbage. All three belonged to the same social strata. The crowd, dressed in a myriad of colours, was a mix of both genders, young and old, and children. The moving human mass was self-centred and emotionless.

Bored, she stepped back and fell in the cane chair. Her thoughts wandered to the previous night.

As a young woman she had hoped that her man would take her in his arms and say sorry, kiss her and make love to her. But like many previous nights, he had fought with her and fallen asleep, leaving her helpless and sleepless. In the dark, she mulled over their relationship, their lives. Even after spending five years together their relationship hadn't cemented. On the contrary, with each passing day their bond had weakened. Neither had thought it to be prudent to tackle the problem in a mature manner. Both had let the differences grow into a huge pile.

"I'm so sorry, honey," he tiptoed into the balcony and whispered. Bending over, he gave her a mechanical kiss.

"It's okay," she murmured, settling for a temporary truce.

Then both came inside. Dhruv had put on his school uniform. She fed him breakfast with her hands and saw him off at the lift. Ved escorted Dhruv to the school bus and after putting him in he returned.

In the meanwhile, Sara got ready and made breakfast. Once Ved was ready, both grabbed a quick bite and left for the office. They drove in separate cars to their workplaces. Until a few years back they had one car in which he dropped her at her office, en route to his. Then they had the same office timings. From home to office was a half-hour journey during which they shared several memorable moments. Often he would touch her hand, or pinch her cheek, or plant a kiss, or look at her with love. Those to and fro drives in the office had acted as glue to their relationship.

As a working couple they were always short of time for themselves, for their son. And the responsibility of managing the house had fallen on Sara's shoulders. His offer of assistance with domestic chores was seldom sufficient and never satisfying. So they had hired Sheela, a woman of short height and fair complexion. The maid, in the late thirties, wore garish clothes, loud lipstick and AD jewellery. She talked more and worked less. Sara was put off by her non-stop gossips, but pretended to listen in order to keep her in good humour. She disliked the maid's leering at men. So Ved was confined to the bedroom when she worked in the house. Sheela did everything except cooking dinner, which Sara did herself because she wanted her family to eat at least one proper home-cooked food.

Thus, this arrangement worked well for four years. But in the cut-throat world of competition where companies worked on tight deadlines and punishing work schedules Sara often had to work till late hours. He was free in the afternoon. For a few months he waited upon her and brought her home along, but later this didn't work out. So she purchased a car for herself. Thereafter they drove to their offices in separate cars.

The cruel fate had snatched the all-important half

hour from them. The glue had begun to melt away, exposing their relationship to outside pulls and pressures.

Whenever she returned home late, she found Ved either reading the newspaper, or watching TV. Sometimes Dhruv was with him watching TV; sometimes the boy did his homework alone, unsupervised. Often he forgot to give Dhruv his evening milk. The moment she stepped inside the house she was besieged by a plethora of problems. She never got any respite until she went to bed. And this routine continued uninterrupted.

Once when she had asked the maid to cook dinner; both father and son had raised a lot of hue and cry over its taste, though she had found the food palatable. Since that night Sara never bothered the maid again. And one night in exasperation, she yelled, "Why can't you guys eat dinner cooked by Sheela once in a while? I also need rest. I'm not a machine."

"Mama, she cooks horrible," Dhruv shouted from the study.

"Honey, I don't mind," Ved spoke, in a flattering tone. "But no one cooks better than you. You're the best chef in the world. Moreover, you know how poor her sense of hygiene is."

"It's better than yours."

"What did you say?"

"You heard it right," she teased.

"Come on, Sara. You can't be so harsh. I'm quite particular about my personal cleanliness," Ved said with a vehement protest.

"Yeah, who knows better than me," she rejoined. "Did you ever smell your socks? I get to while washing. "

The harsh reality hit him hard. The truth was that his socks after two days smelled like rotten eggs, despite foot deodorants. Had he stayed a minute longer, he would have faced more taunts. But if he slipped away from there, he would face her wrath.

"I know you men are the same, wanting a J Lo as maid and a Savitri as wife," she smiled.

"Who wouldn't?" he murmured.

She heard his deep sigh and queried, "Did you say something?"

"Nothing. In case you need my help in the kitchen."

"No, I don't want you to spoil things. You wash the dishes later," she said and went about her work.

After dinner Ved grumbled and cleaned the utensils. It was one work he disliked, but couldn't refuse and annoy Sara further.

In the last few years frostiness had crept in their relationship.

Chapter Nineteen

❄ ❄ ❄

The fiercest battles are not fought on the fertile farmlands, but in the human heartlands, where the battle between wife and the other woman is one of the oldest and bitterest. Often the fate has been unkind to the wife. Once a while, though, it, taking pity on her, does make her victorious, but the victory always comes at a huge cost. In every age, in every nation, in every city and in every street the wife fights this battle every moment of her life; sometimes with the relation's help, but often alone.

And Aparna too fought this battle. Alone.

If the falsehood had feet, it could have walked on until eternity, masquerading as the truth, but it didn't. The circumstances limited its ability to move. In Aparna's case her husband's lies had crawled on for longer than expected. Though frostiness in her life had seeped in during the last winter when Joy had come home on a short leave, she had failed to feel it.

When his love became lusterless and lovemaking a dull chore; she didn't know. Long absences and advancing age, she presumed, perhaps had smothered the embers of passion in the man who is youthful years had possessed unbridled libido that she at times had failed to satiate.

A few months ago while searching his clothes she found a piece of paper in his trouser pocket. It was a verse containing eight lines: a small love poem. For a second she was tempted to entertain the silly thought that he, during his long hours in the jungles of Tripura, had written it for her. But the next moment the reality struck her like a thunderbolt. Neither during year-long courtship, nor in over two-decade married life had he ever hummed a song, or written a line in her praise. How did he do it after so many years? Perhaps it was for somebody else living in the tribal lands. She had no heart to ask him about it, as she knew what his answer would be. She replaced the paper in the pocket.

After dinner he retired to the bedroom. She wound up the kitchen and then sat at the dining table, thinking about those lines that had got etched on her consciousness. Their intensity baffled her mind, their passion pierced her heart. The poem wasn't written in a jiffy. It was spontaneous outpourings of love.

The wife had the bone and flesh of her man to contend with, as the other woman had walked away with his heart and soul. Nothing could be a greater tragedy for the wife than to spend her life with a man whose heart and soul have been robbed by another woman.

During the leave Joy kept to himself. Taking cover behind one excuse or the other he didn't get close to her, physically and emotionally. She was sure he was hiding something from her. What? She didn't wish to guess the worst. And after a few days he was gone, leaving her behind with no memories worth savouring. Wounded, she watched the loneliness come back in the gathering gloom.

Three months later he arrived unannounced. Aparna was excited to see him so soon. She hugged him and cried. Joy remained unmoved. They spent two loveless days.

She felt he was trying to say something to her, but couldn't. Perhaps he was sorry. It kindled a ray of hope in her heart. It gave her optimism to win him back.

But a day prior to departure for Agartala, Joy dropped a bombshell, "I don't feel love for you anymore." Within seconds her blissful world like a house of sand collapsed to the ground. Hopes died a water bubble's death.

"What!" she screamed in rage. "You took thirty years to realize this. And who gave you this realization?"

"I'm in love with somebody else," his voice faltered. "She lives in Agartala. I've transferred this flat in your name and I pledge to give you half my salary now and half pension after retirement."

"And what do you expect from me in return?" she yelled in disgust. A feeling of revulsion filled her heart and soul. It occurred to her then that Joy's interest in her had died long back. His love hadn't waned in a day.

The man waited. Perhaps he fought traces of guilt caused by her presence. It wasn't an easy decision for him to leave Aparna, his wife of over two decades and mother of his two children.

Strange things happened in strange places. And Agartala was a strange place. It was Joy's third posting in Tripura. Three years ago he had come in contact with a woman, social worker who worked amongst the tribal folks, suffering excesses at the hands of the security forces. At the outset he had found the woman snobbish, out to malign the image of the soldiers deployed in the state. A few meetings later he understood her viewpoint better. A few months later he fell in love with her voluptuous body, she with his money.

Love?

They met often and continued with their affair. And one day he married her. He was a year short of sixty; she was twenty years his junior, but such age difference amongst the tribal society mattered little. The financial status of the man did. Joydeep had expected to seek divorce from his wife and settle down with his new wife in Agartala. At an opportune time he thought of breaking this news to his children from whom he expected little opposition. The maximum resistance was to come from his wife who he believed wouldn't give him an easy divorce. So, as part of the plan he transferred the Bangalore flat in her name.

During the night they spoke little. Next morning he was gone out of her life, forever.

For her, it was time for reflection. In the battle between the wife and the other woman, the wife, as often had been the case, had landed up on the losing side. It was a human tragedy of gigantic proportions. Many years ago Joy had robbed her of his heart and soul. Today he had robbed her of his bone and flesh too and walked away. Until that moment she had lived in the hope that one day he would come back to her, his wife of more than thirty years, the mother of his two children. But even that hope was gone now. She found herself sucked into a black hole from where there was no escape.

And she had no wish to escape from there.

Aparna felt her heart ripped out of her body. Before the statue of Lord 'Krishna' she slumped to her knees, held her head in her hands and sobbed. And God watched this irony. While one creator was adored, eulogized, prayed and feared; the other was harmed, humiliated and brutalized. In a brazen act of superiority the immortal creator didn't come to rescue of the mortal half. Cries of despair went on and on, until eternity.

After collecting her courage, she bathed and stood in front of the mirror. Withered breasts, eye bags, chin fat, tummy wrinkles, deep belly button cried out that she was past her prime. However, her waist despite a slim fat layering around it had retained its slenderness. Most of her friends had spread sideways, accumulated a good dollop of fat around the waist and buttocks, and lost firmness of the skin. In comparison, she looked and felt several years younger. What God's injustice it was! While those women lived with their husbands, hers had abandoned her.

As a young bride she often had stood in front of the mirror and each time her heart had filled with pride, gazing at herself; often alone and a few times with Joy, who had spoken a thousand words in praise of her physical beauty; the perky breasts, deep blue eyes, satin skin, taught tummy and long legs.

"You will grow old earlier than me," both had teased each other at every available opportunity.

As time had worn on, Joydeep had acquired more waist-fat, more wrinkles, and more freckles. His voice had hardened. The aging process in her, though, had been slower as she had worked hard to retain her youthful charm. And what a tragedy it had been? A younger woman had stolen Joy from her. It had been heartbreaking, devastating. In the darkness of the night she had shed silent tears and asked God, why hadn't he given a woman the power to retain her youth forever. "No matter what, Aparna I'll never leave you. We will spend after-retirement years travelling and seeing newer places." His words hit her heart and soul like an iron clangour.

A deathly calm prevailed. Aparna's eyes became cheerless and tenebrific. She had a hard look in the mirror and tears streamed down her sunken cheeks in many runnels, over the breasts, into the cleavage and on her hands. And a few tear drops made their way into her mouth, filling it with their saltiness. Her cries mingled with the noise of a broken heart. After some time dried-up tears began to scald her skin. The heart had emptied itself of the humiliation.

She had a hot bath and felt relaxed.

Moments later at the dining table over a cup of black coffee she recollected how Joy and she had shared several wonderful moments at the same table, discussing routine and important things of their life. Never for a second then had it occurred to her that he lived a double life. After their marriage not a day had gone by when she hadn't prayed for his long life. On every *Karva Chauth* and other Hindu auspicious days she fasted for him and their children, and prayed for them. Not once she asked God anything for herself.

Abandoned by husband and ignored by children, Aparna was to fend for herself at a vulnerable stage in her life, to seek succorance in strangers.

If Joy could live his life, why couldn't she live hers? If he could share his longing with another woman, why couldn't she share hers with another man? In retribution, or in helplessness, this idea stuck her mind.

In the night she, for the first time, stared at her total nakedness in desire and felt every part of her body to see if the flame of passion still blazed within her. In what way was she a lesser woman than the one Joy spent his life with? The question haunted her. And only a man could answer that. That moment she thought of sharing her grief with someone and unburdening herself of Joy's burdens. Then she remembered a chance meeting with an acquaintance a fortnight ago. From the visiting card she picked up his mobile number and called him up. They agreed to meet at a restaurant the next evening.

Both reached at the rendezvous on time. The place was dim and half-filled. Both chose a private corner and ordered coffee. The man looked at Aparna. Her face was cheerless and eyes brooding. Perhaps she had called him to share something important. What? He couldn't guess. A long silence ensued until the waiter brought them coffee.

Thereafter, she, fighting back tears, told him about her divorce stopping short of giving him the details. Perhaps it was a deliberate attempt to seek his empathy.

"I'm so sorry."

"Please don't?" her sobs subsided. "Maybe it's my destiny."

"What an irony?" the man spoke in a sad tone. "Our spouses have dumped us. Our hearts are wounded."

"I feel we were destined to meet," she said in a poignant voice.

"Perhaps."

Then they chatted for sometime before returning home. Thereafter, over next few days they met, sometimes at his place, sometimes at hers. Some days later they met at his place. With a surprised look on his face, he opened the door for the lady and ushered her in. It was their third meeting in as many months.

"Please come in," his tone was anxious.

"Sorry, I came unannounced," she sat in the sofa, sunk in thought.

A little later she stole a glance at him. The man wore a black pant, green shirt and red sweater. Behind a sham smile, he hid a broken heart. His eyes were sad, waiting to well up at mere mention of his past. In a two-second glance she saw him brooding.

"Aparna, what will you like, tea or coffee?"

"Tea will be fine… without sugar please."

The man went into the kitchen. She surveyed the living room that was well arranged but missed the hand of a woman. In the unreachable corners the dust glittered against the light. The room cried in the neglect of proper cleaning. The man returned with tea.

"Tea," he handed her cup and then offered her

biscuits.

"Thanks," she managed a smile. He smiled back in courtesy.

"If I may…..," he asked. "Why did you drop in so …….?"

"Why?" she said. "Can't I come to my friend's place? Did you forget you said I can count on you as a friend?"

"Oh, I forgot," he looked sideways.

A lonely heart often sought solace in another lonely heart. There in silence two lonely hearts tried to hear the other's sound. They waited to share their sadness, their bitterness and their loneliness.

"That evening you stopped short of telling your story," she had concern in her voice.

"It's distressing and gloomy."

"Only if you want," she said. "It might lessen your burden."

"All right," he wiped his dry eyes. "Ours was a love marriage. My wife was an ambitious woman. She craved for money, I craved for love. I had limited means. We managed to hold on to our marriage for five years during which I pleaded to her many times that we should plan a child but every time she said she wasn't ready for it. It seems she had planned all along to leave me and waited for the right opportunity. Then one day she met a rich businessman, fell in love with his money and left me, forever."

"I'm sorry."

"These days I read stories similar to mine and I draw comfort that I'm not a lone sufferer," he said with a wooden laugh.

Then they exchanged stolen glances in the accompanying silence.

Her voice, choked with emotion, broke the silence, "Betrayal runs through every tale of heartbreak. My story isn't any different. Joy has left me for a younger woman. Never for a moment did he feel the guilt that he was leaving his wife of more than twenty years. She had washed and ironed his clothes, cleaned his house, and born and raised his two children. The man never realised that the woman had given him hope when he was in despair, given her shoulder when he wished to cry and fulfilled his every desire. And he had used and dumped the same woman like a trash."

She started crying.

"Please don't," he was tempted to wipe her tears, but held back.

"Look at me," she asked between sobs, "Do you think there's no passion left in me? Are younger women more desirable?"

"Please, don't torment yourself," he tried to calm her down.

"I feel like a barren tree who neither can give fruit, nor shade."

Perplexed, he looked at her not knowing how to react to that. Then both fell silent. Dumped spouses sought solace in solitude. Her tears moved him. He came closer and sat beside her. As he bent forward to wipe her tears, the sweetness of her breath hit him, consumed him. Then in a moment of madness, he kissed her. Her lips were wet and hot. She kissed him back. Hit by a pang of guilt, she looked down. He withdrew to his chair.

Loneliness, lying in those hearts in a melancholic sojourn, stirred a few times, but it couldn't gather courage to cross the physical frontier. The orthodox Hindu upbringing held them back.

After a while he broke the silence, "Aparna, your heart is filled with so much of love. I wonder why your husband didn't see it."

"Do you mean it?" she asked, lifting her gaze.

"Yeah." he nodded.

It gave her hope. She hesitated, "Will you marry me?" But fear of a negative response tensed her face.

"Sure," his reply was instant and sincere. "But I need a few weeks to settle divorce dispute with my ex-wife."

"I'll wait."

After a while, she gave him a parting hug and left. No one saw her leave his flat, that's what she thought. But Manjari, who had come there to meet her friend, saw the auntie and became inquisitive. 'Who could she be visiting here?' She wondered. As far as she knew the auntie had no relatives or close friends in the city. Intrigued by auntie's presence in an unknown place, she decided to find out the truth.

Manjari climbed the floor from where Aparna auntie had come down. She had a quick glance at the name plates, all except one bore the names of couples. Who amongst them was her friend or relative was difficult to ascertain. It would have been foolish to ask all of them. So she decided to follow the auntie on her next visit there.

The same evening Manjari rang the bell of Aparna's flat. The owner, with her usual smile, opened the door.

"Auntie, you look sad," Manjari enquired.

"Yeah, the household chores wear me down," Aparna said, settling down in sofa. "Tea or coffee?"

"Tea."

Aparna stood up to make tea. Manjari followed her in the kitchen and there leaning against the counter, asked, "Auntie, did you go out today afternoon?"

"Have tea in peace, darling," Aparna said, with a dry smile.

Thereafter, both drank tea in silence.

"Yeah, what were you saying?"

"Auntie, do you have any relation in the Pacific

Homes?"

Aparna looked sideways and fell silent for a moment. Then gazing into Manjari's eyes, she said, "Are you ready to hear the truth?"

Manjari nodded. Aparna, after clearing her throat, narrated how and why Joy had abandoned her. Manjari heard her. Sadness and anguish hit that young heart with so much force that it made her speechless. Tears rolled down her eyes. And when Aparna finished, she heaved a sigh of relief. A load was off her chest. Bitterness had made way for melancholy. A long tough road lay ahead, but in the company of her male friend she hoped to live out her remaining years.

Chapter Twenty

* * *

At thirty-five thousand feet above the mean sea level every passenger went through a different shade of fear. Yesterday a jet liner had crashed into the Colombian jungles, leaving no survivors. This news was on air on every channel since morning. Those travelling in this aircraft had heard of it and were gripped by a sense of fright, in varying degree. And when the air hostess announced that they could remove their seatbelts, the air inside was filled with relief.

Unbuckling the belt, Vedanta sighed. Until then he, preoccupied in his thoughts, couldn't have a close look at his co-passenger.

"You don't like air travel, do you?" asked a sweet voice.

Intrigued, he turned to the window. A smile greeted him. He smiled back and said, "I guess nobody does."

"I'm Urvashi," she held out her hand.

A surprised Vedanta hesitated for a few seconds.

"Do you find this name a misfit on me?" she asked, bending closer.

"No, no. In reality, you are as beautiful as Urvashi." he collected his nerves as he spoke. "I'm Ved."

He shook her hand. To his surprise, it was warm

and firm. Those long fingers could adore a man's hand better. In comparison his was supple and short, somewhat womanlike. A quick glance at her both hands filled his heart with a tinge of inadequacy. Until that moment he hadn't experienced any such feeling.

She sensed his unease. Vedanta looked as under confident man, who relied on others for support. He seemed vulnerable, and she liked such men. The pause lasted a little longer.

"Your wife is a lucky woman," she said, hiding sadness behind a smile.

"Why do you say that?"

"Sparkle of the ring says so."

"Yeah, she is exquisite, out of this world."

"Should be."

"Should be!"

With a twinkle in her eyes, she spoke, "To get a handsome man as her soulmate."

"Thanks, though, I don't consider myself one," He reddened.

The air hostess cut their conversation short with her customary smile and offered them juice. Cabin crew, comprising three young air hostesses in red dress, wore loud make-up and strong expensive but different perfume. The first air hostess flashed her Rado watch more than her smile, the second adjusted her tresses that tumbled about her face and the third looked stressful as she went about her job in a diligent manner. They with their overbearing presence attracted several young envious glances. The young women travellers had forced their husbands to take the window seat and kept an eagle's eye over them, who pretended unconcerned by to and fro movement of the air hostesses but whenever the wives' gaze turned elsewhere they caught a quick glance of the attractive girls, drew in deep breath to smell the perfume and then looked outside. In this game some husbands had mastered while others were still learning it. The old women passengers gave the air hostesses an affectionate look every time they passed by while their husband preferred to catch some sleep.

The young Urvashi too was peeved about the presence of girls in red whose strong perfumes had smothered hers. It made her feel defenceless and vulnerable. For quite some time she had lost the attention of Ved who seemed lost in thoughts, perhaps in a girl in red. Irked by Ved's inattention, she looked outside the window at the vast blue expanse above and below the cirrus with which floated her anarchic thoughts.

Half-hour later Vedanta's gaze turned to Urvashi. Both exchanged smiles.

"You don't look comfortable wearing the ring," she asked.

"Why do you say so?" Ved had a surprise look on his face.

"It's written on your face," she winked.

"Oh, I'm bad in hiding emotions," he chuckled. "I admire people who wear more than one ring."

"A wife loves to see her husband wear the wedding ring. It assures her of his fidelity. We women love symbols in love."

He nodded in consent.

"Are you a banker?" she asked, after a brief pause.

"No, a software engineer," he said. "It hasn't disappointed you, I hope."

"Why? I'm not looking for a prospective partner to share my life with. I'm a CA......" she stopped to reveal anything further.

"And married to a successful banker," he tried to complete the sentence.

"Does it matter?" she counter-questioned him.

"No."

"Good. It's doesn't matter to me either," her smile was loaded with meaning and mischief. "I've had my share of men. A few of them were nice souls, but married. And I couldn't break their homes. The others were boisterous, self-serving megalomaniacs, who wished to shackle me to their thoughts, their money and their homes, and then use me to satisfy their egos and their bodies. A free bird hates the cage. I want to fly and explore the world. The sky will shrink for my wings."

Vedanta had a close look at her and found a gorgeous woman stranded alone on the wasteland of loneliness, whose vastness was unending and harshness unforgiving. It was doubtful she was there of her own volition. In desperation, she cried for help and if it didn't arrive in time, she was sure to perish.

Urvashi, in a well thought-out move, gazed outside the window to enable him to have a close look at her.

Long face, pointed nose, big blue eyes, thick cheeks and a largish forehead sculpted the woman. Her long hair, tied into a bun, was sure to be waist length. A slim waist parted her body into two halves, each more attractive than the other and in completion for attention. The blue top was an oddity. Perhaps the colour choice was deliberate to attract unnecessary attention. A self-assured woman wore a clever cleavage.

And before she turned to him, he pretended to read the paper.

"Anything of interest?"

"Mundane."

It was a lie any dumb woman could have caught.

"Yours must be a busy schedule," he asked.

"Yeah, but I'd love to work in your company if you

wish to."

"I'm a middle-level executive and I don't handle HR."

"God isn't kind to me this time. He had never been before," there was a sense of loss in her voice.

"Why?"

"Oh, I lost chance to work with an amazing guy," her voice dropped.

"You will get better opportunities."

Smile had returned on her face. Flattery was known to melt many a heart.

"Why? Do you work with geeks?"

"No, imbeciles. Every guy I work with thinks himself to be a Tom Cruise and runs after me."

"Who wouldn't?"

"Would you?" she said, peeping into his eyes.

He reddened with embarrassment.

"Sorry, I didn't mean to say this," was her half-hearted apology.

The silence invaded their space. He fell in deep thought. This wait would be a long one, she knew. Bored, she flipped through the in-flight magazine. But her heart was somewhere else.

The sight of food trolley brought relief on both faces. They had lunch in relative quietude. Destination was a few hours away. Sometimes they fidgeted with iPads, sometimes with cell phones, and sometimes with magazines. Restless hearts sought peace in lifeless things.

In two-hour long conversation Ved and Urvashi had opened up to each other, but a sense of anxiety persisted in their minds. It stopped them from sharing more. The woman found the man protective, the man found woman enigmatic. And each one wished to penetrate the other's fortress.

A woman's heart is the world's most impregnable fortress. Since antiquity, brave men often had fallen trying to reach its ramparts. A few braver made to its gates, but only the bravest reached the sanctum-sanctorum, where Venus reigned. The bravest one got her audience, her love and her kingdom.

Her eyes were closed, perhaps in thought, or in sleep. He too fell asleep.

Of late a young soldier had joined the army on a mission to capture a medieval European Fort, which, it was rumoured, had the riches beyond imagination. Stories of the fort's wealth and beautiful women were frightening and fanciful. Their commander had told them that the women soldiers protected the fort. It had no men folks. 'Come on, we are men and we can defeat those skirt-wearers in no time. Thereafter, the wealth and the women will be ours. Each soldier can take home as many he wants.' He had goaded them.

With renewed vigour the soldiers attacked the fort. The veteran fighters led the assault. The first wave was wiped out as it tried to reach the fort ramparts. Defeat at the hands of women enraged the commander who ordered the second assault, which too was killed while breaching the walls. It was too much of a humiliation for the battle-hardened leader, who led the third assault himself. After climbing over the walls, he shouted and abused the women and challenged them to fight him.

Once inside, he thought he had won the battle. In trying to open the gate he lost his life and those of his men. Through the gate ran out a survivor shouting, 'Run for your lives, if you have any sense left. There are no women in the fort. They are ghosts. They have slaughtered our bravest warrior, our commander.'

Everybody heard it. And then all soldiers except

one ran back to save their lives. The young soldier too, for a second, thought of running away but somehow he held his ground. Back home he had nothing except a small mud house, a cow and a little patch of land. If he returned empty-handed folks would ridicule him and brand him a coward. And he was yet to fight his first battle. The only way for him was forward. He wished to fight and capture the fort and carry away all its riches.

Through half-open fort gate he observed someone gesture to him. Intrigued, he, with sword in hand, paced towards it in fearful steps. As he touched the gate, two masked women opened the gate and ushered him in. Like a victor he was led inside until he saw the queen, the ruler seated on a huge throne. She stood up and came down to receive him. Perplexed, he put his sword back in sheath and took a step forward. She kissed his hand and spoke in reverence, "Come my king, this fort, this kingdom and this woman has been waiting for you to rule."

Many times he rubbed his eyes in disbelief. Before him stood a woman of extraordinary beauty in whose comparison girls in his village were dirty ducklings.

"My soldier must be hungry after fighting. Let's go for dinner," she said and led him to the dining table and made him sit at the head of the table. The servants laid out the meal. After a sumptuous dinner she led him to the bedroom at one corner of which lay the piano. The mahogany glittered. Overwhelmed by the size and décor of the room, he couldn't take his eyes off it. It occurred to him then that someday he would invite villagers to his fort to show them how well he lived. They all would die of jealousy. He had a conqueror's smile.

When he lay down on the bed, his eyes returned at the entry to the garderobe where the queen had gone to freshen up. Every minute seemed a year, as his wait grew longer. Then she appeared in a white silk gown. Her each step brought her cleavage out of the shadow and her breasts out of the silhouette. She walked over to the corner and began playing the piano. The music mesmerised him. Then the enchantress an inch before the bed unleashed her final weapon. A whiff of intoxicating perfume hit him hard as she climbed the bed. A conqueror got the invitation for the final conquest.

Yearning, resting in those young hearts, stirred. Like piano keys, their bodies moved up and down in a rhythm. As a skilful teacher lust played the piano with great feeling, in between striking an octave higher. The pianist continued to play until it got tired. Longing after having its fill slipped away. The bodies fell asleep.

And when the soldier woke up, he asked the female servant where the queen was. She replied that the queen was out to fortify the defences. Could there be another attack, he imagined and ran out. In the corridor he entangled himself with the curtains and fell.

Ved sat up and found himself on a king-size bed in the bedroom with exclusive design and decoration. He screamed, "Where am I?"

A female voice replied from the kitchen, "You are in my house on the sixth floor. Wait, I'll get you tea."

Putting on clothes, he realised he was no warrior but Vedanta and before him stood Urvashi in a negligee. But why her face resembled with that of the queen's? He mumbled to himself.

Urvashi walked in with tea.

"How did I reach here," he asked gnashing his teeth.

Handing him tea, she said, "Last night our flight had got delayed. You had asked me to take you home."

"What have I done?" he asked, staring at the shrunken sheets. The notes of 'aphrodisiac' played all over the place. The top notes were long gone; the heart notes had played a triumphant tune and rested. The field was open for the base notes to display their talents.

Urvashi walked up to Ved and said, "The same thing two adults do on a lonely night. It was a night of bliss, a night of pure love."

"Don't," he shouted. "Don't you dare to call this act of brazen lust as love?" Not a word of his escaped the sound proof walls of that room.

"No, Ved," she spoke in a calmer voice, "Neither for a moment in the present, nor for several in future will I ever think it to be anything but love. In the past several moments you filled my heart with your love-chants and my body with your soft kisses. And this feeling will live with me, forever.

"No. It wasn't love," he yelled.

"Ved," she said in a measured tone. "Don't wind our love into any relationship. Love is free of any boundaries, any bindings. Love is all-enduring, all-encompassing."

"You devil. Don't say a word further," he thumped the table. The anger had begun to surge in his heart.

"Ved, don't you remember, you chanted 'I love you' every minute we made love last night," she smiled a smile of triumph.

"No, it can't be true," he lamented. "I can't do it."

"Ved, please don't torture yourself."

"I'm so ashamed of myself. How could I do it?"

"Don't grieve, you committed no sin," she tried to calm him down. "This secret shall remain secure in my heart, forever."

"But why did I?" his head went in a whirl. The fear filled his eyes with tears of shame.

Ved was the first person she felt pity for. But like him, the pity too had come late in her life and there was little she could do now. Tea had gone cold and so had he.

"A word of caution, don't share this secret with your wife, you will destroy several lives," she reasoned with him.

The room still bathed in dark and in expensive perfume. He stood to leave. A quick pitiful glance later she said in a serious tone, "Let me handle the darkness here, you go out and seek the light. We never met, nobody saw you come here. Bad dreams are best forgotten."

Robbing her of a customary glance, he packed up belongings in the suitcase and guilt in the heart, and stormed out of the house.

She watched him leave. She had let him.

Chapter Twenty One

***

The manifestations of guilt are many and mysterious. In some hearts it manifests itself with passivity, in some with violence; in some with atonement, and in some with revenge. But in Vedanta the guilt manifested in some parts of all these emotions. He had breached the line of fidelity and stood on the side of evil, leaving Sara behind on the side of the good.

Three days later when Ved rang the doorbell, a beaming Sara welcomed him with a possessive kiss on his lips, but failed to elicit the same passion. Dhruv came out running and hugged him, and didn't leave until he got his bribe, the latest PS3, and then ran away with the game to his room.

"How did your meeting go?" Sara asked, picking up the bag.

"Okay."

Avoiding further conversation, Ved ran in the washroom where he scrubbed his body with soap to rid of Urvashi's smell that refused to go away. From every pore the stink oozed out. It in a repeated action he tried to wash it off his body, his mind. After a while when his nerves settled he came out, changed in a kurta and pyjama and joined Sara at the dining table where she waited upon him with his favourite chocolate cake and green tea.

"It seems you had a rough day," she said, pouring tea.

The question arose because he had spent a long time in the washroom. Sipping tea, he spoke avoiding eye contact, "Yeah, there's a road construction going on in Hyderabad and I picked up a lot of dust."

"Good," she winked, showing her unabashed passion-swollen lips.

He smiled a feeble smile. The night was six hours away and he dreaded the moment he would have to surrender to her desires and act himself. After that one-night stand with Maneka he felt he would sully the purity of Sara if he went close to her.

A tempest in the garb of a temptress had struck his peaceful life, whose shards lay scattered from Hyderabad to Bangalore. It would take months to piece them together; it would take years to wash the sin off. How would he walk through the path of fire to cleanse his soul? The guilt of betraying a simple soul had stuck to his heart.

During dinnertime Ved remained silent. Dhruv and Sara did all the talking. They fought with each other to update Ved about their activities of the past few days. The son won the battle and the wife reserved her energies for after dinner tete-a-tete. In a hurry she wound up the kitchen and entered the bedroom. After washing the face, she dried it up with a hand towel and then changed into a pink negligee.

A pint of the night cream she spread over the palms and then rubbed it over her forearms and face, starting from neck to forehead in upward motion. Then she applied his favourite perfume in underarms, at the back of ears and in the cleavage. In brazen longing her breasts perked up.

"Ved, I'm ready," she said in a husky voice, climbing

the bed. Load of hopes was weighing down a young woman. But young man weighed down by guilt was fighting sleep.

"Hi, Sara," he said, suppressing yawns.

For a moment she put her head on his chest and listened to his heart whose pace slowed under the weight of sleep. She jerked her head up and looked at him. His eyelids drooped. A cold shiver of frustration ran through her body that went limp.

"Sara, I'm so sorry," Ved, feigning sleep, murmured. With his back to her he dozed off.

She let him sleep, but was awake herself; looking sometimes at Ved and sometimes at herself. It was unlike him, she pondered, shuffling through the pages of her memory book. Perhaps his dislike for air travel and hectic business deal had sapped all his energy. With prayers in her heart, she slept.

Next morning handing him bed tea, she asked, with concern, "How do you feel now?"

"Much better," he pressed her hand and gave a thin smile.

His hand's reassuring touch reduced worry lines on her face. She felt good and returned to the kitchen. A soft whisper to thank God, before she ate or drank anything was a ritual her mother had taught her.

At the breakfast, she teased him, "It seems you didn't get a good co-passenger in the flight."

"What!" he said, suppressing his surprise. "No, it was okay."

"Oh, my dear hubby suffered a boisterous male."

"Sort of," he mumbled. "Why? Did you expect a female?"

"I know. Manjari tells me all males desire a female co-passenger during air travel."

"And what more your dear friend tells you about

men?" he teased, hiding his mock behind a sham smile.

"Why? It is bad manners to know what women gossip about amongst themselves." Saranga spoke, rolling her eyes in mischief.

"What would my dear wife do if she learnt that her man flirted with a gorgeous woman?" Ved tried to probe Sara's mind.

Within moments Sara's playfulness was gone. Her countenance turned grave. Moving closer to him, she placed her hands on his shoulder and said, "I'll kill the woman."

"And leave the man?"

"Yeah, leave the man to burn in hell," was her instant reaction, "but I can swear by my Vedanta that he will never cheat on me."

She gave a hurried kiss on his passionless lips. Thereafter, both had a quick breakfast and moved out. On the way she dropped Dhruv at the school. Both took turns in this duty. Today was hers. He hired a taxi to the office, as he didn't feel like driving. En route, he noticed couples walk holding hands together, feed each other ice cream and pani-puri at roadside eateries, enjoy a romantic moment at the café, or smooch in the park. Was this public display of love and affection for one another a facade? How many of them, like him, cheated their partners? The question troubled him until he reached the office. It occurred to him then he could share his secret with Manav, his best friend, whom he found waiting in the corridor.

"Ved, let's have coffee. We need to talk," pleaded Manav.

"OK, I'll see you in the café in half-hour," Ved said and moved away. Manav went to the café and waited.

Ved walked past several people who sat in groups of two's and three's on the steps, in the lawn and talked amongst themselves. Perhaps they were taking a break from the office. Sound of their chattering could be heard from a distance. But when he reached closer, he noticed their voices drop in a whisper. They were talking about Saranga and him. He slowed down.

"His wife has left him," a female voice said, in sad tone.

"How do you know?" asked an inquisitive male voice.

"Yesterday when I landed at the airport, I heard the wife talk to her father she was leaving her husband."

"The guy must have bonked neighbour's wife. It's so common amongst folks living in flats," a female rued.

"No, he got laid by a call girl," spoke a male voice, with a glee, "It's so difficult to resist them."

"Nahin yar, his wife had caught him with a male in bed. The guy is a gay," a woman said in half-concern and half-glee.

"No, no. You guys got it wrong. The wife had been humping his friend," said a male voice. "Male are not always at fault, sometimes women also have affairs."

"Come on, you stupid. It's always the man who doesn't get satisfied with one woman," many female voices shouted him down.

"All right, you win, I lose," the male voice surrendered.

The filthy slander refused to die down. Ved looked at each of those dirty faces and for a moment felt liking smashing them with stones until they were reduced to pulp. Then he felt a hand on his back, "Come on, Ved. Let's go."

Manav led him to the cafeteria. In between Ved looked back and felt those slanderous whispers had died down.

"Sorry," Manav said, sitting down. "Forget the gossip. People are people, and they will never change."

"Yeah," Ved spoke, swallowing humiliation with spittle.

"Is there something you are hiding from me?" asked Manav. "I've observed a change in your behaviour for last few days."

Ved looked sideways, avoiding Manav's probing glance. But he couldn't do it for long, as Manav was insistent.

"Yeah, something weird has happened with me last week."

"What?" Manav was curious.

"Manav, I've committed a blunder. I fell for a woman's charms and slept with her."

"Great? I can't believe it, Ved. A faithful husband had sex with a faithless stranger."

"Manav, please don't torment me further," pleaded Ved.

"Relax, Ved. Neither you are the first man to commit adultery, nor will you be the last. So, stop torturing yourself. It's not abnormal to sleep with somebody outside marriage. People do it every day."

Ved listened to him out of courtesy. Opposite him sat a man possessed by evil and spoke the language of evil. It saddened his heart to see his best friend live a life of depravity. Manav was beyond redemption, but he wasn't.

"My dear friend, fantasies are not frivolous. Reality provides us scanty satisfaction on which we can't survive. Hence, fantasies give us additional zest for life. Remember; in the high school we all had a crush on the class teacher, and flirted with her without success. With time the women in our desires changed. As adults, we fantasised about a famous celebrity; dreamed of marrying her but it never happened. Therefore, as long as we don't mistake the fantasy for reality, it's okay. But many of us try to live out their desires and whenever any chance of realising their desires comes their way, they pounce upon it. Adultery is the consequence."

"Manav," protested Ved. "It's wrong for a married man to fantasise about another woman."

Manav smiled, "Ved, I'll narrate you a funny childhood incident. When I was five, I often played hide and seek with my cousins. One day while trying to hide, I ran inside the sari of the auntie who had come to see mother. And by mistake my fingers touched her bare legs. She pulled my ear and admonished me with a huge grin, 'You naughty boy, this isn't a dark room. Go, hide elsewhere.' Ashamed, I ran away from her. During dinnertime everybody in the household talked about that incident and had a hearty laugh at my expense. At that time I prayed the ground below to split up and swallow me. Then father asked them to shut up and thus saved my further humiliation.

Thereafter, whenever the auntie came home, she reminded me of that incident and teased me with a kiss. With passage of time, my awkwardness vanished and auntie's kisses became unhurried and possessive. Perhaps that incident had fed us both with fantasy: She had hers, I had mine. When I reached the age of sixteen, I told her I was a grown up boy and I didn't like her kissing me. Rolling her eyes in mischief, she looked down at me and said, 'I can see it.' Fear of unknown stopped me from doing anything stupid. But that didn't stop her from giving me a coquettish grin whenever we met and I found her lips swollen and greedy. For a brief period she flirted with me but gave up afterwards. Thus, our fantasies remained mere fantasies."

"Did you share it with your wife?"

"No. I didn't have to. The auntie told her everything."

"What was her reaction?"

"When this incident happened I was five. And

when I was married, auntie was past her prime. So the age difference saved me. Since then my wife too makes fun of me whenever she find me in a pensive mood."

"But lustful thoughts about another woman are wrong," argued Ved.

"Lust, my dear friend, is much-misunderstood, much-maligned twin of love. They are inseparable. In mind, both are in harmony but in act lust becomes an evil, a demon; while love moves around with a halo around it."

"Manav," Ved asked. "Did you ever….I mean……?"

"Yeah, I had sex with a few women. It was either paid, or consensual."

"Does your wife know about it?"

"Are you mad?" Manav almost jumped in surprise. "I've no intention of committing hara-kiri."

Thereafter, both friends had coffee in silence.

"Ved, have you told Sara about your one-night stand?" asked Manav.

"Not yet," replied Ved.

"Don't. You will lose her forever. She is too sensitive and possessive about you."

Ved spoke with a sense of surety, "But I'll tell Sara everything regardless of the consequences."

"Ved, Ved……please don't …" Manav insisted. "I think you need to see a psychiatrist."

Thereafter, both left the café.

Chapter Twenty Two

* * *

The insecurity in a human mind provides the perfect ground for the evil to breed and multiply. Threads that hold a marriage together are all the time snapped at by the wind of doubts. The wife always fears and feels the flame of infidelity. Therefore, she, now and then, needs her man's assuring look, and his assuring hug. Her yearnings grow with loneliness; her insecurities with distance. Every woman in love goes through this situation in her life.

And Sara was no different.

It was routine as usual for both. For a day or two on some pretext or the other he avoided sex with Sara, but he knew he wouldn't be able to do it for long. Silly excuses in intimate relationship often ran out sooner than expected. Any refusal could develop suspicion in her mind that he was having an affair with someone else. It was one situation he wished to avoid as long as he could.

Next morning Sara announced that she would be going home in the evening as her grandma had fallen sick and she wanted Ved to go with her.

"What!" he sighed in relief but realising his mistake, expressed an instant surprise.

"Ved, grandma asked me to get you along," she

begged.

"Sara, I wish I could come with you but my boss won't give me leave at such a short notice," he explained.

In the evening he saw her off at the airport and was shocked to see Urvashi waiting in the lounge. After the check-in, Saranga walked up to the sofa where Urvashi was seated. She sat next to her, and shook hands. From a distance, a terrified Ved watched both of them get into animated conversion. Thank God, he wasn't with Sara that moment; otherwise his secret would have been out that evening. He heaved a sigh of relief and returned home.

Inside the lounge, Urvashi and Saranga had got along well in a short time. "My husband and I are software engineers and we both work here," Sara advanced the conversation.

Urvashi, who since adolescence had lived a life of deceit, lied without a twinge of consciousness, "I'm not that lucky. My man works in Mumbai and me here in Bangalore. We meet on weekends. For us it's a long distance relationship."

"How do you manage this, I mean the separation?" asked Sara.

"We endure it," Urvashi replied, with a tear of sadness, which in parts dwelled in her eyes all the time. "Ours is a lonely existence on week days and we get to share our happiness, our grief on weekends. If my heart yearns for him from Monday to Friday, I tell it to hold itself till Saturday. But it accumulates so much of longing in weekdays that one night finds it impossible to fulfil. Loneliness leads to longing, longing to temptation, and temptation to adultery."

"Did you get tempted by anyone, ever?" Sara interrupted.

Urvashi looked the other way and fell in thought. Nobody, no woman had ever asked her this. It was too abrasive, too straightforward a question. Sara couldn't be blamed for it. Such talks often led to such questions. A few moments later Urvashi collected her nerves and her wits.

"To be candid, I did it once but marital vows held me back," Urvashi lied in a convincing manner. "It's foolish to put one's marriage on the chopping block."

Saranga looked askance at her.

Urvashi continued, "Most men I meet are driven by pure lust. Adultery runs in their blood. Since antiquity women have been treated as trophy by men. I guess nothing has changed ever since. By the way, did you ever get……… …I mean……….?"

"Yeah, the man is my husband," Saranga gave an innocent smile. "I'm a bit old-fashioned."

"What's his name?"

"Vedanta. The name is old-fashioned, and so is the guy."

The name unnerved Urvashi for a few seconds. Then she stuttered, "Well, you indeed are a lucky woman. He seems to be a good guy."

"What?" the wife probed, getting suspicious. "Do you know him?"

"No, I thought so," the other woman spoke in a measured tone. "You just said so."

"Did I?" Sara gave a thin smile.

Urvashi had been in similar situations before, and she hiding her irritation, replied, "You said 'he is an old-fashioned guy.'"

"So, an old-fashioned guy is more faithful."

"I guess so," Urvashi said with a wry smile. "You should know better because you live with one."

The announcement cut short their talks. Both shook hands, thanked each other. Urvashi gave Sara 'I know Ved better than you' look and moved to board their separate flights.

Inside the aircraft Urvashi felt uneasy. Meeting with Sara had upset her. Thought that she had slept with Sara's husband made her queasy. God wouldn't forgive her for hurting an innocent woman's heart. For the first time Urvashi felt an overwhelming feeling of guilt. On earlier occasions guilt had stayed in her heart for a short time. 'What had she become?' she pondered. 'A simple girl, who couldn't harm a fly, had turned into an adulterous on the rampage, breaking several hearts.' When alone, she often cursed herself for her present situation. Her memory book was a mixed bag. The bad moments outweighed the good ones. And she feared to shuffle through the pages.

At birth Urvashi, with her beauty and smile, had mesmerised the whole hospital. The old nurse had told her mother that she, in thirty years in the hospital, hadn't seen a more angelic child. Every relation, every friend sang hymns in praise of Urvashi and wished to have a daughter like her.

Born into a rich family, Urvashi was blessed to have a doting Dad and a loving Mom. Her father was a rich landlord in Punjab where the family lived in a palatial house. Theirs was a happy life, envied by folks living within fifty miles around from there.

'This girl will enslave several hearts,' an aunt said, tweaking Urvashi's cheek on her sixteenth birthday.

'Don't curse the child," rebuked the mother. 'Wish she gets the love of the man she marries.'

That wish reflected the pain of an unloved wife, and her fears for daughter's future. But she never shared her sufferings with Urvashi, for the fear of influencing her daughter's mind towards her father. But infidelity chooses its own time to surface up, and it chooses its own audience. A year later it sprang up before an unsuspecting Urvashi. Truth, however, like an onion, peeled off when got soaked in time. Reality was stark and hit her hard like a thunderbolt. She cried when she discovered that her father for years had lived a life of pretence. The truth killed something within her that day. A philanderer father had killed his child's innocence forever. The hero had fallen from the top of a Himalayan peak into the depths of abyss.

Until a few moments ago she had lived in a fortress, guarded by a strongman, who was second to God. And she knew her father wouldn't let any harm touch her. But some men, his father's dirty secret keepers, taking advantage had tried to grope her a few times. It had shocked her beyond belief when his guardian angel hadn't taken any action against those child-abusers. The incident had stolen her nights' sleep. Thereafter, her protection was done by her mother who sent Urvashi off to a boarding school.

In the school the boys swarmed around her like bees, but her dream boy showed little interest in her. It troubled her mind to learn that the boy was in love with an ordinary-looking girl. For days it tormented her and when the nerves settled, she thought of taking revenge on the boy who had spurned her love. So, she took an ugly boy as her boyfriend. The campus ridicule and scorn didn't perturb her. Some days later it had the desired impact. The dream boy dumped his girlfriend, Urvashi her boyfriend. Some unusual circumstances brought them close. In the college where students changed boyfriends and girlfriends more frequently than they changed clothes, this usual event never made any campus news.

With dream boy in her grasp, Urvashi thought that she had the last laugh, but destiny had something else in store for her.

A year later the boy passed out from the school and move away. Urvashi had a couple of years to go. After the school the boy never contacted her, never replied her calls. From the social sites she found out that the boy had picked up a new girlfriend. It broke her down from within, and made her lunatic. From then on her mind was filled with the feeling of revenge for any man who in any way resembled her boyfriend.

Amongst those who suffered her revenge, Ved's resemblance was the maximum. Since Ved had the eyes, lips and nose of the dream boy, he became the victim of her revenge. While other cases hadn't caused her any mental turmoil, Ved had turned her upside down from within. Urvashi would have snatched Ved if he were married to an ordinary woman, but after that short meeting with Sara, her heart was filled with remorse. Sara with her simplicity and innocence had stirred goodness inside her.

This revenge was having its retribution.

Chapter Twenty Three

❋ ❋ ❋

In the gathering gloom of a summer afternoon the smog hanging over the city sky had thickened after the sun had left for the night-rest. The lazy wind had slept through the waking hours. The ambience feigned the rain and fooled the folks.

At home Ved thought about the meeting between Sara and Urvashi. One woman was the builder of his dreams; the other the destroyer of those dreams. One was a simple woman; the other a conniving one. And both women had spent good one hour in the lounge at the airport. What could have transpired between them, churned up his mind? In Urvashi's promise he sought some assurance.

If the day had been a tormentor; the night didn't promise to be any different. The darkness awakened the demon within. The night spent with Urvashi flashed up in his mind again and again, as if that part of the film had been put in a loop. With closed eyes he saw a nightmare; with open eyes a daymare. Though Urvashi had promised to keep their one-night-stand a secret, he knew that the unsavoury past often had the uncanny habit of surfacing up in future, and ruined many a happy married life. And he couldn't risk losing Saranga. For a moment, an idea cropped up in his mind if Urvashi was silenced forever, his secret too would get buried with her, and then he wouldn't have to fear none.

Killing flies, mosquitoes and cockroaches was okay, but killing a human being was a different thing. The very thought of it sent shivers down his spine, and made him nauseous. How could he kill an innocent woman? But a living Urvashi would always remain a future threat to his married life? Who knows, in penury she could blackmail him and demand huge money for her silence; or she could spill the beans to drive a wedge between Saranga and him. A woman's mind was so difficult to decipher by any mortal being.

In the dark, between sanity and insanity his troubled mind oscillated for hours. Sometimes the sanity prevailed and sometimes the insanity. And when the night was past its prime and sleep nowhere near; he walked into the washroom and gulped down a sleeping pill. In minutes he was in deep slumber. The guilt visited him in dream.

After battling for days, his criminal mind firmed up, 'Urvashi will have to die. The history was replete with examples where the kings had massacred millions for the sake of their lover; he was going to kill just one woman.' He thought of hiring a professional killer, but for the risks involved he abandoned the idea. His soul was destined to carry the additional burden of killing Urvashi. He made a foolproof plan, and went over it again and again until he was convinced of it. As planned, he called Urvashi to a secluded spot, where she was lulled to a false sense of security and then stabbed her to death. Disposing the body and the knife off into the river, whose strong current was expected to carry it several miles farther from that place, and crocodiles were expected to finish it off. On a cold December day he sweated like a brick kiln worker.

"Oh God! What have I done?" He screamed and sat up in bed. And then like a child he burst out laughing,

"Thank God, it was a dream, thank God, it …………."

Filled with revulsion for entertaining such an abhorrent thought in his mind, he cried his heart out. Tears fell in torrents. Those were the tears of repentance. But a moment later, the evil within him stirred and argued for ways to kill Urvashi. If she died due to some disease, or lost her voice in an accident; the secret would remain buried forever. As hours passed by, his mind was filled with countless dreadful thoughts about Urvashi. The demons arose to take control of his mind. As he battled them within, he remembered the words the banker spoke to him a few years ago in Kausani.

"Remember, our hearts and minds are pure as long as we want them to be. Deep inside us resides the evil that is put to sleep by God's grace and our good deeds. The first sin awakens it. Then it raises its ugly head, corrupts our thoughts and our ability to reason out things. It corrupts mind, corrodes soul. It gives birth to nightmares, and temptations to commit one sin after another. The mortal beings, thereafter, get caught up in a whirling vortex of sins. In the end, the corroded soul descends into the depths of abyss, forever."

"What's the road to redemption?" he had questioned then.

The Fakir in a pious voice had said, "Atonement. The moment you commit the first sin, confess it to the person whose heart you have broken, without fear of the consequences, and then atone for it. Seek forgiveness without expecting it. This way you will prevent the evil from taking possession of yourself. And remember, time in atonement is critical, because any delay will allow the evil to gain in strength and raise its head."

Vedanta gazed at the ceiling, his mouth went dry and his head burst with a clangour. Then he sniffed a smell fill the room. It was the same dreaded smell of 'Aphrodisiac', which Urvashi had put on that fateful night. He sprayed the room with a freshener, but to no avail. The smell swirled inside the room, first around the bed from where it spread outwards and filled the whole area.

Miffed, Ved smelled the pillows with spittle drops and tossed them out of the window. In fury, he threw everything out of the window and in minutes the room was empty except for the furniture. It gave him some relief. But the smell still filled his nostrils. Bringing hand closer, he sniffed. It came from his body parts. Layers of smell had stuck to his skin like a moisturiser.

The demon was stirring up. It was time to put it down before it took control of him. He ran inside the washroom and stood under the shower, thinking of those sinful moments, and how he had lost his mind and walked into the trap set by the temptress. Urvashi that moment had lost her innocence and become a demon, a powerful demon.

The soap bubbles and the hot water cleansed his body, the tears cleansed his soul. And he stood there until he thought he had got rid of the smell. Emerging out of the washroom, he dried himself with a new towel and dressed up.

It was time to see the psychiatrist. An hour later he was in the clinic of Dr Govind Hari, the city's renowned psychiatrist. After filling up the details, he waited at the reception. The ambience was soothing, and settled his nerves to some degree. His turn came soon after. When he entered, a young doctor stood up and greeted, "Come, Ved. Sit." And then the doctor rang the bell and asked the nurse to get him two black coffees.

"Strange, how do you know I like black coffee?" asked Ved.

"You filled in the form at the reception," the doctor

smiled.

The coffee arrived. They sipped it and chatted about the change in weather and its effect on health. The caffeine and talk steadied Ved's nerves. And after both had finished, the psychiatrist said, "Ved, I'm not a doctor, but your friend. Tell me everything from beginning. Rest assured, what you speak here stays within these four walls. I don't record the patient's conversation."

Then he gave a warm smile, and waited. Nervous, Ved looked around and when he was sure nobody listened to them, he narrated the whole incident, beginning from the time he had boarded the flight until he had entered the clinic that day. And after it was over, his felt a huge load off his chest, he felt relieved. Sound of a deep sigh filled the room.

The doctor heard every word of his in rapt attention. After a brief pause, he asked, "Ved, how do you feel now?"

"Sir, better."

"Is your heart ready to listen what I've to say?"

"Yes."

"Well, infidelity is very much a human emotion, not an animal instinct. Even Gods have fallen to temptation. If Adam hadn't fallen to the temptation of apple, we wouldn't have been sitting here," the doctor paused and waited to see the impact of those words.

Vedanta smiled. It was his first in days.

"Did someone tell you look so handsome when you smile?"

"Yeah, she did. In fact, she still does," Ved's grinned.

The doctor went on, "Ved, you are a good guy, not the philanderer kind. You have committed accidental adultery."

"Accidental adultery?"

"Yeah, the least harmful kind, but it's harmful nonetheless. And like the serious kinds, it has its after-effects. Adultery causes guilt, guilt causes depression, and depression causes suicide. A sensitive person when by chance commits adultery, goes through one or all of these mental conditions. But remedy of this is simple."

"What?"

"Confession, sooner the better. The betrayer must confess his sins to the betrayed. This will help him unburden his heart. I know often the fear of losing the lover prevents the adulterer from walking upon this path, and guilt never vanishes from his heart."

"Thank you so much, doctor. You explained a difficult thing in a simple way. It has lessened my burden and made it easy for me. I know what I must do. One last question, do you advise all patients to confess in the similar situation?"

"No."

Ved had got the answer. He thanked the psychiatrist and left. On the way back, he pondered, and after a long cogitation, he decided to confess his mortal sin to his beloved. The power of truth drove away the fear of consequences.

Chapter Twenty Four

✳ ✳ ✳

The betrayer, casting the fear of consequences aside, moved out to confess his sin before the betrayed. That moment, his heart sought no forgiveness, it sought repentance.

Sara was coming back home and he went to receive her at the airport. Dhruv had chosen to stay for some days with his grandparents, who had promised to bring him to Bangalore. It gave him some relief, as Dhruv wouldn't be around to weather the storm that was sure to erupt after his disclosure.

During flight Sara had been thinking about Ved and how she had neglected him in the last few months. She thought to pamper him with his favourite dishes, spend some romantic night-outs, and then make up for the lost time in bed. In the car, she clung on to him and spoke, "Dadi was remembering you, Ved. Wish you had come to fetch me."

"How is she?" he asked.

"Much better, but she has become frail. The old age is catching up. She was delighted that Dhruv was going to spend a week with her. He too was excited that he will get to hear stories from his great-grandma." Thereafter, they spoke little till they reached home.

As soon as both stepped inside, Ved said, "Sara, I wish to confess something."

"Come on, Ved. You are not in the church, and I'm no priest."

"Sara, this is serious," said Ved, raising voice.

"Can't you wait till tomorrow?" Sara pleaded.

"No, it can't."

"Okay, I'm listening."

"Sara, I've sinned."

"What!"

"Yes, you heard me right. I've betrayed you. I've slept with another woman."

"Oh, God. No……" she wailed and slumped to her knees.

Vedanta ran to get water, and sprinkled some on her face. She regained consciousness and gave him a blank look. Then she trembled in rage, "Why Ved? Why? Why did you do this to me, to your beloved?"

"I'm so sorry Saranga."

"Ved, you sleep with that bitch, and then you come and say sorry to me. And how do you expect me to react? Who was she; a call girl, a whore, or a colleague? Who was she? Tell me," she trembled with indignation.

It made him speechless, it made her furious. Her eyes burned in rage and popped out of the socket. Charging towards him, she yelled, opening her shirt buttons, "Look at me, do you find me lacking in bed? Have I not fulfilled your sexual appetite? Am I less voluptuous than the slut you slept with? Who is she? Is she an Apsara, or an Urvashi who has descended from heaven? By the way, tell me what's her name? …..okay forget the name. Tell me, is it your first time, or a regular affair."

"Sara, please don't torment yourself. It's me who

deserves the punishment, not you. Believe me, it was just one-night stand. I was foolish, I fell prey to it."

"You creep,….bastard, ….. snake sleep with that whore and tell me that I shouldn't torment myself. You disgust me……"

"Sara,……..I didn't………"

"Shut up…….don't………justify your act," Sara howled at the top her voice.

Ved thought it wise to keep shut. The storm was brewing up, and more was to follow. Sara picked up the plate and aimed to hurl at him. He took cover behind the kitchen counter, but she held back and smashed the plate on the floor. Thereafter, she smashed every piece of crockery. In minutes the living room was flooded with broken china and glass pieces. The whole place looked like a battlefield. Hiding behind the counter, he watched the scene.

Then a lull followed.

A fearful Ved emerged from behind the hiding and looked at Sara, who was sitting on the floor and sobbing, "Why? Ved. Why did you do this to me? Our love didn't deserve this fate."

Then she mumbled. Ved didn't comprehend a word of it, but one thing he was sure of that he had caused her immense pain. Within her raged a fire that was burning her down, and the flames reached his heart, but he was powerless to douse them. Helpless, he waited for some miracle. Nothing but God could save him from drowning into the sea of guilt. Then Sara's hiccups started to subside. Ved saw a chance to convince her that it was his lone mistake; otherwise he had been faithful to her. Inching closer to her, he said, "I swear to you, it was my first sin."

"Don't kill my soul," yelled Sara. "You have already killed my body."

"I swear on Dhruv."

"Don't you dare to bring him into this? I don't want your evil shadow to fall on my son."

Then there was calm. Ved thought the storm would follow soon but Sara didn't explode. Sitting on the floor, she cried, and cried, and then she stood up and stormed into the bedroom. The door banged shut behind her. It made him fearful. Could she take any drastic action? Oh God! What have I done? He wept and prayed. "Please God; please don't let anything happen to her. Punish me, instead. I'm the one who is to blame for her condition."

Inside, she cried; outside, he wept. Minutes crept by. The noon passed into dusk and night rushed into the heels of dusk. A few minutes later Saranga, in undergarments, stood before the mirror, and stared at her body, from head to toe. In a deliberate action she ran her hands over her breasts, stomach, waist and thighs, and tried to unearth any extra ounce of fat over there. But after five years of marriage she looked the same. Then she stepped onto the weighing scale, which showed a kilo less than she was before marriage.

A blade, she used for shaping nails, lying on the dressing table caught her attention. In a moment of frenzy, she picked it up and placed it on her wrist. The edge began to hurt. And she was about to press the steel further, her eyes fell on the photo of a smiling Dhruv. Tears welled up in her eyes. The blade fell off her hands. Ashamed, she sat on the edge of the bed and cried, "Oh, God! What was I going to do? How could I be so selfish? Oh God, please forgive me. Oh Dhruv, please forgive me."

She wept—as much for Ved as for herself, pressing his photo to her chest. And when tears dried up, she picked up the suitcase and packed her clothes in a jiffy. It was well past midnight. He stood outside the door and waited for her to come out and eat something. The whole afternoon was frittered away in fighting, and she hadn't eaten anything.

He was concerned for her health. An hour later he saw the bedroom door open and Sara come out it. Without looking at him she went inside the kitchen, made a quick dinner, and brought a plate for him. With her dinner she locked herself in the bedroom and came out the next morning.

"Sara, where are you going?" a worried Ved asked when he noticed her with the suitcase.

"None of your business. I'm leaving you for the good. I'll leave everything that reminds me of you. Wait for the divorce papers."

"Sara, please don't go. I can't live without you. I love you."

"Ved, don't defile that sacred word, as you have defiled your soul," she said, with utter contempt in her voice. "I can't curse you. You are the father of my Dhruv."

"Dhruv is mine too," he pleaded.

"Never dare to lay any claim on my son. He is mine and mine alone. You have lost the right to call yourself his father the day you betrayed me."

Thereafter, she stormed out of the house. He watched her go. With it the repentance carried a heavy price. Perhaps he would never get to see her again. The dreaded prospect killed a part of him. Life would come to such a pass, he had never imagined in his wildest dream. With Sara gone, he was back to the home's brooding silence.

The path to repentance was paved with sufferings and more sufferings. Redemption was nowhere in sight. It was his chosen path and he couldn't complain.

Chapter Twenty Five

❄ ❄ ❄

The light had dimmed. The sun was caged in. The southern wind with it brought in the rain-laden clouds and then massed surrounding winds into a storm. The folks heading home, or elsewhere looked at the sky and prayed. The pedestrians, the bicycle and auto-rickshaw riders, and those travelling on two wheelers prayed the hardest. But this awful weather didn't bother Saranga who that moment weathered the severest storm of her life.

"Dad, I'm coming home by evening flight. Please send the car at the airport," Sara rang up her father, in the taxi.

"Beta is everything okay?" asked Keshav.

"Yeah." She hung up.

A worried Keshav looked for Alka and then told her Sara was coming home. "What?" Alka's mind filled up with random ill-thoughts.

"Don't get perturbed," Keshav tried to calm her down. "Don't tell Amma about it. Let's first hear Sara."

Keshav called out driver in the evening and went with him to the airport. It was his first visit to pick up Sara; otherwise this duty was often done by the grandmother, and sometimes by the mother when the former was ill.

Today Nandini was unwell. During half-hour long drive an optimistic Keshav was unable to drive away bad thoughts from his mind. Sara in her few words had sounded sad, a trait his bubbly daughter wasn't associated with.

The flight was on schedule. The sight of Sara for a second delighted his heart, but as she came closer, he grew anxious. She hugged him but held back her tears. He could sense a storm rage within her heart. "Oh, God not she," he prayed as they drove back home.

Inside the house, Sara threw her luggage away and then ran inside the bedroom. Keshav and Alka followed her.

"Mom, Dad, what have I done to deserve this?" she hugged them both and started crying. Tears came down in torrents. The mother tried to console her wailing daughter. The helpless father, clutching her darling, waited to hear the cause of that anguish.

After some time her cries stopped and she narrated the whole incident. It left them speechless, motionless. The shock was too much to bear. Then it occurred to Keshav that Nandini and Dhruv should be protected from that storm, as both tender hearts wouldn't be able to bear its brunt. After a while, Sara's sobs subsided and she asked mother for coffee. Alka left the bedroom and came to the kitchen. Keshav followed her.

"Alka, Our Sara is under great stress. Don't contradict her. For some time, make her feel we are with her," he spoke, and then returned to Sara.

"Beta, your Dadi's health hasn't improved after you left a few days back. Please don't say anything about this incident."

Sara nodded and said, "Dad, I know. She won't be able to bear this, and neither would Dhruv."

Assured, a distraught father came back to his study. He wasn't sure whether Ved had shared this with his parents. At that moment he was furious with Ved for ruining his daughter's life, but it occurred him that it wasn't time for anger to get better of him, unless he had heard the boy's side of story. He thought of calling up Shashank. As he argued in his mind whether to ring him up or not, his cell rang.

"Keshav, I'm ashamed of what my son has done to our Sara. We feel betrayed and humiliated. Vasudha and I are with you all in this hour of grief. Our heart goes out to Sara. I know what she must be going through this moment. This boy has sullied the family name and image. It's a shame that he's our son," Shashank's voice dropped.

"Please, don't blame yourself," said Keshav. "We are shocked Ved has done this. We trusted him more than we did our son. Pray, God shows a way out of this crisis."

Shashank continued, "I'm not sure whether I should speak to Sara. I can't summon up courage to face her."

"Don't worry, I'll tell you when she's ready but this may not be the right moment."

Thereafter he hung up. Apology from Ved's father had the right impact on Keshav whose anger dissipated. After all, what could the parents do if the son does the crime? He told Alka that Shashank called up and said that his family elders were with Sara in her hour of crisis.

And crisis it was. Now it had turned into a crisis for both families, who had resolved to fight this together and find a solution, until then they thought it wise to let Saranga be on her own.

Nandini after her afternoon nap had woken up and asked for Dhruv, who was out of the house to play with his new friends in the neighbourhood. And when Sara entered with ginger tea, the old woman sat up in bed.

"No, Dadi don't get up. Drink tea from my hands."

"Saranga, my little darling. You are my 'sanjeevani'. Your presence infuses life in this lifeless body," she spoke, with a gleam in her eyes.

"Dadi, don't say that ever again. You will live more than a hundred years." Sara pinched her grandma's cheeks.

"Don't' worry, I won't ask why you have come back so soon. Why don't you join your father's business and stay with us here forever? Then I'll get to see you and Dhruv every day," Nandini said between sips.

"Come on, Dadi. Tell me, who do you love more? Dhruv or me," asked Sara, trying to deflect her Dadi's attention on her puffy eyes.

The great-grandmother spoke without any confusion, "Of course, Dhruv, my little boy. You had a fair share of my love, the boy has got only a little of it. You have heard all the stories that were in my head, but Dhruv, so far, has listened to a few."

"This time, I'm not jealous to hear this."

"I know dear," Nandini had finished tea; Sara took cup from her and replaced it on the side table. "But I see you are sad."

"Dadi, I'm tired."

"Yeah, you look so. If there was something else, you would have shared it with me. Run, get me the newest man of the house," she said.

It was a godsend opportunity for Sara to move away from there. A few more minutes would have brought tears in her eyes and revealed its cause to Dadi. Dhruv rushed inside the house and collided with Saranga, "Mamma, bring my milk to Dadi's room."

A faint smile appeared on her face and disappeared soon after. The boy was ordering everybody in the house. Dhruv ruled the place, which until a few years was her fiefdom.

After dinner Sara was closeted with her father in his study. "Dad, I don't want to go back to Bangalore."

"Nobody is asking you to do so. Amma will be delighted to hear this."

"How much am I worth?" Sara asked, in a sudden and serious tone.

"Come on, beta. For us, you are priceless," was a worried father's instant reply. "For every father his children are priceless."

"No, Dad. I didn't mean that. I want to know how much is your company's worth."

Hers was a troubled mind from which no coherent thoughts could be expected. Keshav was aware of it and didn't know how to deal with her incoherence. But as a father he had to help his daughter to come out of this emotional logjam.

"Oh, Sara," Keshav sighed. "A couple of hundred crores, to be precise about 230 crores."

"How much is mine?"

"Sara," Keshav, suppressing irritation, asked. "What sort of question is this?"

"Daddy, please."

"All of it. Your brother wants none of it. He told me on several occasions."

"Daddy, I'm not greedy," Sara, spoke unmindful of what he spoke. "Dad, I want to join your business."

Keshav sighed. These were dream words he had waited to hear since she had done her engineering, but had put no pressure on her. He had let her do want she wanted to.

"Sara, I'm relieved. You can join the office from tomorrow. The staff will be delighted."

Keshav couldn't hide his excitement and ran to share it with his wife. In the meantime Saranga sat down to write down her resignation letter. It was well crafted, grateful and gracious. The reason was to join the family business. Her boss was sad to lose a great worker, but he wished her well. It had delighted his heart that she, unlike several techies, hadn't hopped on to a different company.

Chapter Twenty Six

* * *

The office air was filled with rumours that were spoken in whispers this moment, but soon their sound got louder, noisier and nastier. The usual office dullness killed, and hence any news about affairs, break-ups and resignations of colleagues lit up the faces of gossip-hungry employees who for days fed on such spicy stories.

In the office Ved learnt of Sara's resignation from a common friend. A hope of reconciliation had faded away, so soon. And then next day news that one woman colleague had committed suicide by throwing herself from the sixth floor sent shock waves in the city. A case of failed love, cried the headlines. The working couple went through tremendous pressures at work and at home, and a spark was enough to drive them to take this drastic step.

For Ved, though, the psychiatrist had precluded the possibility of that extreme step. "As long as there is life, there is hope." The doctor had written those words on a piece of paper and told Ved to stick it onto the mirror. Every day he read those letters the first thing in the morning and drew inspiration from.

A week later Keshav and Alka met with Shashank and Vasudha at a restaurant to discuss how to resolve the crisis that tore both families apart. For some time both families spoke nothing to one another. They waited, and waited.

"We are so sorry," said Vasudha, holding Alka's hand.

"Don't blame yourself. The parents have to suffer for the mistakes of their children. But we've to resolve this. I know Ved and Sara love each other so much that they can't live alone. But Sara is so heartbroken that she isn't ready to listen to anything at the moment. I think we need to give her time to come out of this. Then we can think of bringing them together."

"Dhruv can make this possible. He is our only hope," said Shashank.

"I've a gut feeling things will be all right soon," Keshav expressed hope.

It occurred to Alka if Sara and Ved somehow went to Kausani again, the place could work magic one more time. She shared her view with everyone who concurred with the idea. But convincing Sara and Ved to go there again was difficult and fraught with danger. Then it was decided they would wait for some time before implementing their plan.

With hopes in their hearts they went back home.

At home Dhruv insisted on talking to his Dad, but Sara wasn't relenting. When Keshav and Alka entered the house, Dhruv ran to his grandparents and complained, "Grandpa, Mom isn't allowing me to speak to Dad."

"All right, beta. I'll talk to your Mom."

Then Keshav reasoned with Sara and convinced her to let Dhruv talk to Ved.

"Dad," Dhruv couldn't hold his excitement.

"Oh, my God," cried out Ved, unable to hold his tears. "Dhruv, I miss you every moment here."

"I miss you too, Dad," shouted Dhruv.

Thereafter the father son chatted for an hour about everything they did together. "Dad, speak to Mom," said Dhruv and brought phone to Sara but Ved had hung up. "Dad, Dad…" the boy shouted but realised the call had been disconnected. Demoralised, he put the phone down. But the young Dhruv felt something amiss between his parents. And a few days later, he overheard his grandparents talk about Sara and Ved. The young boy was perturbed to learn that his parents had fought and separated.

That night he insisted that his mother sing him a lullaby. And when Sara tried to sing, but began to sob, instead.

Dhruv said, wiping tears, "Dad has hurt you."

"How do you know, my boy?" she hugged him and sobbed.

"I heard grandpa tell grandma."

"What did you hear?"

"Nothing much, but I can make out Dad has done something very bad to hurt you."

Sara began to cry, "Oh, beta. I didn't want you to know this."

Dhruv stood up and wiped her tears, "Mom, don't cry, please."

It was the most dreadful situation for Dhruv to be in. What a destiny! The young boy was caught in the storm that had threatened to tear apart his parent's world, which until a few days had been blissful like a fairyland.

"Mom, has Dad cheated you?" asked Dhruv.

"Who told you?" she looked at him aghast.

"Nobody, my friends talk about it often."

"You guys have nothing better to talk about in the school."

"We've. This topic comes up whenever a friend is

sad because of the fight at home."

"Dhruv, let's not talk about it anymore."

"Okay, Mom."

After a while the boy fell asleep, the mother kept awake for a long time. The secret was emerging out in bits and pieces, and hurting the young mind. Should she tell him everything? She debated. While her heart said 'no', the mind said 'yes'. The heart lost the battle.

The next morning Sara, when everybody was busy, called Dhruv out and went to the park. Both sat on the bench. Then she told him everything. For several moments Dhruv sat motionless. Then he asked, "Mom, how could he do it? Dad loved you so much."

"Yeah, he did, but not anymore."

"But he said he did when I spoke with him today."

"Please, Dhruv…"

"Mom, don't lose heart. Things will be better, soon."

"How?"

"Wait, let me think," Dhruv spoke like an adult. "Why don't you give him another chance?"

"I can't."

"Let some time pass by and then think about it. Remember, you told me once that Dad met you in Kausani, where he fell in love with you. Somehow I feel you both should go there once again. May be, the same magic can work again, and the place can instil some sense in Dad."

"I don't know. I don't want to talk about it. Let's go to the market and have ice-cream."

"That's a sweet idea to deflect the topic."

"Dhruv, don't play smart with me. I'm you mother."

Thereafter both went to the market and had ice-cream. "Was Ved trying to talk to her through their son?" Sara thought as they walked back home. It infuriated her.

The man without shame commits adultery and then has no guts to feel remorse for it, instead tries to reconcile through their son. How mean of him? She felt disgusted.

The next morning she dropped the bombshell. "Daddy, I want divorce."

"Why beta? What happened? Did Ved say something to you?"

"No, he has nothing to say."

"All right, Sara. Can we talk about it later? You have an important meeting to attend in the office tomorrow. I wanted to discuss it."

"Okay, Papa," she moved to her bedroom. "Let me freshen up."

"Thank God," Keshav sighed. Then he called out the manager and asked him to arrange a meeting. For a while the crisis was averted. In the last few days Keshav had noticed Sara went through mood swings, and Keshav knew what went inside his daughter's mind that moment. It made him to shudder in shock to think of Sara's divorce.

Dhruv spoke with his father daily. In his son, Ved saw his only hope. Children often saved their parent's marriages; it was a well known fact. And Dhruv will prevent Sara from seeking divorce, he was somehow sure.

In the meanwhile Sara got busy with her new job that left her with little time to think about Ved and their tottering relationship. Days passed, months passed.

One day she chatted with her grandma after giving her medicines.

"Saranga, your eyes have lost sparkle. It happens when a wife isn't happy with her husband. What's the matter, darling?"

"Nothing, Dadi. It's the office workload."

"Beta, there's something you are hiding from me."

"Nahin Dadi."

"I know what's holding you back. You guys think any bad news will worsen my health," Nandini spoke, taking Sara's hand in hers. "Don't worry; your Dadi won't die until she sees eternal happiness in her darling's eyes. It's a promise I gave to your grandpa. Remember, you were apple of his eye. He left us all when you were six years old."

"Dadi," Sara put her head in grandma's lap, said between sobs, "Please, don't say this. I can't think of life without you."

"Na, beta. Don't... Your tears will weaken me," Nandini consoled.

Then Sara narrated the whole incident. For a while the frail woman fell in deep thought. It became clear to her why Sara had turned up unannounced. Her heart bled to see her grandchild suffer in silence, alone. Nandini's thought went back to many years in the past. Like Sara, she had then suffered the humiliation of her husband's adultery. It was one secret she hadn't shared with anyone in life. A few years after that incident, she had forgiven her husband and its painful memory too had faded away with time. Now the time had come to share this secret with Saranga. Perhaps it might bring Sara out of gloom, make her see the light at the end of the tunnel.

"Saranga, today I wish to share a secret with you," Nandini said.

"Dadi," Sara raised her head and sat up.

"I had never in my wildest dream imagined that the dark shadow of my fate will fall on my granddaughter's fate."

"What?"

"Keep this to yourself. Nobody in the family knows about it," Nandini resumed. "Nobody knows the whole truth about your grandpa, not even his son. Everybody remembers him as a caring husband, a doting father and grandfather. But I know who he was. He broke the heart of a young bride, like what Ved has done to you. For a year after marriage your grandpa lived a double life. I came to know about his affair by accident. He had a son with that woman."

"Oh, Dadi," Sara said, wiping grandma's tears. "I'm sorry, you had to suffer this."

The six-decade old incident had welled up Nandini's eyes. But the years had toughened her heart. She collected her thoughts and spoke, "For a moment I had thought of committing suicide, but I held back. Keshav was in my womb then. Your father saved himself, me and my marriage. Your grandpa didn't tell me about his affair; I found out myself. And I gave him hell until he repented and promised to break his relationship with that woman. My in-laws supported me in this. Ved, at least, has guts. He has confessed his sin to you, and is repentant. If your grandpa could get another chance; why can't your husband?"

Sara didn't know how to react to that revelation. The grandma had suffered the similar fate decades ago but shown no bitterness. To one and all she had given love, loads of love. The old woman had the heart of gold.

When Nandini noticed Sara in a reflective mood, she said, "I went through the same turmoil years ago, and I'd thought then that this curse would end with me. I never knew that it would skip a generation and hit you. Don't worry, my darling. Together, we will bury this curse forever."

Sara wept and nodded.

With her bony fingers, the grandma wiped off Sara's tears. Then she fell silent. Her mind was flooded with many bizarre and bad thoughts into which she searched for a solution. As she dug deeper into the heap, she found a stone that emitted light. Her face lit up. May be, she had found the answer she looked for.

She stroked Sara's hair and spoke, "I was thinking

why you both don't spend some time together in Kausani. The place might work its magic again. After all, the Fakir's prediction about your future so far has come true. Didn't he say if any miracle were to happen, it would happen in Kausani? And this old woman, with years of experience, is telling you that the miracle is waiting to happen. Ved and you go there and experience the miracle yourself."

Chapter Twenty Seven

* * *

The winter, like a poor child, tried to snuggle into her mother's bosom under the tattered quilt. The dawn fog ensconced in the valley folds became stubborn by the hour. The morning and evening breezes had stolen some of the night's chill, while the day wind struggled to retain the waning warmth. The sun began to lose its sting. The day somehow crawled by. Kausani, in a matter of days, would wait to wrap itself up in the blanket of cold.

The exit of tourists after the Dussehra and Diwali holidays had made the place quieter and its inhabitants sadder.

Vedanta was the first tourist to arrive in Kausani. The car wheeled into the market place that looked like a huge art canvas in which several expressionless faces sat in and outside the shops in groups of two's and three's. At the Chowk he stopped to have tea at his favourite teashop, which had heard his many melancholy notes half a decade ago. Recognising, the owner greeted him with a smile and cleaned a chair for him.

All of a sudden the canvas came back to life. The idling folks began moving, and whispering. Ved smiled. But happiness eluded the local folks. They seemed to mourn the loss of business, which wouldn't return until the Christmas and the New Year, about a fortnight away. And for this small hill station whose lifeline were the tourists, it was a long wait.

The lone traveller had managed to raise only a faint smile on those gloomy faces.

The car, after negotiating the sharp gradient, turned right and drove into the parking. He got out and went to the same hotel and booked the same room, expecting the same people and same warmth. He was disappointed to see the cheerful receptionist missing. Instead, a young man greeted him with a smile. He smiled back and looked around for Rakesh, expecting him to be there.

"Sir, this way," he heard an unfamiliar face pick up the luggage and walk towards the room.

Battling twin disappointments, he followed the man. If Yamini's absence had made him sad, Rakesh's had made him sadder. His heart ached not to find the old surroundings in which he had spent a fortnight there and in which he had found his love, which he, after five years, had lost due to his one night's folly. Another woman would have forgiven her husband, but Saranga wasn't just another woman.

In a fresh coat of paint the hotel, like many others, wore a new look. Some of the hotel staff too had changed.

In new Kausani he hoped to find his old love. With folded hands and closed eyes, he looked at the Holy Himalayas and prayed for divine intervention.

Deepak, the waiter, brought him tea. As he sipped tea, he inquired about Yamini and Rakesh. It gave him great satisfaction to learn that she had got married four years back and moved out with her husband. Rakesh worked in a five star hotel in Delhi.

He said a prayer for both.

Half-hour later after bath and lunch he moved out. His legs took him towards the road upon which he had walked many times during his first visit. The sight of the boulder brought a soft smile on his face. It brought back the memories of the Fakir, the truth seeker.

As he sat on it, the Fakir's voice echoed in ears, "After five years a severe storm will hit your life and tear apart not two but several lives. You will have to come back to this land for penitence and forgiveness. It's tough to predict the outcome but if any miracle were to happen, it will happen right here, in this very place."

If the Fakir's first part of the prophecy had come true, then why the second part wouldn't, he pondered. On the first occasion he had chosen not to believe the Fakir but now he would at his own peril. Hope kindled within him. He wanted to win back Saranga for Dhruv and for himself. His success would gladden several hearts; the failure was sure to kill the spirits of their loved ones. And he would be left with no option but to walk the path taken by the Fakir. For fraction of a second, it brought out the Buddha in him.

A few minutes later a couple with a child strolled passed him. It brought him back to the real world. Under a blue sky for next few hours he relived the happy moments of his previous visit.

The two visits were in a way similar. During the first visit he had met Saranga who had given a new meaning to his empty life. And then he had lost her in the sea of desires. In the second visit he had to rediscover the same Saranga who would refill the void in his life.

As the wind gathered speed, he stood up and walked towards the Anasakti Ashram. It was open. He stepped in. The place was empty but he felt the crowd move around, chatting loudly. In a flash the mystery girl appeared amongst them and then whizzed past him out of the front door. He went in a chase. She got lost in thin air.

Disheartened, he sat under the Deodar tree. The caretaker after closing the door looked around and found a man sitting on the parapet. He went up to him and asked, "It seems you have lost something on your last visit here. I put things left by the tourists in a box. Come and have a look. You might be lucky."

"Thank you," Ved said. "I lost it somewhere else."

"God will help you to find it," the old man's voice had a sense of surety in it.

And before Vedanta could react, the man was gone.

As dusk fell, he returned to the room, where Deepak handed him Yamini's cell number. He couldn't wait to call her up.

"Vedanta," she shouted at the other end. "How are Saranga and Dhruv?"

At the outset he thought of lying but he couldn't, and in brief told her about everything that had happened in his life in last five years. Suddenly her voice dropped. Exuberance was replaced by a deafening silence. Between sobs, she resumed, "I'm so sorry. I can't see sadness on the face of the man, who brought cheers in my life. I can't believe this. God has been unkind to you."

"Don't worry, I've come here in the hope of finding a way out of this storm and I'm sure Kausani won't disappoint me this time either," he spoke with a hope in his heart.

"Will it help if I speak with Saranga?" she asked.

"I don't think so. It might complicate the matter further."

Vedanta was right. A wife battling her husband's affair would be infuriated if another woman, his friend, tried to advocate the man's case. It was better if the couple resolved the issue themselves, without outside interference. She wished him well and hung up. The bell rang. It was her husband. She rushed to open the door.

"Why is my Yami so sad?" Prakash asked noticing her in a pensive mood.

"Go and freshen up. We will discuss it later," she said and went into the kitchen.

Five years ago, theirs had been a chance meeting in Kausani where Prakash, a sales executive in a private firm, had come for vacation. He loved travelling and seeing different places and meeting different people. Lesser known places attracted him the most as they always had small little things left undiscovered and it gave him immense joy to discover those and share them with the world through his blog. Last year he had spent a week in Ladakh and this time he wanted to explore Kausani, about which he had heard from a friend.

As son of a farm labourer, his introduction with poverty had been at an early age. His parents worked on the farms of village landlords on daily wages, and brought groceries with money they earned each day. The family struggled to eat two meals a day. Due to lack of medical facilities his three siblings had died in infancy and as many in her mother's womb. Only two survived; he and a younger sister.

In Kausani Yamini had greeted him, like any other tourist. After a few days both had developed mutual admiration. And as the days passed by, admiration had developed into love and on the penultimate day of his stay, Prakash had proposed to her. She, with surge of million dreams in her eyes, had said 'yes'. After a few months both, with their parents' consent, had got married. She had left job and settled with her husband in Kolkata. A year later they had been blessed with a daughter.

Theirs was a small contented family. Happiness had eluded Yamini for a long time and when it finally did knock at her door, she tied it in the red cloth and kept it in the home-temple. Since then God had been guarding her precious happiness.

"So, who has stolen your peace of mind," he asked, coming out of the bathroom and threw the towel on the bed.

On another occasion he would have faced severe reprimand for this act, which Yamini considered nothing less than sacrilege. She must be quite perturbed to ignore it, he thought. To the kitchen he walked behind her to bring pakodas to the dining table. She got the tea. The dining room was their favourite place to share their daily happenings and plan for things for the next day.

"It's about Ved," she said, pouring tea.

When she was picking up the pieces of her shattered life in Kausani, one fine day Vedanta had arrived like a fresh breeze into her life. She, for initial few days, had tried to attract him to her. In a young man out on a quest in the hills, she fancied her chances. And she thought that her clarity of thought could make inroads into the mind of a confused man. But that wasn't to be. Perhaps she had erred in her judgement and it was reason enough not to admit her love to him. A good friend would have been lost forever and she didn't have many.

This unshared sweet secret rested in her heart.

She gulped down a few sips in quick succession. The warm liquid wetted her dry throat. She told him how Ved's life had been ruined because of his one-night stand. As she began to narrate the details, her voice choked and her eyes filled. Prakash glanced at her and found her face go pale in fear.

He took her hand in his and pressed. His eyes seemed to say, "Don't worry, nothing of that sort will ever happen in our lives. I assure you."

She regained her composure and resumed, "Ved is a

nice person. It pains me to know what Saranga and he must be going through."

"Don't worry; he will come out of this," with these few words, he tried to assure her. More than this wasn't needed. Yamini, he knew, held Vedanta in high esteem and both shared a special relationship that needed no intrusion.

Rest of the evening was spent in silence. A sudden pang of jealousy hit him. Yamini's undue concern for Ved worried him. The man who had lived decades in deprivation suffered from the fear of losing whatever he had. Yamini was the best that had happened in his life and he didn't want to lose her under any circumstance. He knew many marriages had broken down because of suspicion. And he was wise not to let mistrust get better of him. So he respected her need for space and privacy. They had early dinner and went to bed. Tired, he soon fell asleep. She, occupied by worries, kept awake for better part of the night.

Chapter Twenty Eight

❆ ❆ ❆

Suddenness of the showers had surprised both the locals and the tourists alike because neither had expected them. For the first, it was sure to cause damage to the crops and for the second; it meant wastage of valuable time. Paralysed by despair, a helpless Ved lay in bed and watched one full day get washed off by the winter rains. Intermittent thunder and lightning dashed off any hopes he had harboured for a few rainless hours. Bit by bit the darkness engulfed Kausani, converting day into night. And it was sure to be a deep dark night.

On any other occasion he would have loved the rains, but today he felt dampness in whatever he touched. The sheets, the towels and the clothes seemed to ooze water. He called the housekeeping staff and asked them to bring some clean linen and towels. Half-hour later two boys walked in with ironed bed linen and towels, and changed sheets, pillow covers and towels. Standing by the window Ved peeped outside through the glass, hazed by the raindrops and fog. The change of damp curtains would have been an outrageous demand and hence it was dropped. He switched on the blower to warm the air inside. Half-lying on the bed, he ran his hands over the bed sheet. The warm fabric gave him a sense of relief and lifted up his spirits.

The mood continued upward climb until dinner, after which he sat in the balcony and heard the rain buzz in the dark. The surrounding hills had fallen asleep. With limited visitors, the hotel manager had switched off the lights long back. Deepak had left an hour ago. And tranquillity had snuggled under the miles of darkness and dampness.

In silence suffered the beauty of the night. A guilt-ridden heart indulged in the longing for affection. It hoped the last vestiges of its love would revisit and provide succour to its tormenting and reignite the embers of passion. But alas! The guilt had submitted itself to repentance in its corrective care. Like a headmaster, the repentance brandished the stick to admonish and discipline the guilt whenever it erred.

Vedanta had seven days to save his marriage, himself.

A week later Saranga was coming to Kausani, and as desired by their parents both were to spend some time together and iron out their differences. So far all his efforts for reconciliation had been rejected by her, who had refused to yield. Repeated pleas of Dhruv had fallen on her deaf ears. After discovery of his affair Sara had gone into a shock. Every day these heart-tormenting questions swirled in her mind, "How could the man, with whom I shared my heart and soul, seek solace in another woman's arms? How could he bury my love in a night's passion? Were there more women in his life?"

The elders from both the families tried their best to reason out with Sara and pleaded with her to forgive Ved. But their impassioned appeals were met with her stony silence. Then to everybody's surprise one day she agreed to give her broken marriage another chance. In the midst of sighs of relief and smiles was lost the reason for change of her heart. Alka knew whom to thank, and she slipped out from there.

Hundreds of miles away from there in the verdant hills, Ved rued the loss of one full day and found himself clueless how to convince Sara about his love. The more he thought of the sinful night, the deeper he sank into the sea of despair. Hope seemed like a tiny island in that big deep sea, and there was no boat around to sail up to it. He felt unquiet and alone.

If he could unwind the clock, he would have prevented the meeting with Urvashi. But no mortal being had the power to control time. The unsavoury event came back haunting. The woman seated next to him in the plane was a modern-day Maneka. In the flight were seated several handsome men, in whose presence Ved looked ordinary. It didn't occur to him then, but he wondered why had she chosen him? He would never know the truth, because after that night she hadn't replied to any of his calls. Perhaps she had changed her phone number and removed her data from the social sites. All his efforts to trace her had led to a dead end.

If initial efforts were lust driven, subsequent ones were to seek answer to his curiosity. After initial moments of ecstasy, his heart was filled with guilt for betraying an innocent woman who loved him more than she loved herself.

The thought came as a ray of hope in the autumn of desperation and for the first time since his arrival in Kausani, he smiled.

With hope in heart and smile on his face, he went to bed.

The sleep always had a bias towards the poor folks. While the rich did so many things to befriend it in order to get a few hours of it in the night after a day's hard work, the poor did nothing. In this land, though, it treated both, the rich and the poor alike. As Kausani slept in the lap of the frosty night, the flakes all night long fell on the hills, huts, hotels and treetops.

Having slept through the night, Ved awoke early. A strong tea perked him up. He got ready, had breakfast, and then strolled down the road and arrived at the empty Chowk, at one corner of which lay the bonfire ashes around which, under the sack, slept a dog. On hearing the sound of human footsteps, the dog took his head out, looked at Ved with one eye-opened and gave out a lazy growl, as if regretting for mistaking him for an outsider. On many occasions the dog and Vedanta in past few days had crossed each other's path and between them had developed a sense of familiarity that the animal had started treated him as a local man.

These were early hours for the shopkeepers and customers to populate the place. The air carried an unusual chill. The damp fog rested in the gaps, around the corners and in the tree clumps. The mist had curtailed visibility to a few yards and turned chir pines into elongated ghosts. Pulling hood over head, he rubbed his palms to generate warmth and then searched for the path to the intended destination. Through the thinning fog, he spotted a tiny opening and moved towards it.

The narrow track meandered through the forest whose floor was carpeted with dry bronze leaves, with a few fruits thrown around. The mist patches hung midway here and there, waiting for the rains to thicken themselves. Missing were the sun and the wind, perhaps resting after the previous day's hard work. The path, encroached upon either side by dry pine leaves, glistened with dewdrops that had made it slippery. The leaves squelched as he walked over them. The dampness delayed the sound of his footsteps reaching his ears. Anxious, that someone was following him, he looked back a few times, but once he was sure it was his doubt, he shrugged his shoulders and moved on.

His legs, eager than him to reach the place, moved faster than his mind, which was slowed down by a flood of thoughts. And none of them gave him any comfort. From old lady he wanted to seek solution to his problem. Would she be able to do it? It kept coming back until he reached the bend, beyond which lay her house.

The wind smelled of frostiness. The silvery icicles hung from the roof of the bungalow and dripped. The sight made his heart miss a beat. Burdened by negative thoughts, he wandered on. A second later he breathed the familiar scent, felt the familiar touch of the pine. The red, white and pink flowers greeted him at the entrance. It made his heart jump in delight. She was in. He rushed towards the house and stopped for a few seconds in the veranda to catch a breath. The white paint on the chairs had peeled off at places and a few plants in the hanging pots had dried up. Some wooden beams and joiners were breaking up at joints. It seemed the house had aged in the past years and cried for urgent repairs to regain its earlier pristine beauty.

Hung at the entrance was a mirror, which caught his attention. It was a new addition. He looked in it. His eyes fell on the dirty shoes, which he cleaned at the bottom of the trousers, and smoothened his shirt. Grey streaks of hair and dark shadows under the eyes made him look many years older. In comparison, the house looked younger and livelier. Perhaps therein lay a message for him. He waited and thought. Then he knocked at the door.

"Come on, in," the old woman said, opening the door. "What a pleasant surprise. For the last few days I've been remembering you."

A few wrinkles on the face was all the old woman had added in the past years, otherwise she retained the same exuberance and vibrancy in her walk and talk.

Gomati gestured him to sit in the sofa and sat beside

him. Putting her hand on his shoulder, she asked, "Why didn't you bring Saranga and Dhruv?"

"She will follow after a week. An important business assignment has delayed her," he lied.

Getting up, she turned to the kitchen and smiled. He heard her say, "You look tired. I'll get you coffee and then we will catch up."

The ambience of the living room was same; the same curtains, the same paintings and the same furniture. The room was spick and span. He knew her fetish for cleanliness. She had a sharp memory and after so many years she remembered that he liked black coffee.

Within minutes she came out of the kitchen with coffee and cookies. He stood up to help.

"Your favourite cookies," she said, handing him the plate.

Coffee was taken in silence during which they shared a few glances as they hesitated to start the conversation. She felt something was eating him up inside. After removing the cups and plate, she returned to the living room and sat opposite him.

And then for next half-hour he narrated his story, resuming from their last meeting. He hid nothing; she heard everything, in rapt attention. Thereafter, both fell silent; he weighed down by cruelty of the sin and she by enormity of the cruelty.

An ambivert Vedanta had bared his heart out. It did surprise her. Perhaps she, on earlier occasion, had erred in thinking him to be a good man. He had disappointed her, but she had to give solace to the seeker. The look his face sought forgiveness. He responded to all her inquiries with equanimity, and waited for her to dig some magic out of her head of wisdom and give him a solution.

"We all make mistakes," she said, putting her hand

on his shoulder, "If we didn't we wouldn't have been on this planet. I met Saranga for a brief period last time and I must admit she isn't just any other woman. She is out of this world, a woman you don't come across in your daily life. How could you miss this simple fact?"

A pause ensued. He looked at her, and then at himself. Bewildered, he waited on to hear more.

"Vedanta," she resumed, "Women since ages have had a raw deal at the hands of men. They made homes, raised children, furthered the human race and gave comfort to men in happiness and sorrow. But men never treated them as equals. If in the ancient world women were treated as commodity to be won and lost in wars, traded as slaves, housed in harems, abandoned when bore daughters and left to fend for themselves when widowed. Their situation in modern world is nothing to feel proud of. They suffer second class treatment in homes and at workplaces. And what hurts them the most is betrayal by men they love the most and for whom they make every conceivable sacrifice. Marriage for them is a sacred vow, but for most men, I guess, it's an arrangement to continue their lineage. So, when a man betrays the society treats it as a normal thing and people coax the woman to adjust, but when a woman betrays, the hell breaks loose. She is thrown out of the house."

Faltering voice forced her to gulp down a few sips of water. He looked on.

Turning to him, she said, "Remember, infidelity breaks a woman's heart, and a heartbroken woman is hard to be won back. A beloved's heart is tender and betrayal breaks it into pieces. And Sara has the heart of a beloved."

Further words were spoken in such a low voice that Ved couldn't catch anything. Perhaps she didn't want him to hear any of those. Far removed from the realities of today's world, for a woman who led a life of renunciation in the

Himalayas, it was tough to think of any ideas of helping Ved out. Her mind went blank every time she tried to think of something.

"Is there a way?" he pulled her out of her trance.

"Sure."

"What could that be?"

"Penance, sincerity in seeking forgiveness and divine help," she managed a feeble smile.

"Divine help?" he gave her a questioning glance.

"Yeah, you heard me right. Others could have managed with a little of it; you need in abundance, loads of it."

"God save my marriage, God save my marriage........," he mumbled a number of times.

"May Lord be with you," she blessed.

On the last occasion she had blessed, he had found Sara. This time too her blessing would help him find his Sara, he hoped.

White flakes outside the window caught her attention. Like a child she ran out of the house and stood under the open sky. It was season's first snowfall. She shouted for him. He, forgetting everything, joined her. Both palms joined he stood under the sky. In a few minutes it filled their palms with a handful of snow and their hearts with loads of hope.

She looked upwards and thanked God. Her prayer had been answered.

A little later they walked in. She opened the windows. The weather had become warmer.

"This weather is good news for us. Don't worry; God won't disappoint you. Be patient. Go, seek His blessings in snow," she gave him a grandma hug.

It was a message of hope. He thanked and begged leave of her.

Walk back to the room was swift and short.

Chapter Twenty Nine

✳ ✳ ✳

It was a typical night; dark, sad and nippy. And Kausani in all its nakedness shivered under the falling flakes, whose sound broke the monotony of silence. Unabated, snow battered it from all directions, without any mercy. Chione, it seemed, wanted to bury this tiny hamlet for its some past sins. After midnight the fury began to subside. The goddess had realised her mistake that she wasn't in Siberia but in the land of the gods, and for the fear of inviting their collective wrath, she trotted across the niveous landscape and slipped away.

Unmindful, Vedanta lay in the bed. In that lonesome heart surged a mighty torrent of shame, madness and misery churning love that was tormented by guilt and repentance. Subsequent nights, after admission of betrayal to Saranga, ate him up inside. And in those torments, he wished to cleanse his soul. Taking pity, the nights had allowed him a few hours of fitful sleep. Tonight he got nothing better.

The next day he woke up with a heavy head. Stumbling towards the window, he drew the curtains out. The scene outside stunned him. Rubbing his sleepy eyes in disbelief, he thought he were in a Siberian town. A pinch on the arm and the sounds outside convinced him that he was in India, in Kausani.

After freshening up, he rang the call bell. Within minutes Deepak appeared with tea.

Mixing sugar, he said, "Sir, you brought us luck."

"Will I get to keep a piece of it for myself?" Ved asked.

Deepak smiled. Ved had noticed that the boy smiled whenever he didn't understand a particular thing; otherwise he always came up with a suitable reply for Ved's every question.

"This will bring in more tourists here," Deepak said handing him tea. "We are excited about it. The managers have phoned their friends in Nainital, Almora and Ranikhet, and requested them to divert customers here."

"Good," Ved spoke between sips, "So from evening you will get busy and have less time for me."

"No sir," was the boy's mild protest, "You are my lucky customer. Everybody knows here you helped Rakesh to get a well-paying job in Delhi."

"No, no. It's not true," he clarified but in vain.

At breakfast he got the news that the road to Kausani had been snapped due to a massive mudslide near Almora. His heart began to sink. How would Saranga reach this place? He pondered. But his gloom was short-lived as someone informed him that the road via Ranikhet was open. Delighted, he stood up to explore the white expanse.

The higher reaches of town had received the maximum snowfall. Having made up his mind, he ran down the stairs to the Chowk from where he took an upward winding path to the highest peak. The snow rested on the tree-branches and undergrowth. On the forest floor, it shared space with bronze pine leaves, clover, mud and stones. It looked some kind of a fairyland, where the light winked and the winds whispered through the foliage and trees, covered in shades of white and green. The north wind was frigorific. It kissed his face as he moved on and got colder with every yard of climb. The fog had veiled the valley, giving a foot of visibility on either side of the path. Another day he wouldn't come there, but today was a special day.

"Be careful. Yesterday a leopard was seen up there," an old man cautioned him.

"Thank you," he said and without looking back moved on.

Sounds emanating from inside the forest stopped him in his tracks. He strained his ears to decipher them. Amongst irregular bird and animal sounds he heard a faint human voice. Inquisitive, he hurried on.

Immensity of the wild, perpetuity of the silence and perenniality of the anonymity like a holy Hindu trinity reigned in that place. Occasional human visits, though for brief intermittent periods, vexed its eternal tranquillity. The soft beauty of snow in winters added a touch of divinity to the place.

Kausani basked in the warmth of a December sun. The matutinal dew clinging to roadside thistle, broken fences, barks, bushes and grass in the afternoon sun had turned to golden mist. The lazy air swirled, bringing different smell with every motion. The first swirl smelled of melting snow, the second of bletting wild berries, and the third of rotting oak leaves. Once a while, a gust of fresh wind pushed aside all these smells.

Mesmerised, Vedanta moved on.

Unlike the lower slopes where hard pines with knife-edged leaves killed any growth underneath; here under the benign shadows of oak, cypress, soft pines and sal trees several varieties of shrubs, herbs, ferns and clover grew and flourished. Undergrowth made the place subfuscous and cold. On either side of the path lay the brushwood nibbled by goats. The wind smelled of snow, damp and goat droppings. Sight of paw-marks that appeared on the track and then disappeared into the clump of pine, sent a chill down his spine. He froze in terror. The beads of sweat pricked his temples and trickled down. His breathed in short gasps. With shirt sleeve he wiped his face, and waited to regain his breath.

The sun made a brief appearance. He shaded his eyes with his hand, and gazed at the point where the path vanished in the woods.

Not far away under the shadow of a large oak tree, sat an angelic woman resting against the trunk. She was as fresh as the morning dew. The short colourful blouse showed her tanned midriff and arms. The black and red vertical striped petticoat that disappeared in folds and appeared on knees had lifted up exposing her legs. The silver anklets glittered from the distance. Through a thick canopy, the intermittent light falling on her face, covered with a headscarf, dimmed and gleamed it. The wisp of hair escaped her scarf and whipped in the wind. The large gold nose ring paled before her golden beauty. In the right arm was held a twig from which she plucked leaves and threw them, half falling on the ground and half on her lap. Occasional bleating of goats and bucks grazing nearby failed to attract her attention.

As he inched closer he fumbled and stirred the undergrowth. She turned towards him. Enamoured by her beauty, he stood motionless.

"Hey," she rushed and caught him by the arm, "Didn't you notice the cliff below? You could have killed yourself."

"Sorry, I didn't notice it," he spoke, as if he were daydreaming.

"Oh, you were too engrossed in wooing a pretty goatherd," she teased.

He blushed. "Your presence in this desolate place could have shocked anybody."

"Yours doesn't evoke any different thought," she retorted.

"I don't mean to offend but you and your goats are rather unusual to this place," he explained.

"So is the snow this time of the year," the goatherd shot back.

"Yeah, you are right," he extended his hand, "I'm Ved."

"My folks call me Maya." By the light of her smile those words dazzled. Her handshake was warm in that cold weather. It surprised him.

"Is this a reality, or an illusion?" still under a daze, he asked.

"Isn't this snow an illusion?" the goatherd continued.

"Strange!" he muttered.

"Yes, stranger is the location of our meeting and strangest is the situation."

A tormented soul out in the snow to seek solace was more tormented by those words. She didn't wish to prolong his agony. So she kept quiet and waited for him to say something.

"I didn't see you during my last visit. Do you live elsewhere?"

"When was that?"

"About five years ago."

"People see me when they need me," she spoke with a mischievous grin. "This is my native place. My ancestral house is in the valley below. On a clear day you can see it from here."

"Do you often bring you goats up here?" he queried.

"No. Whenever I need to unwind myself, I bring

them to this place."

"So, it's our chance meeting," he asked.

"No, it's planned one. You see me because you wanted to," was her confident reply.

Curious and confused, he asked further, "How?"

"Didn't you come here to seek solution to your problem?"

"Yeah, I did," was his guarded answer, fearing that she knew all about him. But how could she? He argued in his mind. After all, he was meeting her for the first time.

"I know why you are here. We all are humans. We all make mistakes. And we all must get a chance to atone for our sins. Take this out of your mind that neither are you the first person to do what you did, nor will you be the last one. But you can be different from others by repenting your betrayal in all sincerity and humility. Cleanse your body and soul, and rid both of the traces of cruelty you inflicted upon your beloved. When you leave this place your soul should be as pure as this fresh snow."

"Will my efforts convince her of my sincerity?" he asked.

"They should." she spoke in a melancholy tone, "Rancour will melt her heart soon, but hurt might take a little longer."

"How long?"

"Wish I had an answer."

His face fell. Hopes dashed. He was back at the start point. The snow had melted his hopes, and Maya had shown no path. It was a dead end as usual.

"Wait," she thought out loud. "What is Saranga's greatest wish, her biggest dream?"

Vedanta fell silent and his thoughts went back to his first vacation in Kausani. He racked his brains, trying to remember what Sara had said about her biggest dream.

"Yeah, I know what she said," he spoke, unable to hide his glee.

"Well, then go and fulfil it," she untied the knot of her duppatta and took out an herb. "My grandma says this herb relieves a person of all his worries. Boil a piece of this in milk and drink it. It's sure to free your mind. It works, I tried it once."

He extended his hand to take the herb that looked like some Himalayan medicine, used by the saints to cure local folks of physical ailments. If one such herb could cure mental worries, he wasn't sure. But there was no harm in giving it a try.

It didn't occur to him then that they had spent more than two hours together and he could sense she was eager to return home. Though he wished to spend some more time in her company, it would have been unwise to hold her back further. Goats' bleats had become louder and he knew if she wanted to stay for more time, she couldn't.

"I'll walk you till the road head." he said.

"No, thanks. I'll find my way through fog," she stood up to mind the goats. "I've been up and down these slopes several times. Moreover, the goats are my best guide."

"All right."

"It's time to say goodbye," she said, shaking hands.

"When can we see each other next," he asked, anticipating a positive answer.

For a moment, she stood expressionless. Then she said with a rush of smile, "I'm not sure. Do you need to meet me again?"

A last glimpse of her was captured in his heart, forever. She had one last look at him and before turning back, cautioned him, "Don't keep late here. Rush back to your room before dark. This place has leopards."

The goats in search of better grass and foliage had

strayed. Maya looked around and noticed them spread all over the place. The goats who had their tummy full rubbed against the trees. Unlike the sheep, herding goats was much more difficult. She made a loud call and collected them. The bellwether let out a loud bleat and started moving down the slope. The other goats with Maya at the rear followed. He looked in that direction until the fog swallowed her and waited for her voice to die down in the jungle buzz.

The shadows had begun to lengthen and darken. He hurried down the track. Every moment the chance meeting with Maya crossed his mind. Strangeness of the incident troubled him, her enigma engulfed him. There was nobody who could help him to unravel the mystery. Then he thought about the caretaker. The man had retired five years ago, but still worked at the Ashram. Vedanta had a quick glance at him. The man was attired in the same clothes he had seen him on the first visit. The coat had faded at a few places; the pate had lost more hair. Otherwise, the man had the same pride and the same smile on his face.

"Did you find your thing, young man," the old man asked when he observed Vedanta approach him.

"No. I've come to seek your help for something else," he said and then narrated the whole incident.

For a while the old man remained quiet. Wrinkles on his face had thickened. It seemed as though he were trying to recollect something.

"Did you touch her," he asked.

"Yeah, we shook hands twice. Her hand was warm and her smile affectionate. We spent the whole afternoon together."

"Bizarre," the old man muttered.

"What!"

"Nothing," the old man said, collecting his calm. "I thought who could be out there in the cold. But during snowfall some people do behave in a weird manner. I've known stranger things happen to strangers here in the past. So don't worry, she must be a crazy *gaddi* girl out there with her goats."

Vedanta was relieved.

"It's a good omen," said the old man. "She brings good luck." Then the caretaker turned back, and mumbled to himself, "But truth will tear you apart."

With load off his head, he paid no heed to it, thanked the old man and left.

In the market he saw vehicles parked all over place. So Kausani had got what it had been waiting for the last few months. As soon as he reached the Chowk, he breathed a familiar smell.

In the sky above a large cloud thundered. And before he could make a dash for cover, sudden showers struck him with ferocity he hadn't hoped for. Drenched to the bones, he stood under a shed where a dozen half-wet men had taken shelter and waited for the rain to ease off. From their talks he gathered the wait wouldn't last more than half-hour.

The wait got over. With water dripping, he rushed to the room. As he entered the lobby, he sneezed and then kept sneezing until he arrived at the room, which was open. Surprised, he yelled, "Deepak, bring me hot tea."

"Come inside, otherwise you will catch cold," a sweet voice called out.

It was one voice he had been dying to hear for so many months. It seemed as if an era had passed since sweetness of this voice had filled his heart and soul. Opening the door he fell on his knees and cried. Tears rolled down his eyes in torrents.

"Don't," the woman said, emerging from behind the curtain, "Go, take a hot bath and change your clothes. I don't want you to catch fever. In the meanwhile, I'll order turmeric milk."

He sneezed between sobs. She sneezed too.

"Order two glasses," he said entering the washroom.

After some time, he came out and found ironed clothes placed on the bed. But she was nowhere in sight. Was he day dreaming? He pinched himself hard. He put on dry clothes and went out in the balcony. She wasn't there.

A few minutes later she returned followed by Deepak with two glasses of turmeric milk. Without saying a word, they sat opposite and stole glances at each other. And when anxiety had had its moment, she spoke, "Thank God, I came. Don't you remember you can't endure damp weather?"

A feeble smile, a helpless look and a loud sneeze and she burst into laughter. He joined her.

Saranga was back in Kausani.

Chapter Thirty

❄ ❄ ❄

A weary night moved down behind the mountains, shedding its black along. Dark grey patches crept in random geometric patterns in the fading starlight. Dawn painted the clouds in shades of pink and red. The perky twilight had both softness and subtleness. The wind, which rimpled the river waters below, had made the weather clement. The place had serenity of a heaven. And heaven it was.

In her heart Kausani had a sacred place.

Saranga after a fitful sleep of a few hours sat up in bed. Beside her lay Vedanta in deep slumber, as if the man hadn't slept for years. For a moment, she thought he were Dhruv. In sleep, both men looked so cute and their lips half spreading into an innocent smile, but when awake they were so different from each other.

Thin, grey hair had added fragility to his frame. Repentance had shaved off his several youthful years. How could an intelligent guy like him do such a stupid thing and make so many people to suffer? Tears streamed down her cheeks. She wiped her eyes and stood out in the balcony. Through twilight's alleys she took a trip down the memory lane.

It was here she, five years ago, had found her true love in a simple boy, who had shared her dreams, her disappointments, her fears, and her frailties. Then for next one year both had shared a fairytale life, full of love and romance. In the second year Dhruv, their son was born.

The little boy had given a new meaning to their lives.

But her happiness lasted for a few years more. In the fifth year she felt something had begun to miss in their lives. Ved had withdrawn into himself and become reclusive. No amount of cajoling could bring him out of the shell.

And then she discovered what she had dreaded the most; her husband's infidelity. On her return from Bhopal where she had gone to see her ailing grandma, Ved had confessed to her that he had had one-night stand and that was his only sin. Falling on his knees he had begged her for forgiveness. It was one storm that had shattered her citadel of love in which she had lived in the eternal hope that no harm could come to her. The citadel walls had fallen like autumn leaves and the fort lay in ruins.

A heartbroken Saranga had left for her parent's home, leaving behind Vedanta. Earlier, mere thought of a moment's separation shattered them. Now both faced the reality of severance of their relationship. The world that both had built bit by bit lay in tatters.

The dull, grey patches in the sky rushed out and covered the eastern horizon. A reluctant darkness melted away. After many moments of dithering a listless dawn broke. The morning looked sad and dull. Shorn of its power, the sun looked like a moon without patches lost in the wilderness of heavens looking for a place to hide itself.

In this hour of gloom, she missed her grandma. Then she recollected meeting a German woman during her pervious visit. As she couldn't recollect the route to her house, she asked the receptionist about it. The local folks called her 'German Mem' and they all knew where her house was. The receptionist drew the route out on a piece of paper and explained her in detail. Sara had a quick look at it, folded the paper, stuffed it in her pocket and moved out.

The sun had come out. The morning chill had lost some of its sting. To apricity, Kausani had added its own warmth. The wind had lost pace, and weather was pleasant for a December morning.

As she reached the road bend, she recalled everything. Wading through the snow she reached the house and rang the bell. A feeble voice called out from inside and opened the door. "Oh Sara, it's you my child," the old woman beamed.

"So he has been here," she said.

"Catch your breadth, darling," the lady said, "we've a lot to talk about."

"See, I brought you this," Sara handed her cookies.

The woman's face lit up. She exclaimed, "These are my favourites. I haven't had them for years. I'm impressed you didn't forget it after so many years. You know why women are better than men because we never go to any house empty handed."

"Still he's your favourite," Sara complained.

"Come on, Sara. Don't be harsh on the poor soul," Gomati said and walked into the kitchen, followed by Saranga. "The boy is suffering."

"Am I not?"

"I know dear, you both can't live without each other. His suffering is your suffering. You have to end this, you have to end this."

Then she got busy in preparations for lunch.

"Tell me, dear. What will you like to eat?"

"Anything."

"Sara, your grudge is misplaced. You know I love you more than I love Ved."

Thereafter both women were engaged in a desultory conversation. Vedanta was forgotten. They ate rice, lentil and vegetable. Though Gomati had a cook, she preferred to cook herself on special occasions. And today was one of those.

Back in the living room they settled down in the sofa and waited for the other to start the chat.

The burden of opening the bundle of pain fell on the young woman, who thought it wise not to pass on her burden to the elder.

"Did he tell you anything?" she asked.

"Everything."

"How is he?"

"Sad, devastated and a shadow of himself. He has lost kilos and looks like a scarecrow. Remorse has broken him from within. Sara, you can save him."

"Auntie," she smiled, "you are a good pleader."

"No, darling. I think he deserves another chance."

Sara fell silent. Forgiveness hasn't knocked at the walls of her heart, but retribution had made exit long back. A void existed therein. Many thoughts crossed her mind, but she found no solution. Perhaps she expected it to come from some unexpected source.

Gomati gave Sara a loving glance and spoke, "Human beings do make mistakes. What's important is that are we ready to repent for our mistakes, and vow never to repeat them? I think Ved is a well-meaning guy. He could have hidden his sin from you, but chose to confess it to you and repent. And he still is repenting. Without you, he will die. Sara, the boy deserves to live."

"Tell me, will you forgive him if you were Saranga?"

"Yeah, I'll give the boy one more chance," was the old woman's prompt response.

In it Sara tried to find her answer and to some extent she did.

After a great afternoon she thanked Gomati and left. As soon she entered the hotel room she found Ved missing. Where could have he gone? She wondered and then a thought flashed in her mind and she straightway headed to the secluded spot, where they had met for the first time. Half-hour later she was there. A smile flashed on her lips when she saw him sitting there.

Tiptoeing, she came close to him. Ved was so lost in his thoughts that he didn't notice her. Then the still wind stirred and carried her smell to him. Turning back, he asked, "Sara, where have you been?"

"I had gone to see Gomati Auntie. I wanted to come back early but she insisted for lunch," Sara said. "Ved, did you have lunch?"

"Yeah, in the hotel," he satisfied her curiosity. "Come, sit. It's so calm out here."

As she bent down, her hand brushed against his, and then moving a few inches away she sat down. Then they exchanged a brief glance before turning their gaze to the mountains, veiled in a thin orange haze. Intensity of the pervading silence moved their hearts. Repentance poured out of his heart and flowed through his tears, forgiveness poured out of her heart and flowed through her tears. And the sound of their tears tore apart the impregnable silence of the wild. Spontaneous outpourings of emotions continued until their tender hearts emptied the last trace of rancour.

Turning inwards they wiped each other's tears, and gazed into each other's eyes. Like a mountain spring, love began to fill those empty hearts. It was homecoming of his love, after wandering in the woods of temptations for a brief period. The love in her heart for him was pure, egoless and selfless, seeking nothing in return. Its physical manifestation that time wasn't in the realms of their imagination. Perhaps it was buried in the bosom of time.

Between them they shared several moments of silence. When dusk fell they returned to the hotel. If the morning had some misgivings, the evening had removed them. The night was thoughtful, and long.

Chapter Thirty one

* * *

The snow had started to melt away creating a puddle here a plash there. The lower gradients were the first to lose sheen. From the valley floor the heat, like an aging goat, travelled up the slopes. Bryophytes shone with lovely little white flowers. The dry pine grass with snow droplets on its blades revelled in its brief moments of glory. Bigger snow chunks under the shadow of oak tress had a few days of shine left before the sun would reduce them to water in no time. Harshness of a hard winter was still a month away and until then a cycle of good sunshine seemed a certainty.

The snow had lit up the faces of the tourists, but it had brought gloom in the lives of the local folks. For the last few days it had snowed and snowed, turning everything white. The blizzard had snapped the electric lines, plunging the whole region into dark. The local people used crude oil lamps made from used bottles by making a hole in the cap and putting a wick through it. Each room had a niche, inside of which had been blackened by the smoke. These lamps sent out more smoke and less light. The hotels used the electricity generators to run their establishment. Some private cottage owners forced by the power cut had checked into nearby hotels.

The light winked through the gap in the curtains and fell on Ved's face. The heat pricked and woke him up. Beside him a peaceful Sara slept. He left the bed and went to the washroom to brush his teeth. Back in the room he stepped on a stool that fell with a thud.

Sara asked in a sleepy voice, "Ved is the sun up?"

"Yeah," he said, getting close to the bed. "Sara, get up and brush your teeth. I'm going to order tea." Ved then moved out to look for the waiter.

Saranga rubbed her sleepy eyes and left the bed. After a while both sat in the balcony and watched the sun leave the cosy confines of snow peaks and drift in an endless bluish ocean. It looked lonely and lost. With it the new wind had brought in new chill. Ved rushed inside and brought her a sweater. "Thanks," she said, taking it from him.

In walked Deepak with tea.

"Divine," both spoke in unison, taking their first sip.

Then they gazed at the snow-fed mountains on the skyline. They never had a quieter tea ever. The silence had added to its taste. When he had the last sip, Ved said, "Sara, let's get ready. I want to show you something today."

"What?"

"That's a surprise."

"All right."

After some time both, dressed in casuals, went to the restaurant where they had *aloo-parantha*, curd and tea for breakfast. Thereafter they took the road that passed through the town-centre, cutting through the hotels and houses before appearing in the open space. After half-hour stroll they arrived at the bend from where the road vanished into the clump of pines. Scattered were a few village houses on the roadside and on the slopes. Up and down slopes were full of pines and fruit trees, and on open clearings were sowed crops. On the berms and at adjoining areas snow was still present, while from the trees and bushes it had melted away.

Ved held Sara's hand and helped her climb down the stone-stairs and brought her to an open space on either side of which stood apricot, plum, peach and pear trees. Mesmerised like a child, Saranga stood still. Then she, picking up a big chunk of snow, cupped it in her hands and experienced its coldness benumb her palms, but she held it until it melted and droplets oozed out of her fist. When the last drop fell on the ground, she opened her hands. The shrunken palms had gone numb with cold. She put her palms over her cheeks. It brought tears in her eyes. Then she rubbed her hands and when they became warm, she felt them against her cheeks. The tears stopped. Her face beamed with a childlike smile.

For the first time since she had come here, she felt a sense of peace within. Perhaps there was some magic in Kausani that made people forget bitterness. So her and his folks had known all along that if she came here, she would forgive Vedanta.

"But how could they?" she asked herself, "None of them had ever visited this place."

From a yard away Ved let Sara create and enjoy those magical moments. After many months he saw a smile on her face and he wanted to savour this moment in his heart forever. She played with ice, forgetting that Ved was with him. Then the wind picked up speed and for a second she was thrown off-balance. She whimpered, "Ved," and found herself secure in his arms.

"Sorry," she blushed. "I forgot you altogether.

"I loved to see you enjoy the snow."

Then she, leaving his arms, said, "You brought me here for a surprise."

"Yeah," he raised voice in excitement. "Close your

eyes'"

Then he placed his hands over her eyes. The touch sent a shiver of excitement down her body. It was the same feeling she had felt when he had touched her during their first visit to Kausani. Then he walked her a few fields to the east and said, "Open your eyes. The piece of land and the trees on it are all yours."

His hands were off her eyes. For a few seconds she felt black all around and then the surroundings started to become clear.

"What!" She jumped in delight. Her eyes surveyed all around; the pines, fruit trees and crops, and then her gaze turned to the horizon in front. The rays from the sun, setting in the opposite direction, passed through coloured patches in the sky centre and turned the Nanda Devi and adjoining peaks into a golden wonder. The stunning sight filled her heart and soul with ecstasy.

Turning to him, she asked in disbelief. "It's all mine?"

"Yeah, it's all yours. I've given advance to the owner. After six months we will come back and get the land registry in your name."

She paused for a few moments and spoke, "No, Ved. I can't accept it."

"Why Saranga?" he asked, perplexed. "Wasn't it your dream to own a house in Kausani where you could spend summers and winters and after retirement make it a permanent home? I remember you saying that you wished to grow fruits and vegetables on the adjacent land."

"Perhaps, you forgot something."

"What?"

"I said it was our dream, not mine alone," she corrected him. "So how can the land and the house belong to me alone?"

"Sorry, I was selfish," he was apologetic. "Yeah, you said it right. It's our dream, it's our land and together we will build a house on it."

"Ved, it's our dream," she hugged and kissed him. He kissed him back.

Saranga was so excited that she sat down on a boulder and pulled Vedanta to her side and started discussing how she would plan their house; location of the living room, kitchen and other rooms. She insisted for a large front veranda where they could enjoy morning and evening tea. The house should have enough rooms to cater for a large gathering.

"I think we should have enough rooms so that we can call over our folks to assure them that we've come together forever. I'll like my 'Dadi' to spend some time here with us."

"Sure," he assured her. "We will have our house ready by next winter."

"That would be great," she said, wiping her misty eyes.

Thereafter they stayed there for another hour in which they shared their thoughts about their future home. And whenever she felt low he pressed her hand to reassure her of his commitment. Now and then, he noticed, she looked at the land, the fruit trees and the surroundings in disbelief. As the dusk fell they stood up. She bent down, touched the land with her hands and kissed it.

With hands clasped they headed back to the hotel. En route, whenever any rustle in the bushes scared her, he pressed her hand tighter. It made her feel safe and assured.

A thousand mile away the Prasad and the Datta families after dinner discussed about the future of Saranga and Vedanta.

Shashank didn't want to speak with Ved and didn't

have the heart to talk to Sara. He wanted the struggling couple to get enough time in Kausani so that they could ride out the storm. Amongst everyone present there, Vasudha was sure of Kausani's magic.

"Could anybody speak to them?" asked Shashank, who when spoke to Sara's family found himself weighed down by the guilt.

"None." Many voices hummed.

In rushed a beaming Dhruv. Everybody in the room looked at him in anticipation.

"Did you talk to your mom?" asked grandmother.

"Yeah," said the little boy, with a broad smile. "I asked mom how was Kausani and she said it was beautiful."

Dhruv looked at everybody, one by one, and was happy to see their relieved faces. "I'm going out to play," he said and ran out of the house.

The gloom that had pervaded the room until then, made a hasty exit. The glow on their faces lit up the ambience. They, with folded hands and closed eyes, thanked their *kuldevi*. Their prayers had been heard, their fasts had borne fruit. Since Sara and Ved had separated, both families hadn't slept well.

Misty eyes, both the families thanked one another for their support in the hour of family crisis.

The dusk fell in Kausani. The wind was nippy and chirpier. The stars shone bright. The moon peeped through the clouds. In the nests the birds quarrelled amongst themselves. Saranga came out and sat in the balcony. The enchanting ambience held her in its captivity for several moments.

"Sara, tea," Ved walked in.

The sound pulled her out of trance. Taking cup from his hand, she said, "Oh, thanks. I think we needed it after a long evening."

Taking his hand in hers, she said, "Enjoy this divine weather. From tomorrow onwards it will become a dream."

Thereafter both relived the time they had spent together on their maiden visit to Kausani. Under the care of Mother Nature, love resurged in those suffering hearts. Their eyes shed tears in torrents. Neither of them bothered to wipe those.

On the spur of the moment, Sara placed her head on Ved's shoulder, and whispered, "Ved, I love you. Promise you will never betray me, again."

"Sara, I love you too," whimpered Ved. "I'll prefer to die than hurt you again, ever."

Saranga hugged him and kissed his cheek, "You will live a hundred year." He put his head in her lap and lay there for a long time. She moved her fingers in his hair.

A knock on the door cut short their moments of love. Deepak had come to take order for dinner. They opted for local Kumauni food, which was different and delicious. The night was long and reassuring. In each other's arms they fell asleep around midnight.

The dawn light seeping through the window fell on their faces and awoke them. It was a new dawn. With tea mugs in hand, they stood in the balcony and watched the alpenglow paint the surrounding peaks in pink. Early morning chill forced them to place their hands on the mug to get some warmth. An hour later they got ready, had breakfast and for one last time roamed around the place. Thereafter they returned to the room, paid up the hotel bills, got into the waiting car and drove off.

On a clear day the vehicle glided down the winding road. Saranga put her head in his lap and closed her eyes. Vedanta pressed her head to his chest and caressed her hair. In a few minutes the car hit the straight valley road and picked up speed.

On the nearby slope a female voice calling her goats drew his attention. His eyes fell on the figure and he almost jumped in delight. It was Maya. She waved at him and smiled. He looked at her and smiled back. He blinked his eyes in disbelief and when he opened his eyes, both Maya and her goats were gone.

"Oh no!" he exclaimed.

"What happened, Ved?" Sara asked, stirring in sleep.

"Nothing," Ved patted her head.

www.ingramcontent.com/pod-product-compliance
Lightning Source LLC
La Vergne TN
LVHW040001200726
843493LV00005B/1085